AVID
READER
PRESS

NEXT STOP

A NOVEL

BENJAMIN RESNICK

AVID READER PRESS

NEW YORK LONDON TORONTO SYDNEY NEW DELHI

Avid Reader Press
An Imprint of Simon & Schuster, LLC
1230 Avenue of the Americas
New York, NY 10020

First Avid Reader Press hardcover edition September 2024

AVID READER PRESS and colophon are trademarks of Simon & Schuster, LLC

Simon & Schuster: Celebrating 100 Years of Publishing in 2024

Interior design by Ruth Lee-Mui

Manufactured in the United States of America

1 3 5 7 9 10 8 6 4 2

Library of Congress Cataloging-in-Publication Data has been applied for.

ISBN 978-1-6680-6663-8
ISBN 978-1-6680-6665-2 (ebook)

For Philissa

PART I

ETHAN AND ELLA

I

ETHAN AND ELLA MET IN A COWORKING SPACE, ONE OF THE AIRY OPEN-PLAN OFFICES that were common in their city at that time. Ethan had worked there longer and he liked the office, which was on the twenty-sixth floor of a tall building. It was full of plants and full of light and there was a balcony on the eastern side with a rock garden and benches and he would often sit outside, even in the fall and early spring, and this reminded him of his childhood during the pandemic. He remembered windows, high places, the cold.

During those years they lived in a very tall building in a different city. They were meant to live in that apartment for only six months, while his parents looked for a house, but that was not what happened. Life was predictable and orderly until it was not, and in the end they lived there almost three years, from when he was six until he was eight. He learned to read. His parents argued and reconciled endlessly. His great-grandmother, whom he did not remember, died.

The schools did not reopen for more than a year in that city, and he cycled through many different fixations during that time—dinosaurs, self-portraits, Rube Goldberg machines, unboxing videos, Zoom karate, Cosmic Kids Yoga, *Minecraft*, making slime. One of the most durable was folding paper airplanes with his father and then throwing them from their balcony and watching them fly out over the lake. They went through reams of paper and the airplanes were scattered everywhere, which bothered his mother and, for a while, every day, she would insist that they gather them into a pile in one corner of the room. And then, without warning, she gave up and the planes—the ones that did not make the one-way trip over the water—came to rest where they would.

Later, when he would visit his parents as an adult, he would often walk by the old building. And once, several years before he met Ella, he knocked on the door of their old apartment, 22E, and asked the couple living there if he could look around. They seemed much older to Ethan, though they really were not, and the wife was pregnant. At first, they regarded him with some suspicion. But Ethan was charming and soft-spoken, and he seemed harmless and a little lost, like a child. "I spent the pandemic here," he said, and the husband looked at his wife and then said, "Would you like to come in?"

They spent half an hour together. They made coffee and Ethan asked for a few sheets of paper and he showed them how to fold a few airplane models. But none of them flew as far as he remembered.

ETHAN HAD NEVER THROWN AN AIRPLANE FROM THE BALCONY OF THE OFFICE BUILDing, even after working there for four years. He thought about it, though.

He wrote for a website that covered tech trends. He did not like his job very much because his performance was tied directly to clicks and he suspected that the other writers—six of them in all—were faster and funnier than he was. And often when he could not think of anything to write about he would go out onto the balcony to look out over the city or up into the sky and sometimes he would think of the apartment on the twenty-second floor.

It was on the balcony that he first saw Ella. He was sitting on a bench in late November, looking up at the knifelike form of a peregrine falcon as it rose into the sky, when he noticed her standing near the rail on the far side. She was wearing a yellow blazer and leggings and to Ethan she looked cold and very small.

She was facing the opposite direction, so she must have assumed she was alone. He had been watching her for only a few seconds when she took a paper airplane from the pocket of her coat. After quickly adjusting the wings, she threw it out over the city. From where he was sitting, he was unable to see its flight.

When she turned, he saw her face, pale and sharp, like the airplane.

He cupped his hands around his mouth and called out, "I've always wanted to do that."

"Why haven't you?"

"I guess I'm worried it might land on a car and cause an accident."

"You should worry less," she said, and she blew air into her cupped hands and went back inside.

ETHAN DID NOT SPEAK WITH ELLA AGAIN UNTIL SEVERAL WEEKS LATER, WHEN THEY met by chance at one of the office's four kitchenettes. He had hoped they would talk sooner but she was there only sporadically, twice the week of the airplane, once the following week, and then not at all for two weeks after that. By then the episode on the balcony had taken on a dreamlike quality for Ethan, significant but almost forgotten. And when she came up next to him, he did not immediately recognize her.

She was studying a little packet of jerky, turning it over several times in her hands. Her fingernails were alternating shades of pink and blue—newly painted and glossy—and around her wrist were several silver bracelets, which glittered beneath the overhead lights. Everything about her was small. She had small hands and small shoulders and a small, delicate mouth. But her expression was the same as the expression he remembered from the balcony—severe and searching, and her face had a shadowy quality, despite the paleness of her skin. All of this seemed at odds with the fragile, childlike features, the small hands and the fancifully painted nails, and still she was reading the package.

"They don't have any weird additives," he said.

"Oh," she said, glancing quickly to her left. "It's not that."

"What are you looking for?"

"It's nothing. I was just reading the ingredients."

"They're good. I eat too many of those."

She returned the packet to the jar. "I'll have to take your word for it," she said. She turned to leave.

"Excuse me," he said. "Listen, I might have this wrong, but did we meet a few weeks ago on the balcony? You threw a paper airplane. That was you, right?"

"No," she said, after a brief pause. "You must be thinking of someone else."

"Oh," he said. "I thought it was you."

"I don't think so," she said, and instead of the jerky she took a small bag of granola clusters and walked away.

• • •

LATER THAT AFTERNOON, ELLA SAW HIM AGAIN ON THE BALCONY. HE WAS SITTING under a heat lamp, his legs beneath a blanket and his laptop balanced on his knees. It was cold outside, but he did not look cold, which she found intriguing. She was not sure why she lied about the airplane. There was no reason to lie. And now she felt guilty, though when she thought about it there really was no reason for that either because likely enough she would never speak to him again. Ella was a freelance photographer and she was stringing for a magazine that rented a few desks in the office. She would be done with the project at the end of the day and tomorrow she was planning to take her son on a train south to meet up with a friend from college. He did not seem to be enjoying his school of late and he had become increasingly anxious at home and Ella hoped that some time in a more pastoral setting would help him reset. She was not planning to return to the city for a month or so, and even then, unless she happened to take another gig at the same magazine, she would not return to that co-working space.

She watched him from behind her desk. Then she went outside. "Here," she said, handing him an airplane and sitting down on the edge of the bench. "I'm sorry I lied earlier."

He turned the plane over in his hands. "That's okay. I wasn't trying to be creepy."

"You weren't creepy."

"Is this the same plane?"

"No, that one was different."

"Did it fly well? I couldn't see from where I was sitting."

"It started off okay, but then it got caught in some wind and went into a spiral. It was a good one—that design won the world record for distance. This one I designed myself."

"It feels like the weighting is pretty good."

"You know about it?"

"I spent most of the pandemic folding airplanes with my father and throwing them from the balcony of our apartment."

She smiled. "Me too. With my sister. I was lucky not to be an only child."

He nodded. "That's a funny coincidence. Did you grow up in the city?"

"Yes," she said. "I've always lived at the center of the universe."

"The true provincialism of a native."

She laughed, an easy, rolling laugh. The sound of it was bright and surprising because he did not think he had said anything particularly funny. He decided that he would try to make her laugh again.

"Did you know I was lying?"

"I think I wasn't sure," he said. "I'm Ethan, by the way."

"Ella."

They were quiet for a few seconds. Ethan adjusted the wings of the plane. Then he said, "What is it that you like about them? About paper airplanes, I mean," and she thought for a moment and said, "I guess I like them because they seem very free and very light, even when they crash."

ETHAN ASKED AROUND BUT NOBODY ELSE ON THE FLOOR KNEW ELLA. THE MAGAZINE, he discovered, maintained a few different workspaces in that neighborhood; however, the desks in his office were used only by stringers and so none of the people using them in the weeks that followed could say who she was.

It was a culture magazine, which mostly covered life in the city. He realized that he had heard of it because a few years earlier it ran a buzzy, controversial feature about a Jewish theater company doing experimental shows in the southern part of the city, transforming several abandoned warehouses along the water into venues for immersive theatrical experiences called "the Jewholes." But he had only read articles about the article, never the feature itself. Hoping to find whatever project she had been working on—or perhaps something she had done in the past—Ethan went to the website and looked through a few recent features, as well as some of the older, archived content. He did not find any Ellas. "Ella" had been a popular girls' name at the time when they were born and without her last name his search for her byline elsewhere was similarly unsuccessful. And so once again, she began to fade from his mind. Then, one morning, about three weeks later, he went to the magazine's website again and there it was: "To the Underground" by Ella Halperin.

The photographs were in color, but they were shot mostly at night and the limited blue-gray palette made them look almost black-and-white. This gave the series an otherworldly quality and as he scrolled through he had the sense that he was looking back in time. People running to or from something. People waiting to be born anew. Jews.

Particularly striking was an image of a young family, a mother, father, and two small children. They were seated in their living room, at the opening of a large gray tent, mother and father cross-legged and one child on each lap. To their left, where the flap of the tent draped down, was a neat pile of folded clothing and a line of sneakers, along with several gallon-sized jugs of water. The parents were looking straight at the camera, their eyes wide and limpid. The son was looking toward his sister, his expression simultaneously fearful and defiant; the daughter, a few years older, was holding a calico cat protectively on her lap. Below the photo was a brief description:

The Geller family plans to enter the anomaly at the Northlands subway stop at the end of the coming week. When asked about their decision, Sheila and Daniel Geller, both physicians, expressed uncertainty about what they would find but cited concerns about their children's safety in light of newly proposed restrictions. For the past several days they have practiced sleeping in the tent that they anticipate sharing on the far side. In this image, Lauren and Ezra Geller, 10 and 6, guard the family cat, which they will leave with a cousin.

Ethan was stirred by the images and also very pleased to have found Ella's name. But because she was a freelancer, the magazine did not offer any direct contact information. And because she did not appear to have any public social media profiles, he decided to try the "Contact us" form on the website.

> Hi, if possible, please pass along the following message to Ella Halperin. Thank you—
>
> ---
>
> Hi Ella,
>
> It's Ethan from the coworking space downtown. I just wanted to reach out to say that I saw your photo essay this morning. It's so well done, really lovely. I especially liked the portrait of the Geller family. I guess it has a special resonance for me. I'd love to have a chance to ask you about it. Worst-case scenario you get a free cup of coffee. Let me know—
>
> Ethan Block

He concluded with his email address and clicked Send. Then he stood up at his desk and walked a meandering lap around the office. He stopped twice for snacks, though he was not hungry, and both times he nervously chose a small handful of unpleasantly spicy wasabi peas, shaking them in his palm like dice. For the rest of the day he had trouble concentrating. He managed to post once about a video game controller optimized for some of the newer combat systems. But for most of the day he cast around aimlessly and refreshed his email. When Ethan's boss found him outside looking up at the sky, he asked him, with genuine concern, if everything was all right.

"Yes, fine, absolutely," he said.

"Because you're a little behind, you know that, right? I just want to make sure everything is okay. I don't just mean with work. It's not easy for us lately."

"Us?"

His boss lowered his voice. "Us."

Ethan smiled and said, "Yes, of course. I really appreciate it."

"I know you can do this," he said. "You just have to make the decision. There is still the future to think about."

Ethan nodded. He liked his boss. And he wanted to please him. But as he walked away Ethan had the strange impression that their whole conversation was a memory belonging to someone else, a thing of the past, just like Ella.

ELLA RECEIVED ETHAN'S MESSAGE WHILE SHE WAS STILL IN THE SOUTH. SHE HAD NOT thought of him since they spoke and as she watched her son run through a patch of dandelions, kicking their seeds into the wind and sunlight, she tried to recall his face. She found that she was unable to picture him clearly.

Ella had not dated very much since Michael was born, on a warm morning in early fall six years ago. A few weeks after she found out that she was pregnant, Michael's father went north, along with many others, and did not come back. At first she was desperately angry. But the anger faded, perhaps more rapidly than she would have expected, and soon enough she felt emptied out. She had intended to terminate the pregnancy. But she kept on delaying the procedure until one morning she woke up and realized that she did not want to have the procedure at all. She still marveled at this fact. It remained shrouded in mystery.

It was a strange feature of life in their city that babies came home in cabs, on buses, on subways, as though they were people and not small gods. Ella's mother came to the hospital to help her with the labor, which lasted through the night. In her imagination, Michael was born early in the morning, as the sun was rising over the city. This is because the last photograph she took before he was born—a view of the city from her hospital room on the fifteenth floor—was time-stamped at 5:26 a.m. The next image had been taken by her mother—a picture of Michael, still covered in blood, on a scale beneath surgical lamps—and it had the same bluish glow and so the images became entwined in her memory. In reality he was born hours later, at 10:18 a.m., when the sun was already high in the sky. But she remembered him coming at dawn.

Like all children, he disordered and remade her life. When she brought him home, carrying him up three flights of stairs in a detachable car seat, everything about her apartment seemed altered and somehow insubstantial. She said, "This is where you live now. This is your home."

She brought him from room to room. Then she swaddled him in a blanket the way the nurse had shown her and together they lay down on the bed. His eyes were an indeterminate, watery gray and she tried to imagine how she must look to him, blurry and bright. She thought, *For your sake, I would gladly burn the city to the ground*, and then she whispered those words over him like a benediction.

Now, almost six and a half years later, he ran over and rested his chin on her forearm. "What are you reading?" he asked.

"Just an email."

"Are you doing work?"

"No, it's from somebody who liked some of my pictures."

"Is it a friend?"

"No," she said. "Not really. He wants to be."

"I want you to run with me," Michael said.

So she got up and ran.

ETHAN AND ELLA MET FOR COFFEE TWO WEEKS AFTER THAT. THE COFFEE SHOP WAS crowded even though coffee had become more expensive in recent years. The barista practiced making hearts on top of cappuccinos. A woman met a man who was not her husband. People sat and talked about their lives, their work, their children. They talked about the situation and the events and the holes or they did not.

Ethan chose a coffee shop near the coworking space where they met because he thought that might be convenient for her. It was not until after they had made the date that he realized he had no idea where she would be coming from. He apologized as soon as she sat down.

"I wasn't thinking," he said.

"It's okay. This neighborhood is all right. I haven't been over here for a while. Since I finished the project you saw."

"You mentioned you were in the south for a few weeks—"

"Visiting an old friend."

"How was it?"

"It was nice. I only wish it was closer. It's a twelve-hour train ride. We should have flown."

"Why didn't you?"

"You know, I'm not sure. I guess an intuition that the train would be better somehow." She took a sip of her coffee, which she had sweetened heavily with agave.

"Where do you live?" he asked.

"Uptown. We have a little two-bedroom."

"You live with a roommate?"

"With my son."

She watched him as he turned it over in his mind. To her surprise, though he had looked nervous and ill at ease when she first came in, he did not look that way now. He was thinking—calmly, carefully—and as he did she studied his face, brown hair and light brown eyes and a sharp, prominent nose and slightly downturned lips that made him look sad even when he was not. He was handsome, she thought, and though he was a few years older than she was—and though his short, unkempt beard was already showing small flecks of gray—there was a boyishness about his face, a youthful energy tempered by something else, melancholy, perhaps, though she was not sure.

"You have a son?" he said.

"Yes. But not a partner. It's just us. His father went north when there was that radiation hoax at the hole in Canada. He isn't Jewish."

Behind him the espresso machine hissed and sent up a plume of steam. Then he said, "I should know what to ask, but I'm out of my depth."

She was struck by his persistent calm and she smiled. It was a different smile from what he had seen before. It changed her face.

"His name is Michael," she said. "He's in kindergarten."

"Where is the school?"

"He goes to a little Montessori school near us uptown. In general he really likes it, but recently there have been issues. Some of the kids started excluding him. That's why we took a break and went south."

"I'm sorry. I hope things are better now."

"We'll see. He's still the same kid."

"You mean he's still Jewish?"

"Yes," she said. "Yes, that's exactly what I mean."

After a pause he said, "I'm Jewish also."

She laughed. "You didn't need to tell me that."

"I know. Of course. I get nervous around pretty girls."

She rolled her eyes. "How many times have you said that?"

"First time," he said. Then, "You keep kosher?"

"How do you know that?"

"You didn't eat the jerky. I realized why a little later."

"There are some of us who still do," she said tightly.

"I know."

"I grew up sort of religious. I guess there are things that are hard to give up. What about you?"

"I had a bar mitzvah. That's about it."

"Do you still have non-Jewish friends? I mean, from before."

"I have a friend from college, Feng. His family is from Taiwan. We talk once in a while." He tried to gauge her response. Then he said, "So you really do keep kosher?"

"Sometimes. Anyway, that popcorn at your office is pretty good. It's actually one of Michael's favorite things."

He nodded. "Maybe I could bring him a bag sometime."

"Maybe," she said.

• • •

WHEN THEY WERE FINISHED WITH THEIR COFFEE THEY WALKED IN A NEARBY PARK. They found that they had a fair amount in common. They had both attended the same university in the city (their graduating class was one of the last that included Jewish students), though they had never crossed paths. They both had parents in academia. In Ella's case it was her mother *and* her father who had been professors at the university where Ethan and Ella studied.

As they exited the park, Ella told him that she needed to walk farther downtown to meet with someone about a gig and that he could walk with her if he wanted. It was a Tuesday morning and the sidewalks were busy, though less busy than they would have been only a few years ago. On the corner south of the coffee shop they passed a homeless man with a white cat and a sign that read:

alien inside my toenail riding clouds of acid.
red yellow. waterfall inside.
fuck the jews! fuck the jews! fuck the jews!
snake monsters from the holes.
please help a veteran thank you god bless

Ethan dropped a coin into his cup and Ella looked at him with surprise. He shrugged. "He's crazy," he said. "How can it make anything worse?" She nodded and they kept on going south.

As they walked, Ethan told her how much he really did admire her work, that it wasn't just an excuse to ask her out, and she said that she appreciated it, which she did because she believed him and also because she knew her work was good and she enjoyed it when it was recognized as such. She asked him about his job, if he always wanted to be in journalism, and he said he wasn't sure what he did counted as journalism and he told her how it made him anxious because he wasn't fast enough at churning out posts. When they finally talked about the people in her photographs, a few blocks before Ella reached her destination, they disagreed stridently. Ethan thought they were outright crazy. He explained—with an off-putting grandeur that seemed out of character to Ella—that the situation would resolve itself and that the Second Event would fade and things would be fine because they were always fine.

But things weren't always fine, she said. People leave. People run. Other people come and gather power. Or no one has power and maybe that's worse. Just last week, she said, there was a car-bombing across the street from their apartment. You can read about it. The windows shook. And she wanted to say that because he did not yet have children he did not understand that death was unacceptable. But she did not say it.

There was still some tension between them when they arrived at the office where she was to have her meeting. Both of them felt sorry for arguing, because what was the point, really, and to make peace, she showed him a picture of Michael holding a dandelion.

"He's beautiful," he said. "He looks like you." Then he asked, "Can I kiss you on the cheek?"

"Maybe next time," she said, and then she stepped into the revolving door. It turned smoothly, carrying her easily away.

Ethan looked on from the sidewalk as her small, fragile form was blurred by the glass and by the light.

II

THE FIRST EVENT BEGAN IN A LARGE TRAIN STATION IN A MIDSIZED CITY THAT WAS almost in the desert but not quite. The station—165,000 square feet—was mostly underground, including island railway platforms 260 feet below the surface, some of the deepest on earth. It was designed to serve as a shelter as well as a transportation hub and in the event of a major attack the station could house five thousand. Or so the station makers claimed, as they were anxious people, drawn to catastrophizing and the dark depths.

The hole opened some hours after the daily cessation of train service. The only person to witness the event was an employee of the station, an older man—only a few years from retirement—who had worked there for many years. When he was a child his father gave him an electric train set for his birthday, and he grew to love trains and never stopped loving them. He still had the model, which he had maintained fastidiously, in hopes of giving it to his own child in turn. But before long he found himself in his sixties, divorced twice over and childless.

He noticed the growing darkness as he made his way along the platform toward a long escalator that would lift him from the hush of the tunnels to the surface, where the city clanged and rattled into the heat of the night, like an old appliance restored imperfectly to working order. It was always disorienting to rise up into the tumult at the end of his workday, which usually extended into the quiet hours of the night when the machinery of the station wound down and emptied out. Absent commuters, the lower reaches of the station felt extremely remote. The bright tunnels overlaid with pale tile and the glowing escalators framed by arches of steel and glass, illuminated by thin bars of fluorescent light, reminded him of photographs he had seen of the International Space Station. He sometimes felt like an astronaut himself—or he felt how he imagined astronauts might feel—among his friends and siblings, all of whom had children and, increasingly, grandchildren. He had, he realized, lived much of his life as an observer, deeply concerned for the world but somehow apart from it, orbiting the heart of the matter, keeping watch.

The quavering particle looked almost like a broken pixel. He blinked and rubbed his eyes as it spun and stretched and tore itself open. It was the size of a one-shekel coin, an orange, an exercise ball, and finally a person. He wanted to get behind it, but there was no behind it and he turned and turned but it turned with him, lustrous and impossibly black, an eye peering out from a hidden corner of earth and time. For several minutes the station agent stood motionless, as if bound, in the middle of platform one. His smartwatch vibrated against his thigh at random intervals; the metal of the railroad tracks twisted and rose up; a cat, which had no business at such extreme depths, walked along the ceiling. He felt frightened and confused. But as he tried to make sense of the distortions, he also became aware of a strange inner gravity, like the pull of an invisible hand, and he wondered what would happen if he were to step through.

Instead, he boarded the escalator in the center of the platform. He remembered that he was meeting a friend later that evening at a cafe he particularly liked not far from the station. He had not seen the friend in quite a while and he was looking forward to drinking *sahlab* and hearing about his life. But he did look back, just in time to see the eye spin and radiate outward. First it swallowed a building. Then a neighborhood. Then a city. Then a small country.

SOME MONTHS LATER, AS THE BONES OF THE WORLD CREAKED, A MIDDLE-AGED MAN on a small island in the northwest sat at his computer and looked out across a vast, gray expanse of water. He watched the gulls riding the wind and every few seconds one of them would fold its wings and dive down to spear a fish, disappearing beneath the water and then bobbing to the surface. The man first came to the island with his grandfather, who built the house. Then he came with his father, who fished almost as well as the birds. It was a remote island at the end of an archipelago, home to thirty full-time residents and some thirty more who would come to spend the summers, and it was an ancient place, subject to ancient rhythms: the migration of seals and seabirds, the land clenched like a fist in the winter and then bursting with leaves and wild phlox in June, the salt spray that weathered the wood and stripped the paint so that to maintain a house (as the man had done since his father died) was to battle primordial forces. Each summer, when he returned, he found that the seasons had taken their toll, and this, he thought, was true life, remote from the decadence of the city where his sister and brother lived. And, as he aged, it bothered him less and less that he had no one with whom to share it.

Shortly after the Jew hole opened, a blight struck the pine forest that lined the island's eastern shore. It was a foreign disease that had no business on a remote island in the northwest, and the man, along with his neighbors, tried to clear away and burn the infected trees. But the disease continued to spread westward across the sparse grass. In the months that followed he wrote letters to foresters and local newspapers. The blight was a distortion, he wrote, similar to the distortions around the anomaly that he had heard about on the news. And its presence, in such a distant place, only proved that its effects were spreading and needed to be contained by whatever means necessary.

He sent his letters with mournful resignation. He knew that in response there would be scientific expeditions and government agents and press junkets and they would descend on the island and destroy it, as they destroyed everything. But it turned out that he found very little traction. No one cared that the blight jumped easily from pine trees to moss to grass. No one cared about the family of dead seals he found on the rocky beach near his property. And no one cared that before long the disease would swallow the house, the island, the surrounding waters, just as the darkness had swallowed all those Jews. This confused the man and then it made him angry. There were no Jews on the island, of course, and the man knew that this was because the Jews disdained such things, the rhythms of the land, the power of the ocean. The Jews sought to control and then destroy these things and in a fever of inspiration he realized that the hole would expand again because it was hungry. It would consume the Jews or it would consume the world, and the man loved the world.

As the birds fished, the man posted a video about his theories.

Then he made another and another after that, adding them to the still-seething potion of astounded newscasts, breathless posts, puzzled scientific articles, pamphlets of spiritualists and the doomsayers, presidential addresses pleading for calm, scattered reports that the Israelis had had advance warning, that they had known something more, and, it stood to reason, that they had shared their knowledge with Jews everywhere even though Jews everywhere appeared to know nothing and was that not convenient? The first day his videos got thirty-four views. The next day five thousand. The day after that five million. The theories of the man from the island made a great deal of sense to a great many people, because many of them had thought those very same things ever since the anomaly opened, but they had not found a way to put their thoughts into words. This was his gift. He alchemized ghosts and demons and brought them concretely into the world. Soon enough the videos were everywhere. They were as coherent as anything else in those days.

The man remained on his island, seven thousand miles from where Jerusalem had been.

III

WHEN ETHAN WAS TWELVE YEARS OLD, A FEW WEEKS BEFORE HIS BAR MITZVAH, HE was astonished to learn that his parents hated the apartment they had lived in during the pandemic, that the layout was all wrong, that it never felt clean, and that the kitchen floors were uneven and painful to walk on. This is what his mother said, lightly but not without some bitterness. He found it unsettling because he had very fond memories of that place and he did not understand that when his mother said "the apartment" she really meant a whole host of wounds—the end of her career (she had been a political operative), a lost opportunity to move out west to be near her parents, other losses that she could not name but felt deeply. And they left the apartment for a house when the lockdowns ended.

Just before the pandemic, his father, an anthropologist, went to a conference in Berlin. The family made a trip out of it. They decided to rent an apartment, rather than stay in a hotel room, which they thought would be easier for Ethan but turned out to be a hassle. The owner, an older man with bleached hair, was late getting there with the key and the first thing he did when they stepped inside was set up mousetraps along the kitchen counter. During the days, while her husband was attending the sessions, Ethan's mother would push him around the city in a stroller, going inside bakeries or museums, or riding the U-Bahn when they got cold. She was troubled by the still-pervasive shadow of the war and of communism—buildings that remained damaged, plaques all around the city commemorating atrocities, glass windows built into the sidewalks and looking down onto pieces of bombs or other wreckage.

Ethan's mother was not engaged whatsoever with Jewish life growing up. But as she walked without direction with Ethan, she felt hunted. Balancing her phone on the handle of the stroller, she texted her husband:

this place is odd

?

i feel like i'm in the past or something i don't know

how is Ethan?

She sent a picture of him eating a cinnamon roll.

when will you be done?

should we meet you for dinner?

. . .

The ellipsis appeared but the question went unanswered and she had the strange thought that he was gone from their lives, taken, perhaps, or running. Ethan must have seen something on her face, because he tugged on her wrist and said, "Are you okay, Mommy?"

"Yes, I'm fine."

"What are you thinking about?"

"I was just thinking about Daddy."

"Is Daddy okay?"

"Yes," she said. "Daddy's fine. He's still working." And when they came home that afternoon they found two dead mice on the counter. The owner came about an hour later to take them away, his hair now dyed red.

"Poor little animals," he said, as he dropped them into a plastic bag.

When Isaac came back from the conference she was angry with him for not texting back, but also very relieved. The fantasy of his having vanished had become very real for her throughout the afternoon. She was quiet and moody throughout dinner at a nearby restaurant.

Later, when Ethan was asleep, they sat in bed answering emails. Suddenly, she closed her computer and said, "Promise me if we ever have to run away, we'll all run together."

"What?"

She said it again.

"What are you talking about?"

She said, "Just promise me," and he said, "Okay, I promise."

Then he said, "What happened today?" and she said, "I realized that things can come apart quickly." They returned home four days after that, only five weeks before the lockdowns began.

Twelve-year-old Ethan, though he thought of himself as fairly grown-up, knew none of this and when his parents said that they had hated the apartment, his impulse was to argue them out of it.

He had met with the rabbi earlier in the week to start preparing his speech, and as he tried to decide what to say to his parents he remembered their conversation. Although they were not very involved at their temple—they joined only a few years earlier so that he could celebrate his bar mitzvah on time and he really did not understand much of what went on there—he liked the rabbi. She was a kind, gentle woman who was about the same age as his mother and he respected what she had to say because he had a sense that everybody else did. The rabbi explained that the Torah portion for his bar mitzvah contained one of the episodes in which the Israelites complain about wandering in the wilderness and she said that it was important to try to always see the good even in difficult situations. This struck him as a profound and challenging discipline and, with a great deal of confidence, he told his parents that Judaism teaches that Jews should try to be happy with what they have. Then he said it was fun living in the apartment because they got to spend so much time together and they learned about origami and about the physics of flight. He asked his father, if he remembered when they camped out on the balcony in sleeping bags and this made his father cry—his father, who always cried more readily than his mother—and he said, "You're right, Ethan, it was a nice apartment. We were happy there."

ETHAN DID KISS ELLA THE NEXT TIME, ON THE CHEEK AND ELSEWHERE. THEY MET again during the day, for an early lunch instead of coffee, and this time at a place in Ella's neighborhood. After lunch, to Ethan's surprise, she asked if he would like to come back to her apartment.

"To meet Michael?" he asked.

She smiled. "No, he's at school."

On their way back from the restaurant they took a short detour through the neighborhood, which was quiet and somewhat deserted in the late morning. They stopped to sit on a bench and they watched a Jewish worker unload apples from a small truck, an older man in his sixties or early seventies, perhaps a few years older than their parents. A group of children knocked some of the apples onto the sidewalk and then pushed him to the ground when he bent to pick them up. This bothered both of them, though not as much as it would have only a few years earlier. They looked at one another but said nothing. And as they sat on the bench their hands found one another and interlaced. Life happens, even in the narrows.

It was a warm and lovely day. It was only late February but the air felt and smelled like spring and it was invigorating for both of them and it turned them on. And, though neither of them was uncaring, they quickly forgot about the man and his apples. But when they approached the building, Ella pointed to a charred, broken part of the curb across the street and said that was where the bomb went off.

"What was the situation?" he asked. "Did the police come?"

"Of course."

"What happened?"

"Who knows?" she said. "You know how it is. Especially in the Pale."

"When did the neighborhood get that name?" he asked.

"Hasn't it always been called that?"

"No, I don't think so."

She shrugged. "Well, I can't ever remember it being called anything else."

Ella's apartment was in a large hundred-year-old building that held forty or fifty units. It loomed over the street, hiding the sidewalk in shadow. The facade was red brick with gray concrete at the base and the windows were framed with scrollwork that might have once been quite magnificent, but which was badly in need of repair. The front door of the building was set back from the street. To reach the staircase they had to pass beneath a stone archway, and as they did Ella pointed up to a window adorned with rainbows and paper snowflakes.

"That's us," she said.

Her apartment was bright and airy, though rather small. The entrance led into a surprisingly long hallway at the end of which he could see a bamboo plant as well as a jasmine vine growing up around the casing of a window. On the wall were pictures that Michael had drawn, some recognizable and some not, as well as more paper snowflakes strung on chains. Off the hallway to the right were two small rooms and a bathroom and these too had plants hanging in the windows. He liked that she kept plants. He had always wanted to do so himself, but had never managed it.

"You can take off your shoes," she said. "Just be careful of the Legos."

The hallway was scattered with toys—Lego figures, blocks, markers, dinosaurs, puzzles, trucks of various sizes and shapes. Ella kicked them out of the way as they went into the kitchen and living room, which were divided from one another by wooden doors with lattice windows in the center. The table near the kitchen was still set with a half-eaten bowl of yogurt and Cheerios and the couch in the living room was also covered with toys. These Ella brushed onto the floor before they sat down.

"I'm sorry about the mess," she said.

"It's okay."

"After a while you just give up on the toys. You'll see."

"This is a nice place."

"It works for right now."

Ethan nodded.

"Would you like some tea?" she asked. "I have this good Korean tea. And I can put in some of the jasmine flowers."

"Sure, okay."

As Ella waited for the water to boil, she studied him carefully, without giving the impression that she was staring. She knew that he was objectively nice looking, but she was still unsure if she found him particularly attractive. Earlier, in the restaurant, she thought that they would likely have sex but now she was less sure. He struck her—during lunch, during coffee a week earlier, on the balcony in November—as completely without guile. He seemed quite bright. But he lacked the caustic, calculating quality that, in her experience, often accompanied intelligence. She felt very safe with him, which was something that she had not felt in quite some time, and although they still did not know one another particularly well, she felt certain that she could rely on him, that if she called on him—if she really called on him—he would be there. Or he would be dead. This was her exact thought and it disturbed her.

She came back with the tea. After setting the cups on a low table beneath the window, she reached up and picked a few jasmine flowers from along the top of the window and when she did her sweater rose up and revealed some skin at the small of her back. A little more was revealed when she bent over and crushed the flowers between her fingers and dropped them into the tea.

"Here," she said, and then they sat on the couch and drank the tea quietly. Sunlight streamed through the window and the leaves of the jasmine vine were struck green and gold. She moved closer to him and rested her head on his shoulder. After a few minutes she sat up. "You can kiss my cheek now, if you want," she said, which he did, softly and with intention, and then she returned her head to his shoulder and sighed and looked down and saw that he had an erection. When he saw that she saw he blushed and shifted a little and crossed his fingers in his lap.

"Sorry about that," he said.

She looked at him ironically. "Why are you sorry about that?"

"Well—"

"Why do you think I brought you up here in the first place?"

"I don't know," he said.

She laughed and threw her leg over his. Then, with her small hands, she carefully parted his fingers. "I wanted to use you for your body, of course."

THEY DID NOT HAVE SEX. THEY TOOK TURNS GOING DOWN ON ONE ANOTHER, NEITHER of them undressing completely. Ella was initially surprised at how good he was, but after she came she realized, dimly, that she should not have been. He was careful and focused, as he was about most everything. They intended to have sex afterward, but he had not been with anyone in over eight months and he was already very close by the time she took him in her mouth. He only lasted about thirty seconds before he came on his stomach.

"I'm sorry," he said. "It's been a while," and she smiled, sleepily, and said, "That's okay. Maybe I'll give you another chance, Ethan." It was the first time she had called him by his name.

"Also, a therapist once told me that you come quicker when you really like someone."

"You needed a therapist to tell you that?" she asked.

"It made me feel better when I was twenty-two," he said.

She stood up from the couch. "Do you have to go back to work?"

"Not yet." He took a sip of tea.

"I'm going to take a shower," she said. "When you finish that, come lie down with me."

Fifteen minutes later, when they were in bed, Ella reached into the drawer of the nightstand and took out a joint. "Do you smoke?" she asked.

"Not really."

"Do you mind?"

"No, go ahead."

The lighter was on the nightstand on the opposite side of the bed and as she reached for it her small breasts brushed against his chest. When they did he felt himself perk up again.

"Already?" she asked. "Well, just hang on a minute." She took three hits, coughing ferociously after the third. Then she snuffed out the joint and rolled on top of him.

THEY WERE STILL FLOATING SOMEWHERE ON THE BOUNDARIES OF THEMSELVES, HOLD-ing on tight.

"Where were you during the First Event?" he asked.

"Do we need to have that conversation? I guess we do, okay. I was in school in eleventh grade."

"What do you remember?"

"I remember they wheeled in TVs on those black carts and the teachers streamed news websites. I remember thinking, *Okay, nobody is really in charge now.* And I remember thinking, *Where did they get all of those TVs?* I don't know why, but that's what struck me at first. Where did all the TVs come from? Like there must have been a giant room full of TVs somewhere in the basement."

"Did you believe it?"

"Yes. I was in Spanish class and Senora Martinez said something was happening. I went to a Jewish high school and she was one of the few non-Jewish teachers, who taught world languages. She was one of my favorite teachers and I trusted her. She looked shaken but also excited. And then she put it on. We watched for an hour before we were dismissed. I didn't leave right away. Most people didn't. We still wanted to be together, I think. And we just sort of walked around the school, talking and not knowing what to do. I called my parents but they didn't answer until later."

"You walked home by yourself?"

"It was such a beautiful day. Perfect. Warm. And very quiet. We lived right beneath a flight path to the airport but of course there was nothing flying."

"Yes."

"What about you?"

"Sort of the same, though my high school wasn't Jewish. Most of my friends thought it wasn't real for the first few hours. We were sure it was some kind of deepfake. We were skeptical of everything."

"I wasn't skeptical."

"You didn't think it might be a joke? At least initially? It didn't make sense."

"It made sense to me. That's how it is. Also, I had a lot of family in Israel. Cousins that we would visit in the summer. My parents spent several days trying to get in touch with people. But of course no one got in touch with anyone. And then my father went over with the government delegation to study it. They flew into Cairo, I think."

"What do you mean?"

"He was on one of the interdisciplinary teams that went into the Exclusion Zone in the early days when the pull wasn't so strong. He was a philosopher back then."

"He's not anymore?"

"He was forced out with a lot of the others."

"Yes."

over to her and wrapped his arms around her from behind and held her as she sank down onto the floor, where they stayed for quite some time. They were quiet. All was quiet.

Then Ethan's hand, the edge of his little finger against hers, restored her to the present. And as she closed her eyes he whispered something she did not quite hear.

ELLA DREAMT OF A MAN WALKING WITH A TORCH ACROSS A DARK FIELD. HE WAS wearing a thick overcoat, a wool cap, a scarf like a gash, red and wild in the wind. Far in the distance, the lights of a small town. Far behind, a line of trees. And in between nothing. In between the man walking. She saw through his eyes. She was with the man and she was within the man. But she was not the man. She was far ahead, well beyond the lights. What did he know, she wondered, apart from the cold? What did he know, she wondered, apart from the walking. Somewhere the moon, hidden by the clouds. Somewhere an owl, hunting mice and rabbits. From high above she saw the man walk five thousand miles on air. It was the light of his torch and the gentle pressure of his feet that created the earth beneath him, the selfsame patch of ground that carried him on to the lights and chimneys. And always the wolves. And always the bears. And always the Cossacks. And always the dogs. But his father said go, so he went, from Vilna to Shanghai and from Shanghai to Chicago and from Chicago onward, to a place promised but unseen, to a woman named Zissa Botwinik, one of Ella's four great-grandmothers, the only one whose name she knew.

ETHAN WENT OUT TO THE LIVING ROOM AS ELLA SLEPT. OPPOSITE THE COUCH WAS A floor-to-ceiling bookshelf made of white particleboard, sagging with many more books than most people in the city kept at home. The majority were old photography books, nudes and street photography and war photography, some of them reprints of books from over a century ago and some of them, he suspected, originals. He ran his fingers along their spines, delicately and with great desire, as if he were once again touching her body.

Then he walked over to the window and looked out across the city. Somewhere, perhaps two miles south, he saw a cloud of black smoke rising between two buildings. He could not see the source but he could imagine it and when he did he could almost feel his teeth rattle and he remembered last winter when a bomb exploded at a bike-sharing station about thirty seconds after he rode off. He felt heat on his calves, but he kept riding, not looking back until he was a block away, at which point he stopped, breathless, and realized that he was bleeding. The street behind him was mangled and dusky with smoke. There was yelling and the blare of a siren and his body shook. There were pieces of people on the ground. But now, looking out at the smoke from his vantage point in Ella's apartment, his breathing was steady. A person could get used to a great many things, he thought.

Reaching up above the window, he picked a few more jasmine flowers, which he set into a glass of water and placed on the nightstand beside Ella. He kissed her on the forehead. She shifted but did not open her eyes. He noticed again how small she was and he remembered the feeling of her breasts against his chest and once more he felt a torsion of desire. He looked down at her delicately painted nails and he recalled how she turned over the packet of jerky, her eyes squinting slightly, and how she expertly adjusted the wings of her plane. He did not wake her. Instead, he quietly gathered up his jacket and shoulder bag and went downstairs. On his way to the subway he passed the bench where they had seen the Jew struggle with his apples. He saw no sign of what had happened. The vendor, and his tormentors, seemed like ghosts from another age.

He thought again of sleeping Ella, of her jasmine flowers and old books and young son. It was one o'clock in the afternoon and the sun was high in the sky. And as he descended into the station—an express stop crowned with a great glass dome—he felt very light and very free.

THE FOLLOWING FRIDAY, ELLA INVITED ETHAN OVER FOR SHABBAT DINNER. IT HAD been a long while since Ethan had done anything of the sort and he arrived with flowers and wine and cake and a present for Michael—a book of instructions on how to fold 101 paper airplanes. Michael said, "We don't usually fold airplanes on Shabbat," and Ethan blushed and apologized and Ella said it was okay, that they were not all that strict about those kinds of things anyway.

"Did you grow up that way?" Ethan asked, as he followed Ella down the hall to the dining room. Without turning, Ella shrugged her shoulders and said, "Oh, you know," and Ethan said, "Sure," though really he did not.

The other guests were friends of Ella's from college, which was the time in her life when she was at her most religiously observant. She had moved away from observance after graduating—never entirely but very noticeably—which was true of many people she knew, a process of semi-intentional drifting motivated in part by some of the anger she felt having come of age after the First Event, in part as a kind of late rebellion against her parents, and in part because of her general distaste for things she thought were old and parochial and absurd. And though none of this drifting was inaugurated by the fact that she eventually met and dated a non-Jew—a phenomenon that was not so common after the First Event, even among people in their progressive circles—neither was it completely unrelated. It was Tucker who convinced her that it was okay to go to a show instead of to her parents' second seder and that it was okay to put a small Christmas tree in their window and that it was okay that his older brother, though otherwise rather tolerant, had designed one of the most widely used Jewish registry apps that emerged during the surveillance boomtime of her late teens and early twenties. Her friends from college, some of whom sat around the table now, had been concerned and then angry. And despite their having known one another for years, Ella felt somewhat shy and nervous around them, even as she had become very grateful that they had returned to her life after Tucker left and that they had forgiven her, even if she still did not feel as though she needed forgiveness. Now, because they all lived relatively close to one another in the Pale, they got together from time to time on Friday nights.

The two women were Ella's former roommates. At one time they had all been active in Jewish student groups, organizing events when those things were still relatively commonplace on campuses around the country. They had married men who were similarly observant—lithe, thoughtful-looking men wearing kippot and finely knit sweaters—and both couples had children about Michael's age. As the adults helped Ella set the table, the children played hide-and-seek and Michael showed off his new paper airplane book.

Ethan, watching them all cycle through familiar rhythms, felt very much like an intruder, and he was briefly resentful of Ella for inviting him. He must have looked uncomfortable because at one point, on her way to the kitchen to get more forks, Ella touched him gently on the shoulder and smiled, which made his heart jump but did not make him feel more at ease. He realized that she was not the sort of person to give more in that kind of situation and he found this realization simultaneously intriguing and infuriating. She was tough and he liked her toughness and he admired it and he found it lacking.

As they made the final preparations for dinner, they talked about politics. The mayor had recently given a speech in which he proposed phasing out registration apps over the next five years and they were arguing about what it meant and about if it would happen and about whether or not it was really good for the Jews.

He's a friend of the Jews. Not really. Doesn't he have a Jewish sister-in-law? So what? Didn't he approve of public money going to Jewish schools? And to Waldorf schools. And to protectionist schools. Even still. And the dynamics on the city council. And the unrest south of the city. And the rumors about the women who were forced through the anomaly in the park. Where are the police? It was orchestrated by the police. That's histrionic. That's what's real. There is no way of knowing what's real. You sound like one of them. We know another family that went underground. The pull is growing again. Nonsense. You need to open your eyes. And on and on until one of the other women looked at the clock and said, "It's time for candle lighting."

The children gathered. The counter in the kitchen was set with candles, two for Shabbat and one for each child. The women lit and covered their eyes and sang the blessing, their voices blending beautifully. Then they sang a song that Ethan did not know.

It was Michael who went over to Ethan and, very quietly, said, "You look scared."

"I guess maybe I'm a little scared."

"It's not scary," he said, "I'll show you how."

Michael held Ethan's forearm and pulled him gently forward. There were sounds outside—yelling, the low rumble of a train, a siren somewhere. But inside there was a fleeting depth of quiet, rounded off and burnished. The parents blessed their children, prayed fervently for what they could not provide—for light, for peace. When it was time to raise a cup Michael told Ethan to raise a cup. When it was time to wash before bread, Michael guided Ethan's hands. The water was clear and cool. The candles burned steadily next to the sink. Ethan smelled chicken and potatoes. The room was dipped in gold.

"See," said Michael, "it's easy," and then he ran back to the table and sat down with the other kids.

When Ethan turned, Ella was standing very close. She handed him a towel to dry his hands. "Drying off is part of it," she said.

"Oh," he said.

"Michael likes you," she said.

"He doesn't know me."

"I like you too."

"You also don't really know me."

"Yes," she said, touching his face quickly, "I think that maybe I do."

IV

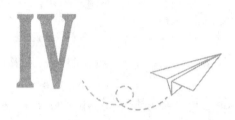

THREE YEARS AFTER THE FIRST EVENT, A MAN NAMED MUSTAFA STOOD ATOP A SMALL hill, raised his binoculars, and looked west across the desert. About half a mile ahead he could see the line of wire fencing that marked the beginning of the Exclusion Zone and five miles beyond the fence he could see the waves of heat and the rim of black, like an oil slick rising to meet the horizon. He had made the trip many times. It no longer filled him with dread. But he always became nervous as he approached the border and he began to wonder, not for the first time, about the ethics of what he was doing. He tried to remember why he was doing it—the steadily mounting costs of his mother's medical care, Khaled's legal troubles, a wedding for Aisha, the byzantine maze of their immigration status—but it was hard to keep things straight and the sun was vicious.

He lowered the binoculars, then drank from his canteen and prayed silently. He was not as devout as he had once been, but he still prayed and often multiple times a day. Now he prayed that the men operating the drones had been sufficiently bribed and that none of them would have a change of heart or a crisis of conscience. Then, he looked over his shoulder at the three Jews—a middle-aged couple with parachutes and duffel bags and a young man with tattoos up and down his arms who carried nothing. "So?" said the young man, coming up next to him on the hill. "Why are we stopping?"

"We should catch our breath," he said. Then he pointed up at the drones that hovered above the fence to the west. "And we have to make sure the timing is right."

Just outside the Exclusion Zone, about one hundred yards from the base of the hill, there was a small metal shed, inside of which waited a dune buggy. When it was time the four of them quickly descended and wheeled it out onto the sand. Gently, but with practiced efficiency, Mustafa strapped the Jews into their seats and bound their arms and legs, all the while praying quietly and asking their forgiveness. There were coyotes who tried to take Jews on foot for a lower fee, but sometimes the pull of the anomaly was overwhelming and the Jews wound up running themselves to death through the desert. It was not always like that. Some of them moved slowly, wide-eyed and mute. But Mustafa had seen runners once, a family of four, the children trailing behind their parents and expiring first and the parents, in their delirium, not even turning back. What drove the Jews to such madness? he wondered. He did not want to see it again. "It's for your safety," he said, tightening the straps. "Not all of you experience it the same way. I just want to make sure you get where you want to go."

"Yes," said the middle-aged man, "we understand. We heard things."

"From this point on we need to move quickly," Mustafa said, and then he put on a motorcycle helmet, lowered the visor, and sped off.

They raced over the cracked, ancient earth. The drones caught the light and winked in the sky, a checkpoint that once admitted scientists and other authorized personnel. It had been years since it was in use. Now it was the domain of lizards and antelope and desert foxes. The woman, twisting her body against the restraints, rested her head on her husband's shoulder. The young man tilted his head toward the sky. He howled with laughter and said, "Let's fucking *go*!" A mile south of the shed they veered right and hurried on to the fence. Every time Mustafa worried that the gap in the fence—originally cut by his cousin, who was also a Jew-runner—would have been repaired by the UN or by one of the other agencies that managed the Exclusion Zone. But it never was. At first, the runners hid the gap with rocks and sandbags and another piece of chain-link fencing, but now it was not uncommon to find it open. Very few people cared. And the ones who did wanted more Jews going through, not less.

They went on, driving easily through a twisted but well-worn path through what had once been a military installation—rock, rubble, twisted metal, rusted-out military vehicles like the husks of great insects, foxes hunting whatever lived inside, swallows flying low, a vulture high above where the drones had been.

The Jews were quiet as they drew near. The couple no longer whispered to one another about their daughter, who had made the trip two years earlier, with Mustafa or with a man like him. They stopped asking aloud about what they might find, about whether or not they would truly come up in another time and place, like the Jewish babies who were buried in the sand in ancient Egypt, only to sprout anew when redemption was at hand. The young man had ceased his wild laughter. Mustafa wondered, as he had many times before, if the distortions made it impossible for the Jews to speak or they simply preferred not to. He did not ask. It seemed a sacred silence and it persisted when, at last, he slowed the dune buggy and removed their restraints.

Many coyotes, on reaching the perimeter, would leave straightaway, but Mustafa always stayed to watch them go down. Sometimes it was a matter of seconds. The pull—either from the anomaly itself or (Mustafa suspected) because of some internal gravity—would be overwhelming and the Jews would race ahead with frightening speed. But sometimes, like today, they moved more slowly, with a dreamlike sense of purpose as if drawn by a gentle magnet, like pilgrims at the Kabah. On those days he would walk alongside them as they made their way to the ridge. His concern for them, irrational and very intense, reminded him of his concern for Khaled and Aisha, when he crept into their room when they were young to make sure they were still breathing. He helped the old Jews with their chutes. The young Jew paused, his face suddenly fearful, his lips twitching. "I can take you back," Mustafa said. "Just say the word."

They all jumped at once. The parachutes burst like popcorn and Mustafa watched the couple sink easily into the dark. The young man, however, dropped like a stone.

SEVERAL YEARS AFTER MUSTAFA HAD ABANDONED HIS SIDE HUSTLE, A JEW IN A BIG city three thousand miles away from the Exclusion Zone opened his wallet and found that his Oyster card had changed. The color scheme was different. There was a new hologram. And it no longer gave him access to the Tube. Barred from entering the turnstile, he went back upstairs to purchase a new one. But instead, as if carried by an unseen hand, he exited the station and sat on a bench in a nearby park. It was fairly early in the morning but the park was already buzzing with energy. People in suits rushed underground or hurried up into the light. Tourists posed for pictures. Street vendors sold coffee and warmed-over rolls. Street performers and chess players began their daily hustle. Drones swerved above the trees. A man sleeping on a bench across from the Jew sat up abruptly and shook off his newspapers like gray plumage. Meanwhile the Jew turned the Oyster card—or what had been an Oyster card—over and over in his hands, marveling at the change. He contemplated the situation, got nowhere, and then he called his wife.

"Look in your wallet," he said.

"Why?"

"Take out your Oyster card."

"Where did you get these?" she asked.

"I didn't get them. That's just how it was when I took it out. They don't work for the Tube anymore."

"What are they for?"

"I don't know. I think we're going to find out."

Instead of going to work, the Jew hurried home, taking a taxi rather than a train. There he held his wife. He felt the otherworldly tremors of their unborn daughter, moving silently between them. And he thought, *There is no such thing as a simple miracle. Soon enough a miracle becomes part of the world.*

THE JEW FOUND HIS OYSTER CARD TRANSFORMED ON THE SAME DAY THAT ELLA MET Michael's father, just before the world ripped again. She was twenty-five and he was also a photographer, older and more experienced. They met covering a protest—a column of people twenty-thousand strong that set out from the northern part of the city and marched south to city hall, where the newly elected mayor was going to make a speech about how and if to scale back the city's Jewish regulations. The shock of the First Event had faded somewhat from public consciousness in the intervening decade and there was a great deal of disagreement about how to approach the city's Jewish population, which was sizable.

In that part of the country, which was generally progressive, there had long been intermittent efforts to overturn some of the harsher measures, which were put in place in fear and haste—exclusionary zoning and frozen assets and restrictions on Jewish involvement in certain industries. These measures had never been entirely popular—the city's educated middle class was, in particular, unimpressed by the videos and conspiracies that had circulated widely in the early days, and public skepticism about the merits of ongoing enforcement was seen, in some circles, as a mark of sophistication, like speaking French or Mandarin. But at the same time, in the years following Ella's college graduation, there was increasing unrest in the city and this contributed to an overall attitude of paranoia that prevented wholesale reform—the occasional Molotov cocktail, protests in favor of lifting the restrictions, counterprotests in favor of keeping them in place, and also a persistent stream of newcomers, refugees from the fires in the west, from cartels in the south, from places farther away full of sand and heat, bringing with them food and language and music, desire and hope and violence, unknowable passions, many of them, so they said, running from the hole that would swallow the entire earth. And the Jews had their hand in all of it, because wherever there are people one finds Jews, passing like ghosts across every boundary, trading border for border, star for star. Everywhere there was trembling, spasms of blood and anger in service of something new, like at a birth.

So although questions about the city's Jewish population had been prominent in the mayoral race, they did not exist in a vacuum. They jockeyed for position alongside other issues—whether or not to resume construction on a semi-abandoned seawall near the mouth of the harbor, how swiftly to absorb the children of refugees into the public schools, when and if to integrate iron dogs, the four-legged, robotic weapons already common in some other cities, more fully into the police force. All of these concerns turned around an obscure, dark nucleus that Ella's father once remarked was similar to the anomaly itself, the shared psyche of a city that was not on the brink but maybe not so far from it. For the city's Jews, it was a relief that for much of the election cycle the Jewish question was only one of many, even if it meant that a return to their pre-anomaly lives was not immediately at hand. But three weeks before the election there were several explosions of uncertain origin and these, for reasons that remained mysterious, returned the Jews to the center of every conversation.

A close advisor to her predecessor and a former police lieutenant, the new mayor had campaigned throughout on the promise that she would stay the course—that the moment, in all of its complexity, called not for rash judgment but for a steady hand on the wheel. On her way to a narrow victory she promised quiet and methodical leadership and transparency, but during her first few months in office she was able to deliver on none of these. Protests swelled. Flyers and graffiti bloomed everywhere. Bridges were blocked. There were beatings and hospitalizations.

Such was the mood in the city on the day of the Second Event, when twenty-five-year-old Ella found herself at city hall, standing up on a bench as a great sea of people seethed and foamed all around her. Although it would become a normal aspect of her work, Ella had never before been in a situation that seemed genuinely out of control, where the possibility of violence was so close to the surface. She was frightened. And she was excited. In the distance—beyond a swirling mass of faces, signs advocating this or that, a man dancing, a man naked, a man throwing fire, a woman wearing horns and skins, a thousand smartphones raised to the sky—the mayor, surrounded by a phalanx of police officers, was trying to speak. She was standing on a raised platform in front of city hall and behind her were the flags of the city and behind the flags of the city soaring was a municipal building, damaged the previous week by a bomb thrown from a motorcycle. She saw the mayor through her viewfinder, a tall woman in a dark blue suit. An enemy of the Jews, in the words of her sister. The mayor raised her fist. She gestured toward the damaged building and her mouth was wide with anger. But whatever she was saying was swallowed by the crowd. Ella saw the platform wobble. The mayor stumbled in her heels and the officers stepped forward. They lowered their masks. The platform shook again. Ella shot the scene. She refocused and shot again. Again. Again. The mayor reached below her podium and, gracefully, strapped a gas mask across her face. She looked like a sea creature, alien and out of place. And then the platform tilted and fell and went under. The people scrambled. The man throwing fire threw fire. Smoke and gas rose up. She saw the batons of the officers rise and fall. She shot.

Blood sprayed. She shot again but she captured only a blur of motion. They were scrambling over the bench. Someone tore her camera from her neck as she fell. She coughed and her eyes teared from the gas and her mouth was hot with salt, her lips wet and swollen. She heard a great roaring sound and then she hit the ground and she looked up and through the haze of violence she saw a silent patch of sky, blue and bright and then speckled with starlings and then black with smoke as something burst and broke and rained down in ash. She heard chanting but she could not make out what was being said. There was blood on her face, in her eyes, in her hair. She struggled to stand, her head throbbing and her vision splotched, but a great weight held her down. Splinters of glass tore into her hands and legs. A police siren, a crush of heat. She screamed as someone stepped on her leg, her stomach, her face. A loose nail found the flesh on her back. Fear crashed over like a great wave. She gasped. She gasped again. Her shoulder burned. She thought he was going to rip her arm from her body. She did not see his face. She heard him say, "Get up, get up." Her head slammed against what was left of the bench as he lifted her. Blood ran from her eyebrow and into her eyes, hot and viscous. "Come on," he said. "It's time to leave." She saw smoke and lights. She heard the insect-like chatter of a helicopter. She heard the thwack of batons on flesh, on bone. "Can you walk?" But she did not hear him. "Can you *walk*?" he said again, this time screaming it. When she nodded he took her firmly by the wrist and dropped his shoulder. With the great weight of his body he pushed through the crowd. He did not stop until they were four blocks east of city hall, away from where the crowds were thick. Only then did he let her go.

"Are you okay?"

She blinked. Everything hurt. Her vision was fuzzy with blood. "I lost my camera," she said.

"Never mind," he said. "That was closer than I like."

She was still dazed. "Thank you," she said.

He looked down at her press credentials. "We have to watch out for one another in our business. I saw you on that bench and I thought, *She's gonna get trampled.* I tried to get to you sooner. Is this your first time?"

"No. Yes. I mean, I've never been in a war zone or anything like that." She still felt foggy. Her lip was hot and swollen.

"Who are you working for? They should have prepared you."

"What could they have done?"

The coffee shop on that street would not serve Jews so he went in to buy her a coffee, and then they found a table in a small public park half a block away. They talked for about ten minutes. He told her that he worked for one of the bigger newspapers in the city and that he was a strong proponent of Jewish rights. "What's gone on in the last nine years has been disgusting. My great-grandfather fought Nazis in France."

"Mine probably didn't," she said. "He was from Odesa."

"It's total bigoted nonsense, what's happened in this city. Around the world."

"People are scared."

"That's not an excuse," he said. "It is strange, though, that everyone seems to be able to spot a Jew these days." He paused before adding, "I knew you were a Jew the instant I saw you up on that bench. I can't explain that. But it's true. Ever since the First Event."

"It's been like that for a lot longer."

"Not like this."

"I was sixteen years old when the screens on the subway turnstiles started flashing a Star of David when I swiped."

"It's terrible," he said. "We need to end that. All the apps and registries should be destroyed."

She rolled her eyes. "Thanks for your allyship."

"I believe it."

Ella shrugged. "The truth is, like you said, you all don't need them." She touched her lip gently and wiped some blood from her chin. "Holes or not, you people could always spot a Jew. Even if you didn't know it."

"I don't think that's true."

"You're not one of us," she said. Then she said, "What happened back there, anyway?"

"Don't you know?"

"No."

He looked at her and narrowed his eyes. "A hole opened up in the city. Or an anomaly, whatever you want to call them."

Ella's heart raced. "What do you mean?"

"Like I said."

"Where?"

"In the park. In that subway station next to the Northlands. And there are others."

"What? What are you talking about?"

"The stories started dropping half an hour ago."

"I was on the subway."

"Can you feel it?"

"I don't know. I don't think so."

"Are you sure? Everything I ever read suggested that Jews could feel the gravity of the anomaly within a certain range."

"I don't know what I'm supposed to feel."

Ella reached into her pocket to get her phone but when she did she found that the screen was shattered and that her pocket was filled with powdery shards of glass. Instead she read the initial coverage on Tucker's phone, her fingers brushing lightly against his as she took it from him. There were holes in subway stations in Paris, in Berlin, in Melbourne, in London, in Toronto, in Buenos Aires—none of them larger than a manhole cover but all of them vampiric, sucking in birds, clouds, light, sound, Jews.

IN THE WEEKS AND MONTHS FOLLOWING THE SECOND EVENT THERE WAS RENEWED fear that what had happened in Jerusalem would happen elsewhere, that the hunger of the anomalies would not subside until cities and nations had been swallowed. But time passed and they were not. Cities with anomalies settled back into their routines, at first uneasily and then with increasing comfort. The distortions turned out to be manageable—localized magnetic disturbances, the disappearance of fireflies, clocks losing, on average, one second per day. People went to work and to school. Subways reopened. The Jews reported visions, but not always of an intelligible sort. A woman saw a plague of locusts rising from a public fountain. A man claimed that his young son aged ten years in a single morning only to shed those years that same afternoon. In many cities around the world the Jews opened their wallets and found that their MetroCard tickets had changed or that new tickets had appeared. Markets developed. The prices of these MetroCards rose and fell. In some places they were scarce and in others they were plentiful and this changed along with the seasons and for reasons both mundane and mysterious. There were rumors about where they had come from—they had been found in an old checkpoint on the edge of the Exclusion Zone or they were printed at a secret facility in the Azores or they were discovered in the sealed cabin of a decommissioned Israeli submarine that had been underwater during the First Event. There were counterfeits and hoaxes. The Jews argued over their meaning and they argued over their distribution and systems were developed and then abandoned and then redeveloped and then abandoned again. In some places they were burned and in other places they were cherished. In the very beginning, before the MetroCards appeared in her city, Ella saw a news segment about a Jewish couple living in an island city on the far side of the ocean who were, according to reports, the first ticket holders on earth. In the interview the man stood next to his wife, who was visibly pregnant, and behind them was a great black sphere. They both smiled as they held their new tickets out toward the camera. "For the subway below the subway," he said. "Proof that ours is an age of miracles." The wife, Ella thought, looked nervous. But she laughed as they turned and they stepped forward together. Meanwhile the end of the world was deferred. There was order and even peace.

• • •

ELLA NEVER TOLD ANYONE IN HER FAMILY ABOUT TUCKER, EVEN AFTER THEY MOVED in together. Neither of her parents would have approved of her dating a non-Jew, though later on, as they supported her through her pregnancy, she realized that their response, had they ever found out, might have been different and more tolerant than she had imagined. Initially, the secrecy was exciting. Even in a city like theirs, dating a Jew, for a person like Tucker, was fairly rare. But over time it started to wear on both of them and they began to harbor resentments. Mostly these were unspoken. But occasionally they burst to the surface in volcanic eruptions of mutual recrimination. He would say she had a haughty, stubborn, and untrustworthy Jewish streak and she would say he was an antisemite like all the rest.

Once they were eating in a restaurant and a man at the table next to them made a nasty comment in their direction. Ella, who generally tried to avoid confrontation, got up to leave, but before she could step out from the banquette Tucker was on him. He dragged the man from his chair and threw him to the ground and bloodied his face before several other men restrained him. Tucker expected her to be appreciative but later that night she told him how much he had embarrassed her. He said she was an ungrateful Jewish bitch and she said he was like a child and that he didn't understand anything about her and he said that she would not let him understand, that she never really let him into her life because she was ashamed of him and because she thought she was better than him and she realized, on some level, that it was true, and they screamed at one another for hours until they were both exhausted and crying and then they held one another and slept and woke up and made love and did not speak of it again. She promised him that she would at least tell her sister. But she never did. And in this way they passed two years until one morning in December they found out that she was pregnant.

They spent the rest of the day talking in circles, orbiting one another but never really meeting. They both felt strangely shy and they did not know what they were going to do or how to feel. The prospect of a child threw the peculiarity of their situation into stark relief and, shortly before going to sleep, Tucker brought up the idea of making an appointment at the Department of Vital Records. It was not the first time they had discussed it and whenever they did they ran the risk of having a vicious argument. But on that night it did not happen. He held her in bed and said that if she were to renounce formally before a judge they could get married. She said that she did not know whether she could go through with it even if she wanted to, which she was not sure she did.

"Besides," she said, "even if I converted, how would that matter? I would still feel the pull. We know by now that conversion can't change that."

"But you might be protected from restrictions. Or something worse."

She shook her head. "And anyway your parents and your sister would still think of me as a Jew."

"That's not true. They would accept you completely."

"But *you* will think of me as a Jew," she said, and he said, "I love that you're a Jew," and she did not believe him even though she knew he was not exactly lying.

They lay next to one another in the dark and Ella watched the shadows move. The world seemed decayed, as if the walls around them had aged immeasurably in an instant. It felt as though their lives were racing ahead of them but that they had been somehow stranded in the past, like an outdated piece of technology, a plug that no longer fit any outlet. And because she was Jewish she was more conscious of it than he. Or, anyway, that was how it seemed to Ella.

She woke up in the still-dark morning and Tucker was standing at the dresser. One of the things that had drawn her to him in the first place was how he moved through the world, with smooth, languid strength, but now he looked nervous—twitchy and disorganized. When he saw that she was awake, watching him, his eyes widened, almost imperceptibly, and a thought came to her, half-formed and vaporous: he was afraid of her.

"There is something going on," he said. "Something with radiation in the water near one of the small anomalies along the border." He paused. "Do you know anything about it?"

"I don't know what you're talking about."

He continued to pack. "Listen. They're sending me north."

"What? Who?"

"They might close the border with Canada. I'm going to be one of only a few photographers on the ground. People are dying."

"You're going now?"

"This afternoon. By train."

"Okay . . ."

"I want you to be careful, Ella."

"When are you coming back?"

"A few days, maybe a week, I guess. I don't know. I'll call you." He walked over and kissed her on the forehead. She blinked, still tired. "Go back to sleep," he said.

When she woke up again the sun was high in the sky. She tried to recall everything they had talked about the night before, but those memories, recent as they were, dissipated quickly. She took a shower—hot and bracing—and she felt as though she had been cleansed in ancient waters. But in the living room she saw that he had left all of his camera equipment behind. And coverage throughout the day revealed that the radiation leak was a hoax.

ELLA'S PARENTS LIVED DOWNTOWN ON THE TWENTY-EIGHTH FLOOR OF THE SAME apartment building in which Ella and her sister had grown up—a tall silver spire that towered over the river. They had both taught at one of the city's larger universities but were forced into retirement after the Second Event. As their idleness stretched on, they began leaving their apartment with less and less frequency, in part because of an ever-encroaching though unspoken fear of the outside world and in part because their neighborhood was home to some of the more stringent mitigations in the city and there were no longer that many places where they could go comfortably. They filled their days with Zoom salons and progressive politics and Jewish advocacy causes, none of which, as far as Ella could tell, had much effect on the non-digital world. This troubled Ella to a certain extent, but whenever she brought it up her mother would make a philosophical point about how digital spaces were as real as any other.

Once, when she was still with Tucker, Ella pressed her on it. They were eating lunch on the balcony and Ella tried unsuccessfully to convince her mother to go for a walk to get coffee at one of the few places around there that still served Jews. The ensuing conversation, which they had had several times before, followed the same beats until, exasperated, Ella accused her mother of intellectualizing and not really engaging with her concerns, which were motivated by love. In response, her mother said something unexpected. She said that staying inside was like going back in time to the days of the pandemic.

"Why would you want that?" Ella asked.

"We were all together," her mother said.

"Growing up, you and Dad told us how horrible it was for parents—for both of you."

"No," she said, "it was really a wonderful time. Only we didn't know it." She paused. "Do you remember how we used to wipe down the groceries?"

"Not really."

"It was such a pain. One time I remember you and your sister were watching TV when the groceries were delivered. You were watching this show about little kids who turn into cute monsters at night when they go to preschool. It was a really sweet show and it was all about friendship and both you and Sophie loved it and I remember thinking how sad it was because you didn't go to school and Sophie had never really gone to school because of the pandemic and you didn't have any friends besides each other. But you guys were just laughing and laughing in the living room while I was on my knees near the door crying as I wiped down a package of frozen salmon." Her mother laughed. "I don't know why I remember that moment in particular. And for a long time it was this awful memory, but it isn't anymore. It's changed."

Far below they could see a column of protesters marching north toward the mayoral mansion.

Her mother turned away from the window and said, "One day you'll look back on this awful time and realize that we were living like God in Odesa."

"I don't know what that means, Mom."

"It means you'll think to yourself, *I would give anything to go back.*"

V

IN THE SPRING ELLA ASKED ETHAN TO JOIN THEM AT HER PARENTS' SEDER. THIS WAS largely at Michael's insistence. Michael started the petition about two weeks beforehand and, even though Ella did indeed like Ethan, at the outset she said no. She found the connection that Ethan had forged with Michael, in only about six weeks, somewhat unsettling.

Ethan had a small, geriatric dog called Lucy and initially, for Michael, this was part of Ethan's appeal. Ella did not know anyone else who kept a pet, and the dog, which he said was the vestige of a past relationship, surprised her. The few times he brought the dog over to their apartment, the three of them would take it on walks through the neighborhood. During these walks, Ella would hang back a little bit, allowing Ethan and Michael to go on ahead, and in this way they developed a relationship that quickly transcended the novelty of the dog and became something solid and abiding even though it was still very new. They already had inside jokes—many of them about her—and traditions that she did not fully understand. For instance, every time Ethan came over he would say, "Hi, boneless," and, inexplicably, Michael would answer, "Don't call me boneless, I'm not boneless, you're boneless, right, boneless?" When she asked Ethan about it he said he was not sure, that it was something Michael told him about from kindergarten and maybe it was from a book. At first she was not entirely certain why any of this bothered her. She knew that Ethan was not dangerous in any way and that his affection for Michael was, at least in part, a reflection of his affection for her. But one afternoon, as Ethan was chasing Michael around a playground while pretending to be a T-Rex, she understood, with a sudden, bracing clarity, that Michael had been missing something important that she was unable to give him and she experienced the trauma of his father's departure anew.

"You really want him to come to the seder?" she said one night while Michael was getting ready for bed.

"Yes, Mommy, I really do. I really like him."

"I know you do."

"Is he part of the family now?"

"No, Michael, not really. He's our friend."

"Is he Jewish, like us?"

"Yes, honey. You know it's pretty hard to have friends who aren't Jewish."

"Daddy isn't Jewish, right?"

"Daddy isn't really a friend anymore. We don't have to think about him."

"Where is he?"

"I don't know."

"I wish Ethan was part of the family. Can he be part of the family one day?"

"We'll see," she said.

• • •

ETHAN WORE A TIE TO THE SEDER, WHICH ELLA FOUND SURPRISING AND ENDEARING. As a consequence Michael insisted on wearing one as well. But he did not have a tie so on the way to Ella's parents' house they stopped at a men's clothing store so that he could pick one out. He chose a blue bow tie imprinted with red pterodactyls. While packing it into a box, the salesman asked Michael if he liked dinosaurs and Michael explained, with a kind of sermonic forbearance, that pterodactyls were not dinosaurs but rather pterosaurs and that they were as closely related to T-Rexes as humans are to kangaroos.

The salesman, unsure of how to proceed, said, "Are you buying the bow tie for Easter?"

Michael said quickly, "No, we don't celebrate that," and the salesman licked his lips carefully and said, "I heard somewhere Jews need ties so that their heads don't fall off." The salesman appeared momentarily confused by what he had said and perhaps he was ashamed that he had said anything at all. Michael, of course, did not know what to make of the comment. But with a child's intuition he sensed in it a strange kind of menace, as if the man had been briefly possessed by a ghost. Ethan was about to say something to the man, but Ella kissed his cheek and whispered, "Just don't," and so instead he swung Michael onto his shoulders and together they walked out into the late afternoon.

"What was that guy talking about?" Michael asked.

"Nothing," said Ethan. "He was being silly."

"Here, let's put on the tie." Ella fidgeted with the bow at the base of his chin, her hands shaking. But she smiled when she backed away from her handiwork. "Grandma and Grandpa will think you're so handsome."

Which they did. When Ethan, Ella, and Michael arrived, about an hour before the seder, they gushed and fawned over him, as always. Ella's father told Michael that doctors often wear bow ties because a bow tie is much more sanitary than a necktie and he said that Michael's choice showed good judgment. Ella's mother gave him chocolate-covered macaroons and a book about Pesach and they sat together reading on the couch.

Ethan and Ella went into the kitchen, which had the hard, gleaming quality that accompanied Pesach cleaning. Ethan started picking at some of the hors d'oeuvres—little quenelles of gefilte fish, olives, orange gelées coated in chocolate.

"I used to love these when I was a kid," he said, taking one of the candies. "I haven't had them in a really long time."

Ella made a face. "My mom always buys them on Pesach. I've never liked them but Sophie does."

"We never really did Passover when I was growing up," Ethan said. "But there were a few years when we had seders and I've always remembered these." He ran his tongue along his teeth and tried to dislodge some of the orange gel. "They have a very specific taste."

She watched him as he took another candy. "You know if my father comes in he's going to chastise you for eating before the seder."

"Why?"

"You're supposed to be hungry for the matzah."

"He gave Michael a macaroon."

"You're not his grandson."

"I'll take my chances," he said.

He smiled—a smile that was both kind and mysterious—and she was reminded at that moment of how little they really knew about one another. Or, rather, she was struck by how little she knew about him. She reached out and rested her fingers on his forearm, as if to confirm and concretize his presence, and she thought of the old Jewish man they had seen on their second date, how fragile he seemed, insubstantial as the children teased him. Beneath the gentle pressure of her fingers, Ethan was solid, unmoving.

Ella had only dated two other men since Tucker left, neither seriously, and she had held herself at significant remove from both of them. But at night with Ethan, particularly after sex, she often found herself talking on and on about herself, about how she disapproved of what Sophie was doing and about whether it was silly that she was still thinking about public school for Michael and about her work and about the families she met who were planning to go through the anomaly in the park. But she had asked him comparatively little about himself. Feeling the sudden weight of this imbalance, she said, "Are you still close with your family?"

"Yes, but I never moved back. They wanted me to."

"All parents want that," she said.

"I almost did, a few months after the Second Event."

"Why didn't you?"

"I don't know. I guess it seemed like a regression. I felt like I needed to make it here."

She touched his neck. "I'm glad you didn't."

"Me too," he said.

She kissed him. "I'm sorry that I don't ask you enough about your life before me."

"You just asked me."

"I know, but still. You know that I want to know you, right?"

"You do know me, Ella. This is me."

"It's just with Michael I need to be careful. There is so much going on that I can't control." She paused and pointed back and forth between them. "So I try to control this. You understand, right?"

He lifted her hands to his face and kissed her fingers.

"Yes," she said. "I know you do."

• • •

SOPHIE ARRIVED HALF AN HOUR LATER AND AFTER SOME COMMOTION—DURING which Ella's parents embraced and kissed their younger daughter and scolded her for not arriving earlier—they all sat down. The table was set with silver and crystal wineglasses that once belonged to Ella's great-grandparents on her mother's side, wealthy people who donated rooms at public libraries and supported artists and collected things like silver and crystal. Their wealth, so said Ella's mother, was squandered by Ella's grandfather—an unwise and unlucky investor—and then shortly after the First Event their name, "Goldfarb," was removed from the rooms because it was too ethnic. Now all that remained of their considerable fortune were a few baubles—a handful of paintings, a ruby ring that Ella's great-grandmother used to wear, a set of Georg Jensen silver, impractical goblets. When Ella and Sophie were growing up, their parents used the tableware for the seder night and it seemed to possess an ancient, haunted quality, like the ruins of a great city. It glittered beneath the overhead lights, concealing worlds. Its brightness was such that Ethan almost had to look away. The dining room table was situated alongside a wide glass window, mirrored against the night sky. As they sat—resting against white pillows on which Sophie and Ella had drawn pictures as children—they could see their reflections in the window, giving the illusion that they were all floating in midair, and they shimmered, festooned by the winking lights of the city, as if shot through with stars. The absurd, extravagant beauty of it all brought tears to Ethan's eyes as he rested his arm on Michael's shoulder. And from deep within this living tableau, Ella's father closed his eyes, raised a cup, and sang: *Kadesh, urchatz, karpas, yachatz . . .*

• • •

THEY HAD JUST EATEN THE HILLEL SANDWICH—MATZAH WITH BITTER HERBS AND charoset—when Sophie started talking about her work in the south.

"We got new templates," she said. "Apparently from a source in the Middle East. Anyway, after they're printed, these new models require much less sanding at the end."

Ethan, seated across the table from her, noticed at once how different Sophie was from her sister. She was tall and muscular and deeply tan. She had a cowboy's energy, savage and propulsive.

Her father grimaced. "Please, Sophie," he said. "I don't think now is the best time."

Ella's eyes darted toward her father, a small, leaflike man with gold-rimmed glasses and a short white beard. Her mother, who was taller than her husband but also slight, reached across the table and brushed some hair out of Michael's eyes.

"I brought one," Sophie said. "I can show you when we're done. If we load them with bullets that have a tungsten core they should be able to defeat most body armor at normal combat range. None of the militias have anything that can withstand the kind of firepower these things can bring." She paused. "Unless it's true they're getting support from the government. Maybe they are."

"What did Dad just say?" Ella asked.

"What?" She looked genuinely confused.

"He said that now is not a good time. I agree with him."

"Oh, excuse me. I didn't realize I needed your permission."

"What's wrong with you? Why are you talking about this around Michael?"

"You think it's better he doesn't know?"

"Know what, Mommy?"

"Nothing, honey. Your aunt is talking about some things related to her work. You don't need to worry about it."

"Is body armor like the armor for a knight?"

"Sort of," Ella said.

"Body armor protects your body from bullets," Sophie said. "In Israel they used to make it for Jewish children."

"Not anymore?" Michael asked.

"Well, it isn't there anymore," Sophie said. "You know that."

Ella leaned over so that her face was very close to Michael's. "This isn't anything you need to think about, honey. Here, maybe you can help Bubbie bring some things in from the kitchen." She forced a smile. "You know it's finally time to eat!"

Ella's mother stood up from the table. "Come on, honey. You can help me put parsley into the soup."

Ethan watched them go without turning around. Their reflections grew wavy in the window. Then they winked out and Sophie said, "What does he think about it?"

"About what?" asked Ella.

"About everything that is happening."

"We mostly don't talk about it. What use is there in worrying him?"

"Didn't you pull him from school over the winter?"

"For two weeks."

"What did you tell him?"

"I told him we were taking a little vacation, which was true."

"You need to prepare him for what's coming. You're his mother."

"What would you know about that?" Ella said.

"I know enough not to get impregnated by some goy."

"You're a child, Sophie, you know that?"

"How long before you realized your shaygetz was never going to help you with your renunciation?"

Their father's eyes widened. "What?"

"Tell him," Sophie said.

"Fuck you."

"Tell him."

"Dad, there is nothing to tell."

"Please," he said. "Let's just not do this now. Be nice to each other."

"I am being nice," Sophie said. "I'm not going to let us end up like those sheep in Europe. I'm not going to die with my cock in my hand. I'm going to die fucking fighting."

"You should hear yourself, Sophie," said Ella. "You sound crazy."

"There will never be an end to it. You understand that, right? Never." Sophie looked at Ethan. "You're fairly quiet. What do you think?"

"About what?"

"About anything."

"I think we can wait and see."

"So it turns out that you're an idiot also."

THEY ALL LEFT SHORTLY AFTER MICHAEL FOUND THE AFIKOMEN AND SUCCESSFULLY ransomed it for a new dinosaur sticker book. Michael, exhausted, was nearly asleep in Ethan's arms by the time they made their way to the elevator. Ella and Sophie had both softened during the meal. They laughed as they helped one another into their spring jackets and their mother, waving from across the room, imagined them as little girls. She remembered when Ella taught Sophie to put on a coat by laying it upside down on the floor and flipping it over her head.

According to an old custom, their father accompanied them downstairs and halfway down the block to the subway station. He insisted on upholding this tradition, despite the danger, just like his ancestors, who defied demons so that guests would not walk out into the night alone. "Well," he said, "it is precisely because of the danger that the tradition exists," and their mother said, "But you're not so young, Joel, what are you going to do?" and, with an ironic smile that had not changed in the thirty-five years they had known one another, he whispered, "Just wait for me over on the couch and I'll show you what I'm going to do when I come back up."

Miriam, now alone, cleared dishes from the table. The brisket was cold and starting to congeal. Everywhere there were crumbs of matzah—on the tablecloth stained with wine, on the floor, on the salad wilting in a wooden bowl, on the sponge sagging beneath its own weight. As she navigated the ruins, she thought about the five of them, down there on the street. Neither she nor Joel had been downstairs in over a month. She wondered if the noise of the city would frighten Michael or if he would sleep through it. Then she thought, *He'll probably sleep through it because he's slept through worse.*

And maybe the streets would be quiet.

But the streets were never quiet those days. They were swollen and angry, an open wound. It was hard to believe there were only forty anomalies worldwide because the world was tearing open all over the place. There were refugees from the west, Jews and Bolivians and Syrians and Californians, men and women with burns, children with cancer, children missing arms, children missing eyes. There were beggars living in tents along the river, selling fish if they could catch them, selling pills or rotting fruit or sex if they could not. There were protests against the police, for the police, neighborhood militias, iron dogs. There were preachers preaching. Everywhere the sound of metal on metal, metal on rock, metal through flesh, the Jurassic hum of drones, delivering, surveilling. And through all of it, people were walking, going about their business, heading to the subways, sitting in restaurants, making friends and enemies. And somewhere there was her grandchild, likely still asleep.

As she slid the leftovers into Tupperware containers, she remembered her time in graduate school when she became interested in the work of a slightly older colleague, who mostly wrote about ethics. She did not know him personally, but she had seen his picture on a book jacket. He had curly hair and a round, open face and a thick mustache. His eyes had a tender, searching quality, his expression bemused and almost childlike. He looked silly and huggable and he reminded her of a Muppet.

As a philosopher he was lucid and stark. She admired the clarity of his work, though it disturbed her, and, walking over to the refrigerator, she recalled a conversation they had when they finally met at a conference. She had attended a session earlier in the day at which he had presented a paper, but she did not speak with him until later that evening when the fire alarm at the hotel went off accidentally and forced everyone down into the lobby. They found one another near the bar, and, when the commotion died down, she said that she enjoyed his talk and he asked her if she would like to sit and talk more.

He turned out not to be all that childlike. He was full of ideas and academic gossip and he was obviously bright and very ambitious and he was charming and self-deprecating, if somewhat caustic. She asked him about his work and when she did his face lit up and he launched into a lengthy explanation of whatever he was working on at that time. She was tired and his presentation, she would always remember, was not especially organized and after a while she decided to give up on trying to follow the content of what he was saying and instead she observed him. She found his passion endearing. She said that it sounded like he really enjoyed his career and he said that he did and she wondered why a person like him, who seemed so content, could produce work that was so severe and uncompromising. She asked him about it directly a little while later, and he said, "Listen, you're Jewish, right?" When she nodded, he told her that he went to yeshiva through the tenth grade and that just before he left to go to public school he learned a story about some ancient rabbis who got together to vote on the question of human creation. After some debate, they decided that it would have been better had people never been created, but, seeing as they were, they might as well inquire into the reality of their situation. That story, he explained, made an impression on him and he said that he thought the rabbis were right on both counts.

"What do you mean?" she asked.

"You should never avert your eyes from anything," he said. "But when you do you realize that life is pretty horrific."

"That's very pessimistic," she said. "Especially for an ethicist."

"Yes," he said. "It is."

"And is that why you got into the business?" she asked.

"Maybe. Probably."

"You know you don't seem like the yeshiva type," she said.

He laughed a bright, easy laugh. "Where do you think I get my ideas?" he asked. And then, because it was spring, he started singing a line from the Haggadah—*This is the promise: That not only one arose to destroy us, but in every generation they arise to destroy us, and the Holy One Blessed Be He saves us from their hands.*

Joel sang the same tune at the seder that night, his voice more or less identical to the voice she remembered.

WHEN MIRIAM RETURNED TO THE LIVING ROOM SHE CUPPED HER HANDS AROUND HER eyes and pressed her face to the window. There was a fire burning somewhere in the north, likely an electrical accident or a small car bomb.

She sat down on the couch and waited for him, feeling a tingle of anticipation as she remembered his smile. Watching the smoke rise into the night, she thought of her childhood, when grandparents seemed very old and when a car bomb would have seemed a monstrous occurrence in their city, exotic and terrifying. The first time she experienced one up close she was nearly fifty, not old but unquestionably closer to the end than to the beginning, and her ears rang and her heart raced and she sat on a nearby bench coughing and shaking. She called Joel and said, *I'm here, I'm okay, I'm okay*, and then she took the rest of the day off work, met the kids when they got home from school, and hugged them as if they were still small children.

Eventually she grew accustomed to spasms of heat and fire. Whenever she heard a bomb she would get down quickly, her face to the sidewalk, her arms covering her neck. If the explosion was close she would feel the heat on her skin and she would choke on dust. Then she would get up and move on to wherever she was going—to see a friend, to get coffee, to meet with a former student. She no longer shook. She no longer took the day (though her days had been taken from her in any case). And now, if they did have to run, Miriam knew that Ella and Sophie would outpace them.

She was not ancient, but her knees hurt sometimes and Joel had to manage his back spasms. And just before the girls left they reminded them once more about the gold behind the bookshelf. "You'll need to take it if we can't," Joel said. "Split it between the two of you if you can't stay together. There will always be a use for gold."

Reclining on the couch, Miriam wondered if he was right about that. What good was gold if everything else went completely to shit? It struck her then that Joel was so much softer than he once had been, wiser, perhaps, but not as sharp, and she knew she had a hand in that. He had always said—in part as an extension of his pessimism—that he did not want children and he maintained that posture for several years, even as they planned their wedding. She always assumed that he would change his mind eventually, or that she could convince him. Still, she had not expected that he would be ready so quickly. He was the one who suggested, only a year after their wedding, that they ditch the condoms. He was the one who insisted they track her ovulation. And as she lifted her shirt over her head she thought, *I led him astray. Now the debt is due, now the promise is being fulfilled.*

VI

A MONTH AFTER PESACH, ELLA HIRED A BABYSITTER, A NINETEEN-YEAR-OLD GIRL named Rachel who came to the city from the west earlier in the year. Ella and Ethan planned to meet up with another couple at a Jewish bar about a mile south of Ella's apartment. As they made their way downstairs, having left Michael and Rachel sharing a plate of fish sticks and watching videos on her phone, Ella felt grateful and serene.

She had been apprehensive about inviting him to the seder. And, though he would not have admitted it, he had been apprehensive about going. But the entire time—as she fought with her sister, as she tried, fitfully, to manage what Michael did and did not hear—his hand had rested on her shoulder and by the end of the evening something subtle but of crucial importance had shifted for both of them. As he carried a drowsy Michael to the elevator, she realized that he was not a guest in her family's life. Her mother, father, and sister were guests in theirs. This realization shook her and shook him and a month later it accompanied them as they turned south, stepped deftly around a charred, crumbling patch of sidewalk, and slipped easily into the warm, dark hands of the city, his fingers resting almost imperceptibly on her hip.

LAURA AND ALEX WERE ETHAN'S FRIENDS. THEY MET AFTER COLLEGE WHEN THEY ALL wrote for the same website and they were his first friends to have a child and own a house outside the city. This had once seemed to Ethan a strange miscalculation, an extravagance, but now, sitting across from Alex, it seemed a perfectly understandable choice. And then, a thought rising like a miasma: *Only not for us, not now*, and, though he did not know where the thought had come from, it lingered and grew wings and seemed to flutter darkly around the room.

About ten minutes after they arrived, the men went to the bar to get drinks and Laura told Ella about how they had recently moved their younger daughter from public school into a private Jewish school that was located in a town north of theirs. They had only met once before, but they were already quite comfortable around one another and Ella felt close to her. She was touched that Laura brought up a topic of such obvious importance and sensitivity.

Laura said, "It was just getting to be too much. I would've done it sooner but Alex believes in public education."

"Don't you?"

"I don't think we can afford to believe in much of anything these days."

"You sound like my sister," Ella said.

"What's her situation?"

"She's somewhere in the south building bombs and printing ghost guns."

Laura nodded. "I have a cousin who went west to join up with one of those groups. I haven't heard from her lately." Laura paused. "Do you ever think about going down?"

"Not really."

"Alex has started talking about it. For Julia's sake. Maybe she could have some kind of life down there."

"Or she could fall forever. Or she could be a victim of any of the hundred other theories."

"Alex has a contact in one of the Jewish research centers in the Pacific. There is new data about the hole in Buenos Aires."

Ella rolled her eyes. "I'm sure there is," she said.

"You don't worry about Michael?"

"Of course I do."

"You know, I held out until last week. Then some kids pinned her down and drew an eagle on her forehead."

"Why an eagle?"

"I don't know. Whatever the reason was, it can't be good."

"What did the school do?"

"You know. What can they do?" She took a sip of her drink and rubbed her forehead nervously. "Alex wants us to go sometime over the summer."

"Come on—"

"He feels the pull."

"We all do, but still."

"More lately."

"I don't know what to say, Laura."

Ella was aware that Ethan's presence in her life had caused a shift in her perspective. Sitting across from Laura, she wondered if her former identification with the Jews who went through (or at least her compassion for their choices) was ever really rooted in a clear-eyed assessment of the situation in their city—the restrictions that only expanded despite promises to the contrary; the increased sophistication of the apps that tracked their habits and commuting patterns and the updates that made it impossible to uninstall them; the court ruling, just last week, that the increased presence of iron dogs in the Pale was a matter vital to public safety because of the Pale's proximity to the anomaly at the Northlands subway stop. Though she did not share her sister's militancy, before she met Ethan she would rattle off these kinds of talking points with sharp alacrity whenever anyone decried the Jews who went underground as fundamentally irrational. Couldn't they see, she would say, just how easily it could all shift, just how easily the corners of the net could be drawn together. But Ethan's general equanimity had altered her perception. She still followed the trendline, of course, much more assiduously than he did. She was aware, for instance, that she had less work in the wake of an anonymous manifesto on "prudent standards of editorial discretion," which was widely circulated, in recent months, among editors of the city's magazines and news organizations. But, with the surprising advent of Ethan, these kinds of things no longer struck her as determinative. She resented the very suggestion that the harsh physics of unknown forces could disrupt the gentle, emerging orbits of their shared life—her increasingly formless days spent cataloging old work and waiting for emails from editors, the surprisingly pleasing experience of picking Michael up from school and going to a nearby bakery to wait for Ethan, who came back to the Pale on most days, even if he did not always stay over. It seemed more likely to her now that her ability to identify with the Jews who went through had not been based on an honest appraisal of *the* situation but, instead, the result of the idiosyncrasies of *her* situation and she found this realization troubling and also freeing. She never thought of herself as a person who *needed* a partner. She had, in some ways, constructed her identity around the conviction that she did not. But it turned out that like many Jews she had a talent for self-deception.

"I just—I don't know what to tell you," she said. "I'm sorry."

"Didn't you do a whole photo series on it?" Laura asked.

"I did, yes."

"Ethan's always been sort of oblivious, but I would've thought you'd understand."

"What would I understand?"

"I don't know, never mind."

They looked away from one another. It was obvious to both of them that the intimacy of their conversation had soured and Ella wondered if it was her fault.

Then, in the half-light of the bar Ella felt herself drift. The music changed. The light shifted and her friend's face was struck gold, as if by the rising sun. Was it still Laura? It was hard to say. Ella smelled cigarette smoke, coffee, chocolate. A woman was singing toward the back, a rich, dark alto. She wore a black dress with long pendant earrings and her lips were painted red. Behind her was a clarinetist, a man playing a triangular guitar, and a drummer. Ella wondered, vaguely, why she had not noticed them when they came in. Then she stopped wondering. Of course they were there, as she was. She had been tired when they left their apartment—so tired she almost suggested not going out after all—but now she felt strangely invigorated. The city fluttered outside, its busy shimmer revealed and concealed by the glare on the window. She blinked, shielding her eyes. Her friend smiled. Ella felt a deep, abiding sense of belonging, whoever and wherever they were. She was at home in the city.

At the table sitting next to them were two men in dark suits. The man with the mustache was saying, "It's amazing—I hate to say it but everything in the west feels distant. It feels like it isn't real. Like it might as well be on Mars."

"I have a cousin in Romania," said the other man. "You met Feige once when she was here."

"I thought you were going to say you have a cousin on Mars. You know I read that through the new telescopes they can see roads and canals up there. They think it's a dying civilization."

"It's probably Jews."

"Why do you say that?"

"Who travels more than us? What's another planet compared to the *galus*."

The man with the mustache laughed and raised his coffee cup. "To the Jews on Mars."

They touched glasses. The other man said, "Feige lost her husband and brother. And my aunt lost her house. She is supposed to be coming here, if she can get here. It's hard to believe."

"I know, that's exactly what I'm saying. And here we are in this beautiful cafe."

"The violence will come here eventually, just like ten years ago."

Ella looked him over, the man with a mustache, as he considered what his friend had said. His face was thin and full of hard lines—a sharp chin and a prominent nose like the busts of Roman generals she had seen in museums. She remembered a photograph that hung in their living room when she was a child, black-and-white and about eight-by-ten. When her mother first acquired it from her brother it was badly damaged—the left side of the face almost completely obscured—but at some point Ella's parents paid to have it restored and then the picture came to life. A handsome, bearded face with clear, intelligent eyes, a strong jaw, and a beautiful Jewish nose—her great-grandfather's. Ella watched him think.

"Maybe so," he said. He tugged on the corner of his mustache and then picked up a small cookie and dipped it into his coffee. "But not today."

As he drank his coffee, Ella looked around.

The light was fading. She noticed that the music had stopped and when she looked over she was unable to locate the woman who had been singing. Her friend was still sitting across from her. Her face was washed in blue light from her phone, as though she had been encased in stone. But she was not stone. Her face flickered and changed. Ella looked to the men sitting next to her. The man with the mustache wound his watch and the other man gestured to a third friend, who was across the room. He came toward them, carrying drinks, and slid into the banquette next to Ella, their legs touching beneath the table. Ella blinked. She tried to reorient herself to the world. Ethan's fingers were moving against her thigh. Someone, Alex or Ethan, made a joke and the three of them were laughing. But Ella missed the joke. She looked down. Her phone dinged and she saw that she had missed eight text messages, four from her father and four from her sister. She looked down but her face did not unlock the screen so she entered her password.

From her father:

Missed call

mom's not feeling well

Missed call

Please stay by the phone

can u talk?

Missed call

Missed call

we're going to st. mary's, Sophie is flying up

From Sophie:

Missed call

Missed call

did you talk to dad?

Missed call

Where are you?

I'm getting on a plane, will you meet me at st. mary's

Missed call

My plane is delayed. Can you call dad?

Ella?

Missed call

Where the fuck are you?

Her eyes widened slightly. She immediately called her father, then Sophie, but there was no answer. She called again. Again. She texted that she was on her way. Then she looked up from her phone like a diver breaking the surface of the water.

"What is it?" Ethan said.

"I—I missed a bunch of calls. I must have been somewhere else. Were you able to see me from over there?"

"What do you mean?"

"When you were over at the bar?"

"I was turned the other way. Ella, are you okay?"

"Do you think it's possible for time to collapse in on itself?"

"What are you talking about?"

"I don't know," she said. "There was a distortion." Then she said, "In any case, we need to go to the hospital."

ST. MARY'S HOSPITAL WAS ON THE OTHER SIDE OF THE CITY'S LARGEST PARK. ELLA instructed the driver to take the fastest route, which meant crossing the park just below the Pale. After a moment's hesitation the driver assented, probably because Ella seemed desperate and also because he was kind. Ethan asked, in an undertone, if she was sure that was wise and she said that he was welcome to get out. She regretted saying that and he regretted asking and they both rode on in silence, first through the bright streets and then through the leafy dark. And when they emerged the hospital rose suddenly from the ground, lit up white like a wedding cake.

At the security desk, Ella gave her mother's name and the guard told them to follow the blue floor decals, imprinted with Stars of David, to the Jewish wing. They hurried through the bright hallways, following the path carefully even when it twisted irrationally and doubled back onto itself. Ethan walked ahead and Ella trailed behind, looking into rooms as she passed. Each one seemed to contain a marble-sized galaxy, families sealed off from the rest of the world, lost in space. She saw an old man being cradled by his wife. She saw a woman sitting up in bed, her arm adorned with IV tubes, her fingers tapping out a silent melody as doctors and nurses hovered around like white birds. She saw a room that was empty and fresh. She saw a room that was empty and covered with blood. She saw a room illuminated by the blue light of a TV screen. She saw a child sitting at the foot of his father's bed, singing, praying, perhaps. They all seemed precious and impossibly distant, united in crisis but spinning off and spinning away, touching one another not at all.

It was not until they reached the Jewish wing that she hurried ahead, rushing past the nurses' station. Someone called out but Ella did not turn back. In the distance, at the end of the hallway, she saw her father sitting in a chair, his eyes closed, his body slouched forward. She went faster, almost running, and when she reached his side she was out of breath. She said, "Daddy, I'm here," and he nodded and said, "Thank you, honey. We're going to be okay." But she knew, from the moment she saw him, that her mother was already dead.

THEY ALL WAITED. ELLA'S FATHER SPOKE BRIEFLY WITH THEIR RABBI AND THEN WITH someone at the funeral home. Eventually a chaplain came to help lower Miriam's body to the floor. He lit a memorial candle and placed it near her head and he encouraged them to open the windows, which he said was required by Jewish law and which he assured them was allowed in the Jewish wing. The chaplain asked if they needed help with funeral arrangements, but Joel said no, that they were fine.

Joel tore his shirt and sat down on the floor next to Miriam. A minute later, Ella joined him, leaning her head against his shoulder. She wished that her sister was there.

Eventually, she asked her father what happened and he said that he did not know, that her mother said she was cold after dinner and that she went to sleep and he could not wake her. He said he waited too long to call the ambulance and that he would never forgive himself. Ella asked him if they were planning to do an autopsy and he frowned and said *Of course not* and *How could she ask that?* And then they were quiet once again. Ella listened to the soft sound of her father's crying and she tried to think of something to say but she could think of nothing. Now and then she was still surprised when her father's religious observance, which had softened around the edges over the years, reasserted itself in full force. She was sorry that she had asked about the autopsy. And she wanted to cry herself but she did not.

An hour later, when the people from the funeral home still had not come, Ella suggested that her father go home to rest. "I'm not leaving her," he said. But he said it without conviction, and Ella said, "She won't be alone."

"Where is Michael?" he asked.

"With a babysitter," she said. "It's fine, Dad. Let me do this for you." And he nodded and she took him downstairs and put him into a cab. "It's going to be okay," she said. "You can stay with us, if you want."

"Don't be silly," he said, and she watched as the cab moved down the street and away into the night.

When she returned to the room, she was somehow surprised to find Ethan still there. He was sitting on a chair next to her mother's body, fiddling with his phone. He looked acutely uncomfortable.

"Can you get me some water?" she asked.

"Yes," he said. "Of course."

After he left the room, she sat down in the chair that he had vacated. It was still warm from his body and she found it simultaneously comforting and repellent. She decided that when he returned she would ask him to leave, but he was gone for quite a while and she began to wonder if perhaps he was not coming back in the first place. She would have understood and she would not have blamed him.

She dozed. She dreamt that there was a tear in the sky and pounding rain made white by the city lights. As the rain fell the Jewish wing of the hospital filled up, not with water but with people, streams and streams of Jews speaking English, French, Russian, Arabic, Hebrew. They huddled together in the hallways and in the hospital rooms, on and beneath the beds. There was a crush of heat, the damp pressure of body upon body. But there always seemed to be space.

Rooms expanded and changed shape and more Jews came. Ella lifted her mother's body so that they were both upright against a wall with the flame floating above. She felt the foundations of the hospital shake. Outside something was whirring, changing, becoming new. The building shifted and they all lurched forward and the hospital was carried away on a swift river. Outside, she could see a great turbid darkness. She could see lights in the sky.

SOPHIE HAD INTENDED TO REST ON THE FLIGHT. BUT INSTEAD, UNABLE TO SLEEP, SHE fidgeted in her seat and paged through the *SkyMall* magazine. There was a solar-powered, portable shower; a kitty litter box in the shape of an igloo; a camera that could be mounted to the windshield of a car; a karaoke machine the size of a small suitcase; a set of razors inlaid with bone; a small, submersible watercraft about the size of a Jet Ski; an iron dog outfitted for civilian use. It had been many years since she had seen an airline catalog. Once, when she was a child, she remembered asking her mother who bought things from *SkyMall* and her mother laughed and said, "No one."

Sophie closed the magazine and pressed her nose against the window. The world outside was formless and void, but for a faint glow along the horizon, perhaps the lights of a city. She thought about the solar-powered shower and about the karaoke machine and then about the one time she had done karaoke, at a bar just south of the Pale on the night that Ella turned twenty-two. They sang "I Wanna Be Sedated," which was a song by an old Jew who died young.

It was hard for her to believe that there was still a market for such things—for suitcase-sized karaoke machines and showers powered by the sun—just as it was hard for her to believe that somewhere, down below the clouds, her mother was dying. But Sophie had been aware for some time that unbelievable things could indeed come to pass. She had seen Jews emerge from the trees around their encampment, looking for children or parents or vanished towns. She had seen their commander heal bullet wounds with her hands.

With who-gives-a-fuck nonchalance, she turned off airplane mode on her phone and, once more, tried to text her sister. But the message would not go through and, as she waited, she drifted off into a tremulous, addled sleep, somehow inured to the strangeness of the world—a world in which there were people who purchased submersible Jet Skis while flying, in which death could come at any moment, in which the light on the horizon was not a city but a plane, not one plane but five, not five but fifty, not fifty but one hundred, not one hundred but thousands, flying now in formation, circling, circling and then diving down, like arrows from a giant archer.

• • •

WHEN ELLA WOKE UP ETHAN WAS SHAKING HER. HE LOOKED WHITE AND GHASTLY AND at first she almost did not recognize him. His face was transformed by fear. She knew that he was talking but she had trouble making sense of what he was saying. She was still surrounded by the inky substance of the dream.

He said, "We have to leave!" But she could not move. He shook harder. "You need to wake up," he said. "Did you hear me?" He fumbled with his phone. "I can't get through to the babysitter."

"What? What's going on?"

"Something's happening again."

"What do you mean?"

"We have to be quick," he said. "They'll be here soon."

"Who?"

"I don't know. Everyone."

"What are you talking about? Ethan, you're scaring me."

"I'm sorry, but we need to hurry. We should be able to get there if we leave now. The buses are still running."

"I told my father I would stay here."

"We need to get to Michael," he said, "right now." Then he said, "All the planes in the sky fell into the hole where Israel used to be."

WHEN THEY GOT BACK TO THE APARTMENT MICHAEL WAS STILL UP, STREAMING CARtoons on Ella's tablet. Rachel, the babysitter, was sitting next to him on the couch, pecking at her phone with her thumb and biting her lower lip. She looked very small and very scared and Ella's first thought was, *Why did we leave Michael with a child?*

"Oh, Ella, I'm sorry, I—I've just been following . . . I know you said only a little TV . . . I . . ."

"It's okay, Rachel."

"We didn't brush teeth yet. We were about to and then—"

Ethan sat down on the couch next to Michael. "Did you guys have a good time?" he asked.

"We had a great time," Michael said. "We played twelve games of Chutes and Ladders."

"Twelve, wow."

"I won seven of them. And then we were going to go to bed, but Rachel said I could watch a little more TV while she read the news. Is that okay?"

"Sure, buddy. That's fine." He looked up at Ella. "Everything is fine."

Ella held out a folded stack of twenty-dollar bills. "You can go, Rachel. Thank you so much."

"I tried to call my boyfriend but he isn't answering."

"We can pay for a cab," Ella said. She was eager for her to leave.

"Can I even get a cab?"

"I guess I don't know."

Outside, a car alarm went off. An ambulance siren. The sound of broken glass. A loud boom. Michael jumped and ran into Ella's arms. He held on tight until the sounds outside faded and once again the neighborhood was quiet.

"What was that?" Michael asked.

"Nothing," Ella said. "Why don't you watch one more episode and then we'll get ready for bed."

Rachel was looking at her phone blankly. "He told me he was going downtown with friends," Rachel said. "But he always answers. I mean—"

Rachel turned her attention back to her phone and when she did Ethan got up from the couch and motioned for Ella to join him in the kitchen. Absently, he filled her teakettle and set it on top of the stove.

"I don't know if we can send her home," he said. "It might not be safe."

"What do you suggest?" Ella asked.

"I don't know. Fuck. I mean, I guess she could stay here? Jesus, I don't know."

"For how long?"

"I have no idea, Ella. Did you get through to Sophie yet?"

"No."

"Keep trying."

"Sophie was on one of the planes, Ethan."

"Are you sure?"

"Yes," she said. "I'm sure."

He was about to say something else, when Michael called to them from the other room. He said he was tired and he asked if, as a special treat, they could all sleep in the big bed together. Ella glanced at Ethan. She touched his arm and smiled weakly. Then she returned to the living room. *Of course*, she would say. *I think that sounds like a really nice idea*, she would say. *But—*

Ding.

A message popped up on Rachel's phone. Her eyes widened and she dropped the phone to the floor.

Ding.

She fell onto her knees.

Ding. Ding.

Then she fell onto her face.

Ding.

Then she screamed.

Michael said, "Mommy, I'm scared. What's happening to

Rachel? Is it because of the sounds? Earlier we heard sounds and she promised me we were safe."

Ella gathered him up in her arms and carried him quickly out of the room.

"I'm scared," he said again, when they were sitting on the bed. "How long before they get here?"

"Who?" she asked.

"The angry people outside."

"We're not going to let them in."

"Are you sure?"

"Yes."

"I'm scared."

"I know."

"How will you stop them, though?"

RACHEL HELPED MICHAEL FALL ASLEEP AND THEN SHE FELL ASLEEP HERSELF. ETHAN and Ella stayed awake for quite a while. Ethan streamed the coverage on his tablet, alternating between the BBC and CNN. Ella loaded several news websites and refreshed them every few minutes. The EU grounds all flights and institutes a curfew. An apartment building in Qatar collapses, though it is unclear if there is a link. Japan and New Zealand close their borders. Refresh. A post from a famous actor, on location in Croatia, sheltering with his wife, sending hopes and prayers. A bomb in Moscow. A bomb in Zagreb. Refresh. A bomb in Cairo. Refresh. Refresh. Probes enter the Exclusion Zone in the Middle East. No data. No data. Refresh. No data. Refresh. No data. Refresh. Refresh. Checkpoints at European train stations. China closes its borders. Italy closes its borders. A recording artist asks a simple question: What's in it for the Jews? Could someone explain? Refresh. The recording artist retracts. She apologizes to anyone whom she offended. The king of England urges calm—Brits will soldier on. France stands ready, #LibertéEgalitéFraternité. Reports of unrest in Buenos Aires. Refresh. Report: Concerns about the security of the Pakistani arsenal. Refresh. New reports of antisemitic attacks in Belgium, Germany. New reports of antisemitic attacks in Norway, Brazil, Singapore. Ella looked up. Refresh. She heard glass shatter. She heard a boom. Another. Another. Closer, louder. Someone outside yelled, "Death to Jews!" She squeezed Ethan's hand, but he did not squeeze back. She squeezed again and he did. Refresh. The National Aeronautic Association suggests links between anomalies and instrument failures, spokesman says there is no evidence of pilot error. Report: Video tracing the heritage of all the pilots garners three million views, four million, ten million. Refresh. The Man on the Island posts again. Refresh. #HolesNotReal trends. A politician posts that unreleased intelligence suggests a Russian hoax, a Chinese hoax, a Jewish hoax. Report: Physics professor at MIT suggests that magnetic disturbances near holes may have contributed to plane malfunctions. A news anchor dies on the ground in Syria. A statement from the UN condemning any and all acts of antisemitism. A post from the secretary general: We stand united against bigotry in all its forms. Refresh. Iron dogs maul Jewish protesters in Paris. Police investigating. Increasing distortions around the hole in Melbourne, watches not keeping time, rolling blackouts. The Australian Jewish community reports siege-like conditions at a synagogue outside of Sydney. Refresh. Report: Anomalies growing eight centimeters annually, twice the previously measured rates. Refresh. "No Cause for Alarm"—National Academy of Sciences disputes growth claims. Explosion rocks Mumbai. French minister condemns violence, urges journalists not to jump to conclusions. #Notmyneighbors trends. #TheworldisfullofJews trends. Refresh. A post from a Viennese minister urging leaders to take up the Jewish problem. Video meme of people wrapped in Israeli flags travels the world, one hundred thousand uploads, five, two million. Profile pictures change to Stars of David. Profile pictures change to black holes. Refresh. Tens of thousands head north. Militias, formed after the Second Event, remobilize in Mexico, Nova Scotia. Refresh. Canada pledges neutrality. Canada pledges to disband extremist groups. Report: Canadian minister offers to supply guns to the militias. A recording artist posts a hip-hop version of the Israeli national anthem. Refresh. All borders close. Refresh. Flights grounded worldwide, #silentskies.

WHEN HER PHONE RAN OUT OF BATTERY ELLA CURSED AND SMASHED A GLASS IN THE sink. Then she sank to the floor and cried. Ethan held her for thirty minutes. He said that tomorrow they would call about funerals and figure out what to do, but she knew that was bullshit, that there was nothing to do and that, whatever happened, she would not be able to mourn her mother or her sister.

ELLA FELL ASLEEP AT TWO O'CLOCK IN THE MORNING, BUT SHE WOKE UP TWICE, first at three and then again at four thirty. She was both exhausted and wired, and the second time, assuming she would be unable to fall asleep again, she got out of bed and walked down the long hallway to the front door of the apartment. Unthinking and frightened, she put her eye to the peephole—the white fluorescent light, the empty stairwell, nothing, nobody. She took a step back. Her heart pounded.

Behind her, on the small love seat she kept beneath the window on the far side of the entryway, she could hear the soft sound of Rachel's breathing. She was wearing sneakers, her beautiful legs, too long for the love seat, curled up beneath her like a child's. When Ella saw the sneakers, she was filled with a sudden maternal concern—its force and power almost overwhelming—and she knelt on the floor and gently unlaced and removed Rachel's shoes. She stirred but did not wake. Her cheek was glowing from the light of her phone and in the photograph Ella could see the moonlit remains of a Jewish caravan, after the iron dogs had finished their work, along with a text that read, *Weren't your parents heading east towards you?* Looking away, Ella squeezed the phone carefully until the screen went dark. She took a blanket from the arm of the love seat and draped it over Rachel's body and then she turned and walked back down the hall, pausing briefly at the door to the room where Michael slept in Ethan's arms. She considered waking Ethan but decided against it. She thought, *Who knows when or where they'll sleep next*, a thought that seemed wild and irrational upon reflection. She steadied herself along the wall and kept walking. The living room, silvered by the streetlamps outside, took on a strange, lunar quality, and as she made her way to the couch she felt as though she was traversing the surface of a distant world. She was alone. She slept.

WHEN SHE WOKE UP IT WAS MIDMORNING. MICHAEL WAS SITTING AT THE KITCHEN table, drawing and chattering away about dinosaurs. With sunlight streaming in through windows opposite the kitchen, the room seemed stitched through with fire.

Ethan was standing at the stove ladling batter into a skillet. Neither he nor Michael noticed her immediately and she stood watching them. Michael was talking about a dinosaur called cryolophosaurus, a favorite of his because it was unearthed in Antarctica, and coloring furiously.

"Ethan," he said, "did you know the name means 'frozen crested lizard'? Because it was found in the ice!" and Ethan, not turning, said absently, "I didn't know that, buddy, that's pretty cool."

A few seconds later, Michael looked up from his drawing and saw Ella standing in the hallway. He said, "Mommy, can you go back to sleep? I just want to have special pancakes with Ethan."

She smiled and walked over to kiss him on the forehead. "But I want special pancakes too," she said. "Can you share them with me?"

She went to Ethan, who was still facing the stove, and wrapped her arms around him, resting her chin on his shoulder.

"Good morning," he said softly. His whole body was tense and his hands shook as he flipped a pancake, on which he had made a smile out of chocolate chips. The pressure of her chin was hard and definite. He felt better now that she was awake.

"Where is Rachel?" she asked.

"She was gone when I woke up. She left her bag. I found her number in your phone and I tried calling, but she didn't pick up."

Ella nodded. "What are we going to do?" she whispered.

"We can decide later," he said.

"When?"

"Let's just have this morning," he said. "Then we'll see."

Ella made coffee and when the coffee was done, so were the pancakes. The three of them sat together and Michael told a stream of knock-knock jokes, the majority of which made no sense. After each joke, Michael's whole body shook with laughter and this made Ethan and Ella laugh as well. Beneath the table, Ella's hand found Ethan's and he squeezed gently.

Ethan remembered once, when he was a small child, he had a nightmare about the Tasmanian Devil from a Bugs Bunny cartoon.

Whirling around their apartment, it slobbered as it chased him and eventually it scratched his hands, leaving red marks across his knuckles. He knew that if it caught him it would kill him and instead of helping him his parents laughed at him for being afraid. He did not often remember his dreams but this one he remembered with perfect clarity. He awoke, horror-stricken, just before sunrise, and got into his parents' bed, where he would sleep at night for the next two weeks. During that time he would ask them, over and over, if they would save him if a dangerous animal got into the house or if they would laugh like in the dream and they said that of course they would save him and that there were no dangerous animals where they lived and this always made him feel better, at least temporarily. But now, as he listened to Michael's laughter, he once again felt himself surrounded by the dark plumes of a nightmare. They were all laughing now and Ella's legs were shaking beneath the table. But Ethan felt as though someone had ambushed him, a monster sprung from a hidden closet. It was not over in an instant. He did not wake into the light and the dream did not fade. It was thick and sticky as tar.

He said to Michael, "That was a good one, buddy," and he watched him laugh, his shoulders quivering and his head tilted back.

He thought of the Tasmanian Devil and the scars on his fingers. Under his breath he whispered a little prayer. He was grateful that once, long ago, he had learned to move through life terrified.

WHILE MICHAEL WATCHED UNBOXING VIDEOS ON ELLA'S TABLET, ETHAN AND ELLA went into the bedroom to talk. Or rather, they meant to talk. Instead they sat next to one another on the edge of the bed and read the latest on their phones. There was more unrest in the southern part of the city. The mayor made a statement. After twenty minutes of scrolling, Ethan and Ella remembered one another and words started pouring out. It was as though they had emerged suddenly from great depths. Outside they could hear the whir and clatter of iron dogs.

Ella said they should get out of the city. He could work remotely, if the website would still pay him, and at least Michael could be outside without worrying about what might explode. Ethan did not see a point. He said they were as safe here as anywhere. Safer. Things would settle down. She would find work again. He said she had a responsibility to take pictures, to show people what was going on. *But no one seems to know what is going on. We'll find out. But what about going underground? The mayor said . . . The mayor said?! . . . The mayor said?! The mayor is a Jew-hater. So what? How can you say so what?* She said they should not just sit around. She said he was free to do what he wanted. They fought. They said things and took them back. They kept scrolling. They refreshed their inboxes. They kept making calls.

Ethan spoke with his parents at about ten o'clock in the morning. It was different where they were, quieter. After the Second Event, the city where Ethan grew up emptied out, losing almost a third of its population and nearly all of its Jews. Ethan had tried to convince them to move east, but he had been unsuccessful and after a while he found himself unable to argue about it anymore. His parents were both very patriotic. His father had enrolled in the ROTC in college and he served a few years before going on to graduate school. These were some of the best years of his life and they instilled in him a sense of belonging and duty. He loved the country and he loved his city and unlike the others he would not leave. Still, today, the morning after the Third Event, Ethan's father awoke to find that their credit cards had been declined, that their online accounts were locked, that the local bank—a small community bank where they had kept their money for years—refused their withdrawal request.

"Do you remember Frank Preston?" his father asked. "He always kept a bowl of Tootsie Rolls on his desk. Well, he still works there. He's like eighty-five years old. He's the one who refused the withdrawal. He was really apologetic. But he refused. Can you believe it?"

"I can believe it," Ethan said.

"I'm sure it'll get sorted out," his father said. "Just like last time."

"Have you and Mom thought about what you're going to do?"

"Have you heard about the tunnels? How all the holes are connected underground?"

"I've read some things. None of that has been confirmed."

"Do you think it's real?"

"I don't know. What's real, anyway?" Then Ethan said, "Dad, be careful."

"I'm always careful, Ethan."

"Does Mom have enough of her pills?"

"Yes."

"Get cash as soon as you can."

"Okay. Ethan, it's going to be fine."

"I'll talk to you soon. I love you."

"I know that, Ethan. Thank you. I love you too." There was a long silence. The timer timing the length of the phone call kept ticking away.

"Dad?"

"I'm very proud of you, Ethan."

Ethan did not respond.

"Did you know that?"

"What have I done, Dad?" Ethan was struck, all of a sudden, by the smallness of his life.

His father asked, "How are Ella and Michael?"

"I guess they're okay, considering."

"You have a family now," his father said. "Do you understand that?"

"Oh, Ella, she's just—"

"Don't finish that sentence. You have a family now."

"Okay, Dad."

"I want you to say it."

"I have a family now."

"Do you understand what I'm saying to you?"

"Yes."

"I'll see you down the road," he said. "Maybe I'll see you down there. But you don't come back here."

THEY SPENT THE REST OF THAT MORNING AND EARLY AFTERNOON AT HOME, PLAYING board games and folding airplanes and refreshing their newsfeeds. Ella spoke to her father around midday and they decided that he should come up to stay with them, at least until the initial spasm of unrest subsided.

Checkpoints had sprung up overnight like moonflowers. They bloomed darkly on satellite maps. They grew like lesions on highways and on bridges. The subways were running, but not reliably. The harbors were blocked by Coast Guard vessels. The skies remained empty, apart from drones, which hovered over the rivers like prehistoric insects. Ella said that if Joel was going to go uptown he should make the trip soon, that he should not wait even another hour. Joel said that he would bring the gold.

Throughout the day Ella called over to the hospital to inquire about her mother but no one answered. At the funeral home there was an answer, but they could not give her any information about when or if they would be able to pick up the body. There was rioting in that part of the city and there were reports suggesting that some of the rioters made it into the Jewish wing, either by chance or because that's where they were going.

ETHAN LEFT AT ABOUT TWO O'CLOCK IN THE AFTERNOON. MICHAEL CRIED WHEN HE said that he was going and, as Ethan was tying his shoes, Ella also said that maybe he should just stay after all.

"I should at least go back to get clothes," he said. "I'll be quick. I promise. I bet I'll make it back before your dad gets here. And then we'll figure everything out."

As Ethan got ready to leave, Michael sulked quietly near the door. His hair, soft and dark, fell across his forehead, and his eyes, which were pale blue, were teary. He asked Ethan if he was really coming back or if he was leaving for good.

"I'm coming back," he said. "I promise. I'm just going home to get some clothes and my computer. And I can bring back some treats. There is a great bakery near my apartment. How about some really good cookies?"

"I don't want any cookies."

"Okay, no cookies."

"Will you bring Lucy?"

Ethan, still kneeling, looked up at Ella. He had not thought about the dog once over the past day and a half. "It might be hard to bring her here," he said. "She'll be safe at my apartment."

Michael considered this. "What if you get lost somehow?" he asked.

"Here," Ethan said, picking up a plane that they had flown down the hall earlier in the day. "You throw this from the balcony and wherever I am it will find me."

"Really? I don't think that's real."

He smiled. "Try to believe it."

"But how do I know you'll be back?" Michael said, almost crying again.

"I'm telling you I will be. I wouldn't lie to you, Michael. There is nothing I won't do to get back here tonight so that we can all play another game of Chutes and Ladders."

"You promise?"

"I promise."

"You'll really do anything?"

"Anything."

Suddenly Michael's eyes were clear and his voice was steady. "So if you aren't back that means you're dead?"

Ethan and Ella shared a quick glance. He tried to hold her there, but she looked away.

"Yes, Michael," he said, "that's right. If I'm not back that means I'm dead."

VII

THE CREDIT CARD ON ETHAN'S PHONE WAS REJECTED, SO, LOOKING AROUND FURtively, he ducked underneath the turnstile and made his way quickly down to the subway platform. Most Jews avoided the subways in the years since the Second Event, but Ethan rode the trains often, commuting most days to the office building where he and Ella had met. He did so entirely without fear and he believed that the hesitancy of others reflected superstition or even capitulation and sometimes he would try to argue them out of it at parties or over dinner. But as he waited for the train he felt the strange interior pull of the anomaly—always present but generally easy to ignore—with a kind of violent urgency and for several seconds he had to steady himself against one of the steel pillars.

The station was mostly deserted and he waited on the far northern end. He was worried that he would have nowhere to run, should it come to that, but he also thought it would be safer because no one could come at him from behind. Then he laughed nervously as he realized that he had no real frame of reference for anything that was happening to him. When he was with Ella and Michael, only a few minutes earlier, he had felt oddly composed. But now he felt cluttered, disorganized by a nonspecific and all-embracing fear.

The platform trembled as the train approached. His fingers twitched. His body coiled. He was exposed and vulnerable. He was lost to himself. Way down in the dark he felt an animal's freedom, exhilarating and strange. If he had to run he would run until his heart burst.

He got onto the last car of the train and found that he was the only passenger apart from a man on the far side beneath a blanket made of plastic bags and duct tape. When the train jostled, the man hardly moved and Ethan thought that he might be dead. He wondered what, if anything, he should do about it. He noticed that his phone was still getting service and thought briefly about calling the police. But he had a vague and tremorous intuition that involving the police in anything that happened between now and when he planned to return to Ella's apartment that evening was not a very good idea. *Better to keep moving*, he thought. But still he watched the man, who was possibly dead, and so he did not initially see the three others who got on at the next stop, two men wearing army-green hoodies and black boots and a third wearing a red T-shirt with a band insignia on the chest. They sat down directly across from Ethan and looked at him with careful, measured suspicion. When Ethan noticed them, about halfway between where they had gotten on and the next stop, he shifted slightly in his seat and then got up and walked to the opposite end of the car. The man beneath the plastic bags was breathing after all and a few seconds later he opened his eyes and sat up. His whole body shook with laughter.

"Fuck the Jews," he said. "And their sky lasers. Am I right, my man?"

Ethan looked over his shoulder. The three men were still sitting, though they had turned their heads. The one in the T-shirt narrowed his eyes. Ethan had never walked between subway cars before but once he turned he did not hesitate. The handle trembled in his palm and the door slid easily. In came the wind, the heat, the bone-crushing weight, the scream of metal, the black ground beneath the city, the godlike thunder of the wheels, the tumbling violence, the ancient monsters, the world unmade. The wind stung his eyes. He squinted but he did not look back. He went out into the half-darkness. His legs wobbled and blood leapt into his throat. He saw the blur of lights. He steadied himself and stepped through.

The women in the next car regarded him warily. He made eye contact with one of them and then quickly looked away. He was acutely aware of his body, the pulse in his neck, the rapid movement of his chest. Steadying himself, he cupped his hands around his eyes and looked back through the glass. The three men were now standing opposite one of the side doors and he could see them laughing. Meanwhile, one of the women in the new car approached him from behind and tapped him on the shoulder. Ethan twitched and said, "Get away from me, lady."

"It's okay," she said. "We're opposed to all of this. Stay here with us."

"Opposed to what?"

"You know."

"I'm not sure," Ethan said. "Look, I don't want to cause any problems here."

"Exactly," she said, turning to her friend. "This is what I have been saying to you. Why would the Jews want any of this? For God's sake, the biggest hole swallowed up their whole country."

"Jews will sacrifice anything to get a leg up," the friend said, sitting down on a seat opposite Ethan but looking past him. "You know none of the Israelis died in the First Event."

"That's ridiculous," said the other woman.

"It's true. They can travel through from hole to hole. They've got like a network down there. That's how they are. Why do you think so many are going down there?" She glanced up at Ethan. "That doesn't mean they deserve what's happening around here, though. It's not neighborly."

The train slowed and Ethan lurched forward. Hanging onto one of the overhead straps, he saw the three men exit onto the platform and hurry toward him. He waited until he was sure that they were getting on again and then once more he stepped between the cars. He calculated how many stops were left. Seven, if he decided to walk a mile after he got out. Yes, he thought. That was the only thing to do. He would keep moving. The world spun. He passed through two doors, three doors.

In the fourth car he waited. The three men were two cars behind. They were not walking between cars while the train was moving so Ethan thought that he could stay comfortably ahead of them. The fact that the train ultimately ended did not enter his mind. In his imagination it stretched forever.

The fourth car was considerably more crowded than the first three. There was a family of five, a couple resting on one another on the far side near the door, several people traveling alone, a pair of subway employees sharing a pole in the center. He had the impression that he was looking at them from a great distance. His ears were ringing from the sound of the train. He felt like he was still between the cars, even as he sat.

When the train came to a sudden halt Ethan felt a wave of nausea. The voice on the intercom said, "I'm sorry, ladies and gentlemen, we are delayed because of a police investigation at the upcoming station, we hope to be moving shortly."

Ethan's breathing was labored and for a few seconds he was certain that he would vomit. But he did not vomit. He swallowed, wiping sweat from his forehead, from his neck, from the curve of his nose. Then, pressing his cheek against the cool of the window, he tried to compose himself.

In his head, he heard a song that his father used to play when he was growing up about a lonely, angry man who wishes for an alien invasion because he wants to vaporize the world. At the end he crawls over rubble and bodies to ascend into the sky. It was a frightening song and he had never understood why his father, a very social person with a great many friends, liked it so much. Now, he realized that what he did not know about his father—what all people never come to know about their parents—was vast, and that the difference between them was almost unfathomable. How could love survive such a chasm, he wondered, and not only survive but thrive so that it became not just one love among many, but an orienting principle, a cipher through which the secrets of the world were simultaneously concealed and disclosed, a commanding, shattering presence. So it is between parents and children. The intimacy is shrouded in great mystery.

He thought of Ella, hunched nervously over her phone, Sophie with her ghost guns, his father trying to get money from Frank Preston, who was once his friend. He thought again of Michael. What did he really have to do with the boy? Why was it that it was the promise to him that was keeping him upright, helping him blink away the fog, forcing him to run? *Seven more stops*, he thought. *Only seven. Seven is nothing. A mile home is nothing.* He would be fast and light. But he was exhausted. His neck was tight. His stomach throbbed. What if they came for him from two cars down? How would he fight? What would he say? How would he beg? What would he do when it became clear that there was no escape?

Could he break a window? Push the emergency button? The clarity he had experienced only seconds before was pounded by waves of anxiety and confusion. It was pulled under. But still there was Michael, still there was Ella, down there in the shadowy froth. He heard his father's voice. "I want you to say it." And he said it, softly. "I have a family now." He would say it even if they filled his mouth with blood.

He shook himself. He felt extravagantly, cartoonishly out of his depth, as though he had arrived on a distant planet. He decided that he would not allow himself to be caught. He would die first.

He tried to make a plan. The train had stopped near the junction of a decommissioned tunnel and he started thinking about whether or not he could get down safely. If he climbed out between the cars he could probably lower himself safely onto the tracks. But where would he go and why? It seemed possible but not necessarily safer. He peered out into the tunnel, which was strung with caged lights. They cast strange, spidery shadows and illuminated inscrutable lines of graffiti, mysterious and runic, as if remnants of a distant and long-vanished world.

The voice on the intercom said, "Once again, we thank you for your patience, we should be moving shortly," and a short while later Ethan felt the wheels grind. The train seemed to struggle. Then it rolled, slowly. Then it raced on.

At the next stop the three men got within one car of him. He could see their faces, hazy and distorted through the window in the door. They hovered, wraithlike, above a sign that read PLEASE USE EXTREME CAUTION WHEN OPENING THE DOOR WHILE THE TRAIN IS IN MOTION. There were six more stops after that and he decided that he would keep on moving. He would try to stay one car ahead until he reached the front of the train, at which point, when the side door opened, he would sprint north along the platform and reboard the train at the far end. He did not consider leaving the subway altogether. Who knew what he would find on the streets?

When at last he reached his station, he was breathless. He had lost track of the three men somewhere along the way and, looking around wildly, he realized that he was no longer sure if he was being pursued. He went up as fast as he could, ascending two, three stairs at a time, stumbling, smashing his shin, cursing as he felt blood run into his sock, still moving, thinking about Michael, thinking about Ella, as behind him he heard someone laugh, heard a voice that was carried to him as if by magic saying, "Look at the Jew run."

ETHAN SPENT ONLY ABOUT THIRTY MINUTES AT HIS APARTMENT, ENOUGH TIME TO throw some clothes and toiletries haphazardly into a suitcase and to leave his dog in a cage outside the door of his neighbor's apartment. Lucy was a small animal, a dachshund mixed with something else, and she was very old, the last remnant of his relationship with Priyanka, a relationship that occupied his midtwenties and that he once thought would end in marriage. Soon after they broke up she moved out west to take a job at a tech company and he kept the dog. They promised to visit one another in six months to see what was what. But six months became a year and a year became two and then came the Second Event.

Ethan was not overly sentimental. He was not the sort of person to show anyone pictures of an animal. But he did care about the dog, particularly in light of Michael's affection for her. And apart from his parents and a few friends from that time in his life, it was his longest-running relationship. Had someone asked him, two or three days earlier, if he would ever consider leaving the dog outside the door of a woman whom he barely knew, the question would have seemed too far-fetched to answer. But his neighbor always struck him as kind and he was confident, though not certain, that she would take care of the animal.

ETHAN'S GREAT-GRANDFATHER HATED DOGS. AS FAR AS HE KNEW, THE ONLY REASON to have a dog was to bite a Jew. By the time Ethan was born his great-grandfather was well over ninety. But he held him once, just after his bris. They said, "Here, Lazar, this is your great-grandson," their faces, almost indistinguishable, hovering around him like bright spirits, their voices muffled as if carried from a great distance. The old man, his eyes clouded with cataracts, could hardly see the infant. But he could smell him—soured milk and fresh skin and laundered cotton—and he could feel the gentle pressure of the tiny fingers as they held on, reflexively, to his thumb. For an instant, he felt a wave of love and concern for the child and when he did the old hardness rose up in him once again, the clear, merciless kind of love he learned when his own father, half-forgotten, forbade him from eating for a week so that when the Russian army came they would not take him. There were so many things the little Jew needed to know, things that were slipping away from him. And, with a spasm of desperation, he tried to tell him, even though he could not find the words.

ETHAN MADE HIS WAY QUICKLY DOWN THE STAIRS OF HIS APARTMENT BUILDING, HIS suitcase bumping awkwardly behind him. The dog yapped. Ethan did not turn around. When he was in the entryway he paused to glance at his phone and saw that there was still no service. He turned airplane mode on and off. Nothing. The dog barked louder. He leaned his shoulder into the door and swung the suitcase around as the door opened. It was midafternoon. The sound of the dog faded as he hurried away.

He planned to take the subway back, but by the time he reached the station he found that the trains were no longer running. A crowd was gathered around the station, some of them carrying posters and bullhorns, some of them waving flags, a few that Ethan recognized and many that he did not. He was half a block away and he did not get closer. A few police officers were trying to disperse the protesters. They were yelling and hitting people with clubs and two of them were unloading a pair of iron dogs from the back of a car. Soon, Ethan thought, they would activate the dogs. Soon, he thought, there would be tear gas. He had a surgical mask below his chin and he raised it over his nose and mouth, but he coughed nonetheless. Then he felt the heat of an explosion. He fell quickly to the ground, lacing his fingers behind his neck and squeezing his eyes shut. Shards of concrete scraped his hands. Something slashed his arm and he screamed.

When the ringing stopped he could hear the people yelling. He could hear a siren, the chop of a helicopter, the sound of more clubs on windows, on flesh, on bone. He was afraid that he had been blinded but when he opened his eyes the world was bright and clear. He started north, the wheels of his suitcase spinning with gravel and broken glass.

He decided to walk along one of the main avenues. This raised the likelihood of his getting caught up in something, but he reasoned that it was safer than being cornered alone on a side street. The avenue was half-shaded and canyon-like in the midafternoon. It was thick with people, overturned fruit stands, rotten strawberries, little fires, trash, a halal cart selling chicken over rice, a man selling candied almonds, a woman standing on top of a bombed-out car preaching about what was to come, a man sitting in the center of the street with two cats and a sign that said, DYING OF JEWISH RADIATION, PLEASE HELP.

Ethan walked alone for a few blocks and then joined up with a group of people who were also heading north. After his experience in the subway, he was grateful to be walking with others. Most of them were wearing green and blue—ostensibly some kind of uniform—and, though he was not certain, he thought that they were probably armed and perhaps heavily armed. They were flying a banner that Ethan could not immediately identify—not that he was able to identify many of the flags that flew increasingly around the city in those days, the flags of neighborhood watches and fraternities and militias. Based on their colors he thought that they were likely deniers—committed to the idea that it was all some kind of grand hoax—and so probably they were unconcerned that he was a Jew. But, looking around quickly, he did not think any of them were Jews themselves. And he did not ask. When he got back he could tell Ella about it. Because of her work she knew about a lot of the groups, the larger ones anyway, and she held them in universal disdain and had funny things to say about them. She would make a joke about him marching with the green and blue, whoever they were, and she would laugh her bright, easy laugh that always took him by surprise, like sudden rain. Just ahead he saw a group of men smash the window of a white van with a pipe and then pull the driver out onto the street. As they kicked him, Ethan looked away and he tried to imagine exactly what he would say to Ella, a lodestar as he looked north.

They did not make particularly quick progress. The police had set up checkpoints every few blocks, funneling everyone into narrow columns bounded on either side by temporary steel fencing.

At each checkpoint everyone had to turn down a side street, walk twenty paces, cross the street, and then cut back, just like during the Thanksgiving Day parade. The purpose of the checkpoints was unclear. There were no turnstiles, no scanners scanning phones or watches, only officers and iron dogs. The dogs, gun-black and dull, were mounted with rifles on either shoulder and they were controlled by small black tablets in the hands of the officers or by nothing at all. They moved with twitchy, lifelike precision. The officers watched and laughed and for the most part they seemed to be waving everyone along, except periodically when they would pull someone aside for questioning or to ask for a bribe or to bloody their face. These encounters seemed random to Ethan, falling mostly (but not entirely) on single men. They did not appear to be targeting Jews, which made their violence seem utterly inscrutable—inhuman, elemental, and, therefore, unstoppable.

After passing through several checkpoints without incident, Ethan turned to one of the people walking next to him and asked what it was all about. She was a big woman, taller than Ethan, with thick, tattooed arms. Her left eyebrow was pierced with a stud, on the end of which there was a small red jewel. On her back was a large military-style backpack, covered in blue and green patches.

"You mean with the checkpoints? They set them up overnight."

"The mayor didn't make any statements."

"Yeah, well. Who knows where they're getting orders. Maybe it's just so they can shake people down and kick the shit out of them. They don't need an excuse for that. Anyway, they know better than to fuck with us. They fuck with us and we're going to war. Reactionary fascist fucks."

"Where are you all going?"

She looked at him suspiciously. "Why do you care, Jew?"

"Oh, I'm sorry. I don't know. I was just making conversation."

She laughed. "Relax, I'm fucking with you. I used to date a Jew."

"Oh. I see."

"Man, you Jews have no sense of humor."

"We invented stand-up comedy."

She laughed. "Again, I'm fucking with you." Then she said, "We're going to the mayor's mansion. We're going to make it clear where things stand, you get me?"

"I appreciate you letting me walk with you."

"How far are you going?"

"About four miles."

"Up into the Pale?"

"I guess so, yeah. If I can make it."

"You can make it. We'll get you there. You just stay with us."

"Thank you."

"You respect the green and blue, brother?"

Ethan decided it best not to ask what she meant. Likely the answer would have been unintelligible anyway, one of the complicated policy statements common to groups like Sophie's.

"Absolutely," he said. "No question about it."

She nodded. "One marble. One destiny," she said, looking north.

Thirty paces behind, Ethan heard someone scream. He turned back and saw that a police officer had his knee on the back of an older man. He saw the man's legs twitch and blood came from his nose, his ear. Another man yelled, "God save me," and leapt at the police officer, clawing at his face and trying for his gun. A shot. Another. Another. A quick burst of bullets from an iron dog. Ethan looked back but he had trouble understanding what he was seeing. He was unmade by fear.

"Come on," the woman said, grabbing his arm roughly. "Now is not the time to gawk. We need to keep moving."

"Why are you helping me?"

"We're Earthlings. You'd help me, right?"

Ethan blinked.

"You would," she said, and she pulled him on.

Overhead a flock of starlings speckled the sky. They were high and silent and the sun was bright. Along the median the trees were all in bloom.

THERE WERE TWO MILES OF PEACE. UP AHEAD THERE WAS A CHECKPOINT AND BEYOND the checkpoint the park, a green jewel.

Ethan, for reasons that he could not understand, remembered how Priyanka used to love the park, and how she once gave Ethan a hand job underneath a blanket on one of the larger fields. Around them was a froth of people—a softball game, children with Hula-Hoops, bubbles floating up, a group of women doing tai chi, friends sharing a joint, friends sharing wine, children running from their parents, perhaps someone else getting a hand job, someone else getting fingered, surely someone else getting a kiss. These were the ones he could see before he closed his eyes. But there were others, hundreds, thousands blurring into color and light, like ripples across still water, and the apartments and office buildings enclosing them inside a jagged, enveloping bite, the glory of the city, the jaws of life. Her fingers encircled his cock while a softball player circled the bases, while the ball spun in the sky, while the bases encircled the grass, while the streets encircled the park, while the city tumbled along its endless orbits, while the earth spun and the stars wheeled, while the great sphere of the universe turned around them, faster, faster and forever, or so it seemed then. Forever the warmth of the sun on his face. Forever the touch of her fingers. Forever the high, clean air. When he came she smiled and wiped her fingers on the grass. He was twenty-four.

Apart from the cab ride to St. Mary's, it had been a number of years since he was in the park. It was closed entirely following the Second Event, while the national and local officers assessed the threat level. Fourteen months later, when it was clear that the smaller anomalies did not produce the same kinds of distortions as the big hole in the Middle East, the park was reopened. The mayor publicly went for a jog and members of the city council, two of them Jews, hosted a pancake breakfast at the southeast corner, where lawns and sculpted trails opened out onto several grand hotels. But apart from a few select attractions like the zoo and a large Ferris wheel, the park never recovered—not the southern reaches, strewn with manicured lawns, ballfields, and bicycle paths, nor the Northlands, where the park seemed to slip off into a valley of time and the gardens gave way to twisting paths cut with roots and streams and bedrock. It became the province of thrill-seekers and criminals and smugglers and those with nowhere else to go. The gazebos and gardens and bandshells were overgrown. There were coyotes. Some said the raccoons behaved strangely. Ethan did not know anyone who went there.

Ethan found himself daydreaming as they approached the checkpoint. He imagined himself years in the future, dancing with Ella at Michael's wedding. He could hear the music and he could see the revolutions. They would jump and clap and clap and spin. They would lift a chair. Two chairs. The couple would shriek, losing hold of the scarf, but it would make no difference. Still they would spin. Still they would howl. To life! To life! And then heat and then pressure and then something burst. Ethan staggered. There was blood on the ground. The policeman at the checkpoint said something into his radio. There were people lined up against the side of a building. The world spun. Ethan held the wall. Were they still dancing? The circles broke and herniated and life spilled everywhere. A line of officers in riot gear moved forward, shields shining in the sun. They moved in a blur of light. One of the officers shouted, "Get back in line!" before lowering a gas mask. Everyone had masks, like in the early days of the pandemic. The men and women in blue and green were milling around. Overhead were drones, birds, a helicopter. Ethan blinked. His eyes burned. He saw people on balconies looking down but they faded into light and noise. Someone shouted, "I'm not a Jew!" Smoke. Gas. Rubber bullets. Dogs. Iron dogs. The big woman pulled him back and crushed him against the wall. "You stay with us," she said. "Do you hear me?!"

"I can hardly see," he said, "something happened to my eyes."

"It's the gas. It's always the gas with these fuckers. Pull your mask up. We'll take care of it." She pressed something into his hand. "Take this."

"I don't know how to use it."

But she was gone, seized by the undertow and pulled under. The barricades fell. The helicopter was joined by another. More drones. More dogs. Someone threw a Molotov cocktail and Ethan felt glass on his legs, in his legs, blood in his shoe. He ran. Ahead of him a man in uniform held out his hand for him to stop, but Ethan spun. The man swung his baton. He missed. He missed again. And Ethan staggered forward. There was a gash on his eyebrow and blood ran into his eyes. He coughed and spit. Next to him there was a car on fire. He heard a goat bleat. He heard a cat yowl. A police officer stood on top of a van, waving his arms as if trying to take flight. He fell to his knees as a group of protesters rocked the van from either side, one, two, three, four, and over. He went into the crowd and Ethan could no longer see him. Ethan still had the gun, printed in green-and-blue plastic. It looked like a toy but it did not feel like a toy. It was too hard and too heavy. It was a thing for use. His legs and chest burned. The checkpoint was gone. No one was chasing him. Somewhere inside the smoke he saw a dog of flesh, not iron, its insides hanging down as it twitched and fell. The wind picked up. Through a fog of pain and nausea he thought, *The wind will clear the smoke and by then I need to be somewhere else.* He leaned over and emptied his stomach. Ahead of him he saw a mother walking with two children. "Stay by me," she said. "I'm not going to let go." There was blood on her arm and her fingers twitched. "I won't, I won't . . ."

Ethan thought to give them water but he had no water. The wind was cool and fast. Magnolia petals swirled and settled. Stumbling, he ran for the park.

HE DID NOT STOP UNTIL HE WAS HALF A MILE IN, AT WHICH POINT HE SAT ON A BOULDER and investigated his injuries. His head throbbed and there were some pieces of glass in his leg, and when he took his phone from his pocket and turned the camera on his face he saw that his left eye was nearly swollen shut and there was a deep gash on his forehead from which blood dribbled down his face like dark fingers. He tried to understand what was happening to him. He was exhausted but still twitchy with fear. His legs ached and it hurt to breathe, but as he stood up he found that he had no trouble supporting his weight and when he was quite sure he was not dying, he climbed down quickly and kept on, walking first along one of the main promenades near the edge of the park and then cutting in deeper and making his way across a series of gardens and ballfields. He saw overgrown roses, late-blooming tulips, dahlias, a rusted-out soccer goal, a baseball bat covered almost entirely with moss and hardened clay. Then he passed beneath a large stone arch and the light changed. In the distance, to the south, he could still hear the muffled sounds of the city churning. He could hear the wind and the sound of his own breathing and the ringing in his ear and his shoes as they scraped stone.

After walking for about a mile, he made his way across one more soccer field and then ascended onto a clay path surrounding a large reservoir. He planned to circle the reservoir from the east before cutting northwest toward the Pale. He thought this would give him a reasonable vantage point from which to spot anything dangerous. But when he looked around he saw no one. He was alone.

He estimated that it was about a mile and a half between the reservoir and Ella's apartment, but it had been so long since he was last in the park that he was not really sure. Looking down at his legs, which were splotched with blood, he was suddenly aware that he was still holding the blue-and-green pistol that the woman had pressed into his hands. He had never held a gun before and he was struck by how heavy it was and he thought to put it into his pocket or to slide it into his belt like in the movies, but then he realized that he did not know how to do that safely and he worried about shooting himself. He decided instead to pack the gun away in his suitcase, which was singed and covered in soot but otherwise intact.

As he walked on, his head tilted and his eyes drifted listlessly around, not really seeing much of anything. He could no longer hear even the faint sound of the city beyond the trees.

There was no chatter from the police helicopters, no buzz from drones, only the quiet, nimble flight of birds, the sound of a duck as she led ducklings along the edge of the water, the sound of his feet on the clay. And then there was no sound whatsoever.

He thought about the hole, somewhere up ahead. He could feel its pull, the invisible hand that would drag all things in and under.

• • •

ETHAN SKIRTED THE NORTHLANDS, STAYING INSTEAD ALONG ONE OF THE MAIN ROADS north through the park, and reached the exit as the sun was setting. The evening, soft and warm, finally began to settle over the city. Dark clouds gathered in the west.

Before stepping out onto the sidewalk Ethan turned back. On the border of the Pale, the thick trees of the Northlands gave way to a more open area, crisscrossed with bike paths and dotted with a few small playgrounds. It had once been full of hot dog carts and people selling lemon ice but it was empty when he passed through, apart from a single man in beads and torn clothing performing devotions at the memorial to a famous musician who died in the previous century.

But now, as he turned east, he saw a large glass structure that looked like a solarium. It was lit up inside and Ethan saw tables full of customers, men in suits and bow ties and women in long dresses, waiters pushing carts loaded with pastries, fruit, cheeses, the green of hanging plants, the glint of steel urns. There were musicians—a clarinetist, a drummer, a man playing a triangular guitar, a singer in a dark, flowing gown. He could hear the music—the rich, smoky voice of the vocalist and the bright wail of the clarinet. A horse-drawn carriage pulled up in front of the cafe and a young Jewish couple stepped down. There had been a fair number of horse-drawn carriages when Ethan first moved to the city, but they were regulated into nonexistence a few years later by the city council. He could not recall the last time he had seen one. He watched the couple as they went inside. They disappeared into a sugary froth—laughter, music, light. He thought, Who were these Jews who lived so well at such a moment? Then he turned again and left the park behind.

Ella's apartment was only a few blocks away and Ethan walked with his eyes on the ground in front of him, fighting with the suitcase as the wheels caught on damaged chunks of sidewalk, jammed, and then finally broke. He cursed and his voice bounced between the buildings and rang out. The suitcase looked startlingly decayed and Ethan realized that he really had no idea what had happened to him since he left Ella and Michael earlier in the day. He tried to piece it together but everything was jumbled up and absurd. How long had it been? He remembered what Ella had asked about time collapsing, but, to his surprise, he could not fix the sound of her voice in his mind. Already the memory was thin and it hurried away from him and once more the past broke through the filigreed cage that kept it at bay. It no longer spoke the language of clarinets and confections and rich fabrics. It was a monster, wheeling pell-mell through the city and the city towered over him and he felt as though he was traversing a vast canyon. He heard the labored exhalation of rocket fire, but he saw nothing. He dragged himself forward, pulling the suitcase behind him.

The clouds opened—driving, wild rain. His eyes stung. His clothes, tattered and dirty from the walk, seemed to run from his body in great silver streams. He sought refuge beneath an awning. But the awning, torn and singed around the edges, provided very little cover and so he continued on, almost running. The sewers were clogged with leaves and crumbling concrete and other detritus—plastic bottles, burnt rubber, torn tire treads, a stuffed elephant. He passed an older Jewish couple, huddled together on a stoop sharing a poncho. He passed a woman pushing a stroller in which a baby was screaming, but the sound of the child was drowned out by the roar of the rain. Water flowed easily up over the curbs as if rising from the ground.

Ella's apartment seemed to emerge gradually and then all at once, like the prow of a ship. Many of the apartment buildings and streets in that part of the Pale looked the same—the result of a furious period of redevelopment a century earlier—and because the exterior was more weathered than he remembered he thought that maybe he had taken a wrong turn. The bricks all around the entryway were loose and toward the top there were several apartments with boarded-up windows and on the boards were symbols and words that he could not make out. But, lifting his eyes, he saw the rainbows and the paper snowflakes. He saw movement in the window, a vague form blurred by the rain and he remembered when Ella first invited him back, how they passed beneath the stone archway and how she pointed up to the window and said, "That's us."

LATER ON, IN THE DARK, ETHAN ASKED ELLA IF IT WAS A CAR BOMB. "WHAT DO YOU mean?"

"The outside of the building. The boarded-up windows."

"The building is fine. It's just like it was earlier in the day."

"Are you sure? It looked different when I came up. It looked older."

"I heard there was a bomb twenty blocks south."

"But I saw it."

"Maybe you were dreaming."

"I don't think I was dreaming." Then, "Have you ever seen things?"

"What kind of things?"

"I don't know, Ella. I saw things."

She held on to him. "I've seen things too."

"When?"

"In the bar just before everything happened."

"What did you see?"

"I can't explain it."

"Tell me."

"I saw another generation. They were just like us. And then they were gone."

IN THE MORNING THEY WOKE UP EARLY WHEN THE SKY WAS PALE AND THICK WITH birdsong. There had been explosions and sirens through the night but now the city outside seemed strangely quiet, blank and anesthetized, as if after a great snowfall. Ethan and Ella rose very carefully, so as not to disturb Michael, who had climbed into their bed in the middle of the night, tangling his arms in Ella's hair. They made their way slowly down the hall. Ethan's ankle throbbed and he winced as he walked and Ella helped him along.

Joel was already awake and they found him sitting at the kitchen table, streaming the news on his phone. Neither Ethan nor Ella could see the screen, but the voice of the newscaster filled the room like an incantation as he cycled through stories about how the world was coming apart. There was a new piece of anti-immigration legislation in Spain; reports of increased behavioral changes near the anomaly in southern France; a recently released study offering projections about when the anomalies would cover the majority of Europe; a rumor that one of the smaller parties in the Irish parliament was prepared to topple the ruling coalition over some minor issue related to Jewish registration; a document detailing an incident during which thirty-four United States marines heard a voice from one of the anomalies demanding Jews as tribute.

"Dad," Ella said, "how long have you been awake?"

"A while," he said.

Ella walked over to him, leaving Ethan on the far side of the room, and rested her palm on her father's shoulder. With his right hand he reached up and interlaced their fingers and with his left he opened a picture of the four of them, Miriam, Joel, Ella, and Sophie, which Ethan had taken just before the beginning of the seder and in the half-light it shone gently. Ethan, from the entrance to the kitchen, had the impression that he was watching them from a great distance. It was an illusion, a trick of the early morning. It persisted. Joel rose—"*El maleh rachamim, shochen ba'meromim*"—his voice bending along an antique scale and blending with the sound of the birds. It was a tune Ethan did not recognize in a language he did not understand. But as the city came to life outside he knew, at once, that he was hearing a prayer for the dead.

PART II

THE PALE

VIII

IN THE EARLY DAYS AFTER THE THIRD EVENT THE INTERNET WAS AWASH IN POSTS— solidarity, sympathy, rage. The Jewish mayor of a midsized city in the west gained three hundred thousand followers in twenty-four hours, even as Congress created a commission to study the Jewish question, even as the head of the National Academy of Sciences went on television to say that the testimony of the marines must not be dismissed out of hand and that the strong connection between the Jews and the anomalies, confirmed by over a decade of research, will require difficult choices going forward. When asked if the Jews were to blame for their own misfortunes, the scientist said that he would not go that far. When asked if he thought all Jews would one day need to pass through the anomalies, he said that he himself had Jewish ancestry on his father's side. Meanwhile the violence continued throughout the city, not everywhere or all at once, but spasmodically, as this or that militia occupied this or that office building, as the police built wire cages and detention centers outside of important subway stops, as the iron dogs malfunctioned or did not. Every night political leaders posted videos urging caution, urging restraint, urging kindness. Every night another video assuring all Jews that they had a home. Every night a bomb somewhere. Every night a protest. Every night a vigil. From the Pale they saw flags flying from high balconies and atop buildings across the park—Israeli flags, city flags, American flags in only blue and white. After sundown, one of the tallest skyscrapers in the city, a towering office building that rose into the sky just south of the park, illuminated select windows in order to spell out WE ARE ALL JEWS. But as the summer went on the flags were carried away on the wind. Or they were torn down. Or they were burned. Internet posts were replaced and replaced again. A month after the checkpoints went up the building's windows changed to JEWS LIVE IN ALL LANDS and in the Pale the Jews were left to wonder what the change could mean. They argued about it—at home, in schools, on the streets, in the synagogues. But no one could agree and there was no one to ask. Leaving the Pale through the checkpoints was no longer so simple and soon enough it was nearly impossible. The procedures were byzantine, the barriers mostly impenetrable, and those who knew the answer, if there were such people, were on the far side. Then the second message faded as well.

Life stopped but time stirred. It was most evident, at first, in the breakdown of appliances, the cabinet door that required a piece of duct tape to ensure it stayed closed, the dishwasher that left oily streaks on all the dishes on the bottom rack, the blender that only worked on speeds two and five, the hinges on cabinets that loosened and broke, the internet connection that slowed to a crawl. It was impossible to stream videos during peak hours. And then there were no peak hours. And then, throughout the Pale, there was no more new content to stream.

Ella's smart fridge stopped functioning after about a month and online ordering stopped shortly after that, which caused shortages and a week of riots and this led to further restrictions. The city constructed a large warehouse adjacent to the checkpoint on the southern border and stocked it with groceries, clothes, approved electronics, medical supplies, soap, and hardware. It was managed by a series of rotating officers, who also served as points of contact between the newly formed neighborhood council and the city government. The managers were bureaucrats, as far as the Jews could tell, but they commanded a small group of guards and they wore police-style badges and, in addition to managing the flow of goods, they also oversaw passage through the checkpoint. Before long they began distributing ration cards as well, along with a new paper currency, styled the Standard Palemark. Luxury items like wine, drones, and new computers were smuggled up through an abandoned subway station at the northern border of the Pale or across the park from the eastern part of the city, and these things were relatively plentiful, or not, depending on the mood and temper of the manager at any given time, and the managers rotated in and out and their moods were as inscrutable as the weather. Meanwhile the weather rolled on. Meanwhile the Pale sank further into itself.

The drainage sewers on side streets remained clogged with debris and when there was heavy rain the streets would fill with water and children would go outside to play with their friends. Sometimes they would not wait for rain and the older children on the street would open a fire hydrant. Sitting in their living room—pecking away at their laptops when the internet was available—their parents could hear them as they played. They would go over to the window and look out on the high arch of the water and the children kicking up rainbows and somewhere, in all that water and all that light, laughter. For the younger ones, life in the Pale was remarkably normal at first and in some ways more pleasant than it had been before. They made friends. They learned to read. They started learning to code. They went to school, just as they had gone to school before, only the children and teachers were nicer to them. They did not understand, at first, that the lives of the adults around them had changed radically. They only knew that now everyone lived together, grandparents, aunts and uncles, cousins, which was wonderful and exciting, and then when they did come to understand it more it did not seem strange because it was all they could remember. Their parents were grateful that they were happy but they were also conscious of the fact that the happiness of the youngest children created a certain distance between them—their experience of that time being so different—and this troubled them and they comforted themselves thinking that their children were young and maybe it would end and they would remember none of it. But for many of them this was not comforting. If they had work, they worked. If they did not, they borrowed or begged or bartered, navigating the strange, insular economy created by the Palemarks, which were increasingly the only kind of currency anyone had apart from gold. They argued about how much they should tell the children and about what they should know and about what they already did know, and each family made choices, as families always make choices, eventually coming to celebrate or regret them.

The skies were quiet, apart from the war planes that periodically and inexplicably ripped over the city. Meanwhile people continued to see and experience things, visions either private or shared. Some people called them miracles, but what is a miracle? There was the time that a great airship appeared in the sky, dipping briefly below the clouds, and then climbing out of sight. There was the time when all street signs changed to Yiddish. There was the time that a pack of wolves came out of the park. There was the time that three square blocks were swept up in a wedding party, though nobody knew the bride or groom. There was the time when parents panicked because a beggar who slept by the river came to a meeting of the newly formed neighborhood council to say that he saw twenty children playing by the water and that they all became fish and swam away. There was the time that mountain goats appeared on rooftops across the Pale. There was the time when the cantor at a synagogue wore a white miter hat that vanished and reappeared throughout the service. There was the time when winged creatures appeared in the sky. There was the time when all the trees bled. They did not last long, the miracles, and many assumed that they had something to do with the anomaly in the park, though no one could say what. They were fleeting and unstable. They did not take place beyond the checkpoints, where the city went on with its life, the convulsions having subsided into a timorous calm. As they became more and more commonplace the Jews began to ignore them. It was possible, they learned, to live with a great many things and no one talked much about what they saw or did not see. In any case, what was there to say? Jews had been through worse. They had seen miracles more magnificent.

The non-Jews left, for the most part, before the start of the first school year. It was not an injunction. It was an understanding, deeper and more powerful than law, and after the exodus was complete the population of the Pale was smaller by two-thirds. The streets, which in that part of the city were accustomed to a constant thrum of activity, became quiet and eerie. Garbage trucks continued coming through checkpoints, but less frequently, and the excess trash, combined with the relative quiet, lured raccoons and a coyote from the park. The children were frightened of the raccoons but the coyote became a mascot and they named him Lazar Wolf and spotting him at night was considered a great accomplishment.

Beth Israel hospital was understaffed but not dysfunctional. Some of the doctors organized a six-week course to train nurses, aides, and other paraprofessionals and this was well attended, especially by those who were out of work, and it was offered quarterly. In this way the hospital was able to keep up with need, for the most part, though there were some exotic cases that they could not handle and then families had to apply for a dispensation to cross the park and go to St. Mary's. When the dispensations came through, a city ambulance would arrive to take the Jews away, an occurrence that became increasingly fraught as time went on, as the streets became quieter still. The public school buildings, which had been somewhat overcrowded in recent years, now had ample space. They received funding from the city—a controversial decision of the city council—but there were staffing shortages. As entering the Pale through the checkpoints became increasingly difficult, teachers from outside came less and less. And then, following Thanksgiving, they did not come at all, apart from a few activists who wanted to "raise awareness." An ad-hoc school board was set up and parents were enlisted to teach lessons or mini-courses.

The main funeral home in the Pale was destroyed during an early riot and so the dead were honored at a community chapel housed in a corrugated metal warehouse adjacent to the southern checkpoint. A rabbi set up an office there and he conducted the funerals as the guards looked on. The services followed one another with only minor variations because all are alike in death and because nothing else was possible. To the families he would say, "May you all be comforted among those who mourn for Zion and Jerusalem." Then he would nod to the guards and they would carry the body away through the checkpoints, for burial, so they said.

• • •

FOR ETHAN AND ELLA THE CITY BEGAN TO TAKE ON A HAZY, DREAMLIKE QUALITY. ON warm nights during the first summer, after Michael was asleep, they would go up onto the roof of the building and look south toward midtown, a conflagration of light and life that seemed strangely still at such a distance. Sometimes they saw smoke rising. Sometimes a helicopter flew low across the skyline. But mostly the city beyond the Pale seemed motionless. If the neighborhood council had recently managed to procure an allotment from the dispensaries, they would share a joint and fold airplanes and watch them disappear into the night and it seemed to both of them that the planes carried an impossible weight of memory and hope out over the scarred streets. But they never spoke of it. They talked about Michael, mostly, and about her father, who seemed frail of late. They kissed. And sometimes, if it was very late, they made love on the roof, shyly at first, until each time they overcame their inhibitions and they were slicked with desire and then she would lower herself onto him, her small breasts pressed up against his chest, the warmth of their bodies sealing them away inside a private darkness.

The subway started running again about a month after the Third Event, though it did not serve the Pale. It bypassed all but the first station at the southern border, which was, in any case, only open to checkpoint personnel and to cops and to subway workers and to members of the neighborhood council when they received a dispensation to travel south. But they could hear the subway cars as they passed beneath them, the dark growling of the past.

One night, when they were on the roof, a drone flew west from the park and hovered directly above them for three minutes. They were both a little bit high and when they saw the drone they became quite nervous. They stood very still for about thirty seconds. Ethan whispered that they should get downstairs out of sight. But

Ella, after an initial surge of paranoia, burst out laughing and raised her middle finger to the sky.

"Come on," he said. "What are you doing?"

"I'm telling whoever is watching us to fuck off." She tilted her head back. "Fuck off!"

"Let's go down," he said.

"No," she said. "Look, it's doing something."

The drone descended forty feet, its white frame struck aglow by the city lights. It rotated one hundred and eighty degrees and came to hover at eye level. A smooth woman's voice said: "WE APPRECIATE THE COOPERATION OF ALL JEWS DURING THIS DIFFICULT TIME. WE ASK THAT YOU NOT LEAVE THE PALE UNLESS GRANTED PERMISSION AS SCIENTISTS BELIEVE THAT THE MOVEMENT OF JEWS MAY CAUSE THE ANOMALIES TO EXPAND FURTHER. PLEASE CONTROL YOUR SOUL'S DESIRE FOR FREEDOM. HUMANITY THANKS YOU FOR YOUR SACRIFICE." They did not move. The blades spun. The drone trembled. Again: "WE APPRECIATE THE COOPERATION OF ALL JEWS DURING THIS DIFFICULT TIME. WE ASK THAT YOU NOT LEAVE THE PALE UNLESS GRANTED PERMISSION AS SCIENTISTS BELIEVE THAT THE MOVEMENT OF JEWS MAY CAUSE THE ANOMALIES TO EXPAND FURTHER. PLEASE CONTROL YOUR SOUL'S DESIRE FOR FREEDOM. HUMANITY THANKS YOU FOR YOUR SACRIFICE."

A FEW WEEKS AFTER THE CHECKPOINTS WENT UP MICHAEL GOT INTERESTED IN PRImates. Neither Ella nor Ethan knew what, if anything, had given rise to Michael's new fascination, and its sudden intensity startled them. During the weeks when it was still possible, he downloaded hundreds of monkey videos and watched them over and over. He also found as many books about them as he could and paged through them until they were falling apart. For several months, most every day he would write and illustrate monkey guidebooks and prepare presentations that he would deliver to Ella, Ethan, and Joel during breakfast or after dinner, or he would go to the library and read them to whomever would listen—other children, parents, librarians, or the custodian, an Eritrean man who was one of the few non-Jews still living in the Pale. The head librarian happened to be an older Jewish woman who had worked at that branch of the public library for many years, which meant that the library was one of the few municipal institutions that continued its work more or less as usual, even after the checkpoints went up. Joel would bring Michael there many afternoons and he would always read a book called *Lemurs of Madagascar*, until one day—*the best luckiest day of his life!*—the librarian gave it to him as a present.

That evening, as they were working on a thank-you card for the librarian, Ms. Herzog, Michael asked if he could have his birthday party at the zoo, and without really thinking, Ella promised that they would make it happen and that he could invite as many friends as he wanted. She told him that even though the zoo was closed to Jews at the moment it would certainly open again by the time of his birthday and Michael lit up and hugged her and said that that would be the best present. Later on, as gently as he could, Ethan questioned the wisdom of promising something they were not sure that they could deliver. But Ella said he was being alarmist and needlessly negative and of course they would be able to have a party at the zoo, of course things would be different by then, of course things would change. The city had experienced these kinds of spasms before and things had always settled down. Ethan disagreed and said that they should at least consider the possibility that the situation was substantively different. He reminded her that when they first met, their positions about the state of things had been more or less reversed and he asked her what had changed and she said that she could ask him the same thing and their disagreement metastasized over the course of several days and eventually culminated in a vicious fight. Ella said that if he thought life with them was hopeless he was welcome to leave for the underground at any time and she said that he had glommed onto their family in a moment of stress and that he was using them for who knows what. He said that she was ungrateful and that she had become willfully oblivious and self-hating. She said that he didn't know anything about Jewish life or Jewish identity, that when she met him he had been indistinguishable from any city shaygetz, no matter who his friends were now. He said that she was a cold, resentful mother and why not do everyone a favor and head north to be with Michael's father and the other Jew-haters in Canada. She said he was an unserious, frivolous person. He said she was unlovable and careerist and self-serving. She said he made her want to die, that she was going to go up to the roof and jump off, that she couldn't live with him and her father and Michael anymore. He said if she felt that way then they would be fine without her.

They continued screaming until Michael woke up, frightened, and asked if the bad people from outside the Pale were coming to get them. If so, he said that they should all try to be nice and quiet so that maybe they would not notice them. Ella said, "That's a good idea, honey," and together they walked Michael back into the room they all shared. He fell asleep in minutes, his soft, easy breathing warming the space between them and restoring them, at least in part, to one another. But over the next few days they fought several more times, increasingly aware that their disagreement about whether or not to promise Michael a party reflected a deeper and more profound breach between them and a surprising inversion of their former tendencies. Neither of them was reacting to the situation in the Pale as they would have predicted. They seemed alien to one another and to themselves.

In Ethan's mind, Ella's blindness to their circumstances was mostly a product of her professional situation, which was, on balance, a great blessing. During one of the lulls in their weeklong conflict, Ethan recalled the days after they first met, how he had searched for her name online and finally found her photo essay about the Jews who were going underground. He had been moved by the sensitivity and the urgency of Ella's work, even as her apparent perspective—that the choices of the people in the photographs were intelligible, if not entirely warranted—seemed outlandish to him at the time. He had thought her a radical, which intrigued him but which was also foreign to his sensibilities, and thought her radicalism was bound up in her photography. But now, ironically, her work had precisely the opposite effect on her. Soon after the checkpoints went up, Ella secured a job documenting life inside the Pale for a progressive magazine in the city. And because she continued to work regularly, if remotely, with non-Jews, it was hard for her to imagine that the harsh restrictions would last much longer. The magazine that bought her photographs often organized virtual retreats and team-building exercises and meet-and-mingles for their stringers, and Ella joined these frequently and with more enthusiasm than Ethan ever would have predicted. She would sit at her computer with a glass of wine, when wine was available, and she would laugh and laugh and Michael would ask, "What does Mommy think is so funny?" and Ethan would shake his head and say he didn't know. And any day she expected that something—she could not say what, precisely—would change, and that when it did they would reclaim their old lives like soldiers returning from war.

For Ella, meanwhile, Ethan's increasing fatalism was mysterious and disquieting. When they first met, his sense of himself as a Jew was attenuated and slight, a minor inconvenience like passing rain. He was unconcerned about the state of things in the city and, like a lot of the deeply secular Jews that she knew, he thought that the real danger lay in the shared delusion that they were in some kind of grave danger. They had argued about it more than once. But this perception had been altered, somehow, by his journey back to the Pale on the day after the Third Event and Ella could not shake the feeling that the person who returned to them that evening was not quite the same as the person who left earlier in the afternoon.

He, along with many others, lost his job a week after that, and in the days and weeks that followed, Ella had to remind herself often that his was the more common experience, that her own situation was unique and lucky. By midsummer, having little else to do, Ethan had become actively involved in a number of community initiatives. These included sitting on the school board, which was in the process of figuring out how to open schools in the fall, and also joining an ad hoc committee—really a subcommittee of the neighborhood council—that was tasked with monitoring and trying to increase the flow of information into and out of the Pale. This they hoped to accomplish by finding and destroying some of the government surveillance boxes shortly after they were installed and by trying to jam the drones that hovered over the checkpoints. The committee would meet in what had once been a sixth-grade classroom in one of the middle schools that had fallen into disuse, and then they would roam around the Pale at night, sometimes making progress, but often enough (at least as far as Ella could tell) spending much of the night drinking and planning and talking politics at a bar called Isaacson's. There were Jewish separatists and new-Zionists; secularists who advocated for working with the city authorities; Israelis who had been abroad during the First Event and who observed Yom Ha'atzmaut as a day of mourning; militants who advocated for an uprising; orthodox rabbis who advocated quietism and acceptance, as they had centuries earlier; *ba'alei teshuvah*, the newly religious who preached about God's wrath and about repentance and fasted on Mondays, Thursdays, and Sundays; a group that called themselves the Rabbits and urged Jews to give in and head underground. Ethan would come home, sometimes a little drunk, and he would be on fire with this or that argument, arguments that were, to Ella's mind, invariably tired and exasperating and beside the point, because there was no point that she could see apart from trying to carve out a little life for Michael, insofar as she could, and that meant keeping her job for as long as possible, promising him a party at the zoo, trying her best to believe that there was still a future for them in their city, the only city she had ever known, because there certainly did not seem to be a future anywhere else. Increasingly, however, she found herself drawn into the past. She remembered when her father would come into their room before bedtime, how he would recite the *Shema* with great emotion, lingering over the verse about "teaching the words to your children." And she remembered him visiting her in the hospital, just after Michael was born. "Listen, Ella," he said, as he sat on the end of the bed, "now your job is to make sure it doesn't all end with you," and she watched with fascination as he stood up and carefully adjusted Michael's pink-and-blue-striped hat. She knew from her mother that he had once professed a desire not to have children at all and as Ella tried to make sense of Ethan's behavior she pictured her father standing over Michael's bassinet and she thought, *Well, people change, sometimes in dramatic ways.*

It was true Ethan made friends this way—going to meetings, drinking at Isaacson's—in particular Moti Shafran, whom he had only known for a few months but with whom he was already quite close. Moti was a coder from Israel who had gone on a work trip when he was twenty-three, two days before the First Event, leaving behind his wife and infant daughter. He spoke of their disappearance without bitterness, which struck Ella as strange and she did not entirely trust him. In addition to sitting on the tech committee, Moti formed a neighborhood militia called "From Their Hands," or, informally, "Moti's Crew," a group of men and women who started printing guns and making Molotov cocktails and doing business with the smugglers who met them in the Northlands or who came up through a subway station on the northwestern edge of the Pale, appearing suddenly, like harried commuters. Some of them were activists but most of them opportunists, and they accepted dollars and sometimes Palemarks but preferred gold or silver, which members of Moti's Crew gathered from abandoned apartments. And in these things Ethan was a partner as well.

All of this—the meetings at the school, the vandalism of city property, his involvement with the smugglers—was unsettling for Ella. She understood that the activities meant a great deal to Ethan and she was grateful that he had something to occupy his time, but they were not things she had imagined he would do. He was such a gentle person, quiet and careful, and this was among the things that she had initially found attractive about him. But one day at the end of June he suggested that Michael learn how to handle a gun safely and when she said that she did not think that was such a good idea he brought her into the bedroom, took his tattered suitcase down from a high shelf in their linen closet, and removed the green-and-blue pistol from the outer pocket.

"Why do you have this?" she asked.

"Someone gave it to me on my way back here," he said. Then, sensing her confusion, he added, "On the day I went down to my apartment."

"A member of a militia?"

"I don't know who she was."

"I believe it's the colors of a group called the Earthlings," she said. "They have some theory about the anomalies and aliens."

"Well," he said, "I guess it's ours now."

"I want it out of the house."

"The schools might require shooting lessons starting in the fall."

"There is no way I am letting Michael do that."

"What are we going to do, then?"

"I don't know, Ethan."

"We need to plan. What about going through?"

She looked at him intently. "What about it?"

"Well, you did that whole photo series on people preparing to go underground."

"So what? You said yourself they were crazy."

"I think we should talk about it."

"We have no idea what's actually down there. Maybe it's nothing."

"It can't be nothing."

"Why not?"

Ethan walked over to Ella and gently took the pistol from her hand.

"I just know it somehow."

"That's insane, Ethan. I don't want to discuss it."

"We need to discuss it eventually."

"It would be too hard for my father."

"That can't be the only reason we don't talk about it," he said.

"Well, anyway, it can wait until after the party at the zoo," she said. "You'll see. We'll have the party and you'll feel different."

THAT AFTERNOON, WHILE ELLA TOOK MICHAEL TO A PIANO LESSON, ETHAN MET MOTI at Isaacson's. They sat at a small table near the window and looked out onto a large square. In the center of the square was a subway station that had been a major transit hub in that part of the city. In the months since the trains stopped serving the Pale, the station itself had become a kind of public monument and meeting place—rabbis preaching from overturned crates, militia leaders registering volunteers, men and women selling fruit, soap, electronics, shoelaces, live animals.

Everywhere the smell of rotten bananas and apples crushed into the sidewalk, everywhere people and faces, everywhere birdshit. The domed glass structure that enclosed the entrance to the station was covered with pamphlets; advertisements for lectures and musical performances and meetups, notices about lost items; tear-away coupons offering violin lessons, housekeeping, medication; flyers with faces of missing children, missing spouses, missing parents; coded messages about smuggling runs; political ads; cartoons; instructions for building bombs; prayers in English and Hebrew; all of them overlapping and rippling in the wind. And now, as Ethan looked out, one of the flyers came free and traveled up into the sky.

"It's a mess out there," Ethan said. "Look at this guy—" He pointed to a man who was singing and whirling and trying to draw passers-by into a wild dance.

"It reminds me of the shuk in Jerusalem. Did you ever go there when you were a kid?"

"No."

"There were always guys like that dancing around."

"Why?"

Moti shrugged. "Some rebbe taught them that when they danced they could kick away the evil in the world. Apparently some of them danced right down into the hole."

"Says who?"

The waiter, a skinny man with a mustache, brought drinks along with some pickled tomatoes. "I can't believe they still have these," Moti said, pointing to the tomatoes.

"Nobody ever liked them. And I'm pretty sure I've seen that guy throw them back into the bucket when people don't eat them. I don't know why he puts them out."

"Sam tells him to do it."

"I guess so."

"Sam is a zealot when it comes to those tomatoes."

"I'm sort of developing a taste for them."

Ethan watched as the waiter went back behind the deli case, which held only liquor. The floorboards, which bore the deep imprint and glossy patina of thousands upon thousands of steps, squeaked beneath his feet as he walked. Before the checkpoints went up, Isaacson's had been a cafe and appetizing shop. It had been in operation for nearly a century. For many of those years it was a popular tourist destination, and Steve Isaacson, the great-grandson of the original owner, was a prominent resident of the neighborhood. But about a month after the Third Event, customers arriving on a Friday morning hoping to buy lox or chubs or onion rolls or schmaltz herring, found the grate down and a sign that read: LIKE MANY JEWFISH BEFORE ME, ISAACSON HAS RETURNED TO THE OCEAN. A few days later looters came and made off with the lox and most of the remaining herring. A week after that a man named Sam

Kramnik came looking for the last of the fish, but all he found were buckets of pickled tomatoes and several cases of booze in the basement—bourbon, mostly, but also gin, vodka, schnapps, and arak. The booze had been overlooked and the tomatoes nobody wanted and the whole place still smelled of fish. But Kramnik had just lost his job at a financial firm in the city and, like many others, had spent the last few weeks in an aimless, agitated haze. So without asking anyone's permission (there was no one to give it), he tore down the grate and reopened Isaacson's as a bar. After only a short time it became something of a neighborhood institution, its success, as far as Sam Kramnik was concerned, tied inextricably to the pickled tomatoes, which seemed to multiply in the brine and never ran out. Isaacson's was always busy. People who had work came after work and people who had dates came on dates and the vendors in the square came when the market closed and sometimes the border patrolmen came for free drinks or to see if they could fuck a Jew one way or the other. As was the case wherever there were large gatherings, there was almost always drone surveillance outside, and if Kramnik was there he would sometimes drag a bucket of pickled tomatoes outside, throw a few at the drones, and yell, "See, motherfuckers, little miracles happen everywhere!"

Ethan bit into a tomato and winced. "You know this will prevent scurvy for like a whole year."

"Are you going to sea?" Moti asked.

"There is less and less fruit coming through. You never know." He took another small bite and then pushed the plate aside. "I still say he throws the tomatoes back and that's why they never run out."

"It's as reasonable a theory as any of the others." Moti laughed. "Well, whatever is going on with Kramnik's tomatoes, we're not going to allow people to starve. We're going to take the fight right to them."

"We can't win, you know."

"You're a fatalist."

"I'm not."

"Okay, listen: It's 1975 and there are some Soviet generals in a war college and they're briefing students on the inevitable conflict with China, and one of the generals explains that they are going to be outnumbered ten to one. One of the students, distressed, says that the situation is hopeless. *Not true*, replies the Soviet general. *Just look at the Yom Kippur War. Three million Jews defeated thirty million Arabs. Sure*, says the student, shaking his head, *but where are we going to find three million Jews?*"

"That's funny," Ethan said.

"You're not laughing, though."

"I'm just saying I don't see the point in pretending we can do something we can't."

"So you're some kind of accommodationist now?"

"I'm keeping my options open."

"Ella's rubbing off on you."

"You know, she used to be a radical. She had views similar to the Rabbits. Less extreme."

"What happened?" Moti asked.

"I'm not sure," Ethan said. "She wants Michael to have a normal life. It's hard to know in advance how you will really respond to a thing. Look at me."

"I see a limp-dick dabbler."

"You're lucky I never take you seriously," Ethan said.

Moti threw back a shot of arak. "Have faith in the cause, *achi*."

"I don't know how you drink that stuff."

Moti blinked slowly. "It reminds me of home."

Ethan nodded. "How old would your daughter be now?" he asked. "Twenty-one, I guess."

Moti was quiet.

Then Ethan said, "I'm sorry. I don't know why I asked you that just now."

"It's okay, *achi*. Anyway, look, we need to go into the park again."

"Yeah, okay."

Moti got up and stepped toward the door. "Wait," Ethan said. "You mean right now?"

"Kyle said there is some stuff coming in from the East Side that we'll want to see."

Ethan said, "Do you even know who we're meeting?"

"The text was from this smuggler who lives somewhere east of the park," Moti said. "I've met him a few times. He has interesting things for sale. He comes with his wife. We'll see. They're Jews, actually."

"Really? How many can there be outside the Pale at this point?"

"I don't know. They must have made an arrangement of some kind early on. I think the husband worked at City Hall. They were on an exemption list."

"I didn't know those still exist."

"They aren't the only cryptos."

"I don't understand why we call them cryptos," Ethan said. "Everyone knows they're Jews."

Moti stood in the doorway and shrugged. "What can I tell you? There are Jews everywhere, just like they all say."

Ethan and Moti left Isaacson's and rushed across the street. The Pale had cooled in the late afternoon and a pleasant breeze swept west from the park. At the northeastern corner of the square, opposite the entrance to the subway station, there was a teenager standing in front of a folding table. On the table there were pairs of tefillin and prayer shawls, along with several prayer books, and whenever a man would pass by he would say, "Excuse me, are you by any chance Jewish?" He could not have been older than sixteen and he seemed oblivious to the irony of the question and also to the irony of Moti's response.

"No," he said. "No Jews here today."

KYLE BENTON MET THEM JUST OUTSIDE THE PARK, THE SHIRT OF HIS GRAY UNIFORM untucked and his sidearm hanging haphazardly off his hip. He was sitting on top of a large boulder—common in the northern part of the city where the bedrock was exposed—and when he saw them he waved and shouted something they could not quite make out. After hopping off the rock, he sauntered down a small hill and into a narrow corrugated-steel vestibule that had been set up near the entrance to the Northlands. Then he opened up a tablet and, with swift fingers, redirected the drone that was monitoring them from just above the trees. The three of them watched as it buzzed out over the park and landed softly in a field about a block south.

Kyle turned back. He had a soft, doughy face, with a rough beard that was beginning to go gray. As Ethan and Moti walked forward, Kyle stepped out of the vestibule, slid his baton from his belt, and raised it above his head.

"What the fuck do you hymies think you're doing? You know the park is restricted this week."

"Come on, Kyle," Moti said. "I'm not in the mood right now."

Kyle brought the baton down hard, missing Ethan's arm by a few inches and sending little pieces of gravel flying. Ethan jumped. Kyle laughed and adjusted the holster of his pistol.

"You're an asshole," Ethan said.

"I thought you Jews loved assholes," Kyle said, making a hole with the thumb and forefinger of his left hand and sliding the index finger of his right hand in and out.

"Fuck off, Kyle," Moti said, and Kyle, suddenly no longer smiling, said, "Careful, kike. You never know what a big goy like me is capable of."

"I've got a pretty good sense," Moti said. "Look, you said to be here on time. We're going to be late now."

"It's always business with you people, isn't it? Let me give you a piece of advice. There is value in the human touch."

"That's what you have?" Ethan asked. "The human touch?"

"Absolutely. Ask Abby. She's a Jewess who comes to see me here in the mansion." He smiled and pointed toward the vestibule. "In exchange for smartphone cases. She sells them on the street."

"You're disgusting," Moti said, handing him a fifty-dollar bill. "Come on, let's get to the station."

The three men went along a paved road and then turned left into the Northlands—a lush, heavily wooded section of the park that stood opposite the Pale to the east. The Northlands had an almost tropical quality at the height of summer and they walked on a hiking path next to a narrow stream.

"It's quickest this way," Kyle said. "And it minimizes the chances that we'll be picked up by any drones."

"You know," Ethan said, "if the goal is for us all to go down through the anomalies maybe you should just open the park all the fucking time."

Kyle laughed. "You're in the Pale as much for your protection as ours. That's why the park is restricted. We're straightforward, man. We don't have that devious Jewish streak. Besides, if everyone wanted you to go down, we'd just make you go down."

"Then why allow the Rabbits to go through at all? If you're all so concerned about our well-being, I mean."

"That's a question for the politicians, not for me."

To the south a drone buzzed east above the reservoir.

"Anyway, can't you get a handle on those?" Ethan asked.

"No," Kyle said. "I think the drones are controlled by someone out west at a military installation. I can't do anything about it."

"Then what good are you?" Moti asked.

The Northlands had never been maintained with the same fastidiousness as the more stately sections of the park to the south, but in the years since the Second Event it had become even more wild. It was abandoned, more or less, and what remained of the hiking path was swollen with moss and milkweed and wild lilies and violets. Kyle started talking about unrest in the suburbs west of the city, but Ethan did not really listen. The trees crackled with the sound of cicadas, as if being consumed from the inside by an invisible fire. The air was thick with mosquitoes, struck alight where the afternoon sun split the trees and made their swarms appear to Ethan as golden snowflakes, twirling and dancing. As they walked, Ethan watched the water. He saw the tadpoles and the water striders and the slow-moving turtles and the jeweled dragonflies and then he looked up and saw a tanager, a waxwing, and two mockingbirds and he recalled that many years ago he briefly dated a woman who was an avid birder and he remembered that she took him on that very path, cataloging the birds she saw in an app on her phone. *Another life*, he thought. But then suddenly he felt as though she was walking beside him—the girl with the birding app—and he felt untethered from time and from circumstance, just like the birds themselves. Momentarily free.

Eventually, they turned off the path and cut through a thick tangle of bushes before emerging once again onto a paved road. In the distance to the south Ethan could see the edge of the reservoir and to the east, on the edge of several overgrown ballfields, was the subway stop—a staircase leading underground, over which spread a copper archway, now a dull green, embellished with flowers and small animals. When they arrived, they stood beneath the arch. The station was one of two such stops that used to service the park—the other being the stop at the zoo two miles to the south—but it fell out of service after the Second Event, when the anomaly opened just beyond one of the turnstiles. Grass grew up from between the cracks in the staircase and the archway was thick with ivy. Ethan and Moti sat down at the top of the staircase and looked down into the dark.

Kyle, standing over them as he leaned against the banister, said, "Be careful, it's close."

"Why didn't you ask them to meet us someplace else?" Moti asked.

"Because nobody comes here," Kyle said. "Well, except for the ones who do. You Jews can feel it, right?"

Ethan and Moti said nothing.

"Of course you can. It's right beyond the turnstiles down there. Just like in the pictures from the Exclusion Zone, but smaller. You can stretch it out, though." He smiled. "Like Abby's asshole but a lot darker. Why do you think the city put such a top-notch guard in place?"

Ethan said, "Can we see it?"

"You want to get your dick wet? You Jews are sick." Kyle laughed. "Sure, go ahead and have a look." But Ethan did not move.

Moti looked down at his watch. "We are on time," he said. "*Nu*? Where are they?"

"Relax," Kyle said. "You need to learn to relax."

"We're exposed here," Moti said.

"Trust me," Kyle said.

"Trust you?"

"We're friends, right? Okay, so trust me."

Kyle sat down next to Ethan and Moti on the stairs. He put his arm around Ethan and he laughed when Ethan's body went stiff. After a few minutes, Ethan turned to Moti and said, "Did I mention to you that Ella is still telling Michael that he'll be able to have a party at the zoo?"

Moti shook his head. Kyle looked as though he was about to make some kind of comment, but instead he lowered his eyes and said nothing.

THE SMUGGLERS ARRIVED ABOUT TEN MINUTES LATER, HEADING WEST ACROSS ONE of the ballfields—a woman with short hair and several earrings in each ear and a man with a beard and pale skin and delicate, child-like features. With them, to Ethan's great surprise, was a boy about Michael's age.

When they approached the stairwell Moti rose to shake their hands. The woman glanced at Kyle suspiciously, told the child to stand behind her, and then turned to her partner.

"Noah, what's with the guard?" she said. She was obviously frightened and she shifted uncomfortably, adjusting the green backpack that hung loosely from her shoulders.

"He always comes, Alice," said the man. "He's going to take his cut."

"He's freaking me out."

Noah nodded. "Let's be fast."

The woman handed him the backpack and he reached inside and took out a manila folder. He handed it to Moti.

"What's this?" Moti asked.

"MetroCards," Noah said, "for the subway below the subway."

"No," Moti said, quickly closing the folder. "We're not in the market for anything like that."

"You could sell them, if you want."

"That's not what we're about," Moti said. "Go find some Rabbits to buy them."

The man looked at Ethan. "Does he speak for you?"

"How many?" Ethan asked.

"Three."

"And how much?"

"Two hundred each. Dollars, not Palemarks. Plus whatever you have to pay him," he said, pointing to Kyle. "If the subway exists they're worth a lot more."

"Does it?"

The man shrugged. "Have you been through to look? You know what I know."

Ethan opened the folder and ran his fingers across the edges of the MetroCards. In the right-hand corner there were holograms that changed as he moved his wrist, alternating between doves and lions, unstable as rainbows and full of color, images of great beauty.

AS THEY WALKED BACK TOWARD THE PALE, ETHAN THOUGHT ABOUT MICHAEL AND Ella. Ella would be making dinner when he got home and Michael would be at the table near the kitchen, playing a game with Joel or reading one of his primate books. Ethan wanted to be home.

When they reached the vestibule at the entrance to the Northlands, Kyle collected his fee. Then he gave each of them a fist bump and climbed back up on his rock to smoke a joint. Looking down on Moti and Ethan, he said, "Oh, by the way, you don't want to go to the zoo anyway. There is something going on with the animals lately. The polar bear swims around and around in these nonstop circles. The giraffes won't eat. They're putting Prozac into all the feed."

"What happened?"

"Who the fuck knows. The parks department thinks it has something to do with the anomaly up here. But they won't say that."

"So? What do they say?"

"Well, naturally they blame all of you."

WHEN ETHAN GOT HOME HE HID THE METROCARDS ON THE TOP SHELF OF THEIR closet, inside a pair of boat shoes that Ella never wore. Then he went into the kitchen and kissed Ella on the back of her neck.

Without turning, she raised her hand and pressed her palm to his cheek and he smelled jasmine. He told Ella about meeting with the Jewish smugglers.

"Did they have anything interesting?" she asked.

"No," he said quickly. "But they had a child with them."

"How did they seem?"

"Scared," he said.

Ella nodded. "Yes of course," she said. "It's hard for me to imagine how they make it work. I heard there is a community of cryptos living just outside of the city in the forests along the river. And then an even bigger one in an abandoned indoor waterpark one hundred miles north."

"I don't know where they live," Ethan said. "Still somewhere east of the park, I guess. Moti thinks they must've been on an exemption list early on. That's probably right."

"Will you meet them again?"

"I don't know."

"What's in it for them?" Ella asked.

"Money, I guess."

"It can't be only that."

"Well, they're Jews. Maybe they care about us," Ethan said.

Later, before going to bed, he took the MetroCards down once more and watched the holograms change. Ella and Michael were already asleep, the bedside lamp casting shadows across their calm, distant faces. With his back turned he could hear the soft sound of their breathing. Standing in the closet, he wondered about how it would have gone without them. Would he have been pushed up into the Pale during the first organized wave of relocations? Would he have fled the city to the refugee camps in the south? Would he have gone further south to join up with one of the Jewish militias? Each of the possibilities surfaced and then faded away. He could not follow their many permutations, remnants of paths-not-taken that seemed to extend into the darkness in an infinite wake. What did they matter now?

Behind him, Michael mumbled something in his sleep and shifted his body against his mother's. Ethan reached up and slid the MetroCards back inside Ella's shoes. He tried not to think about them. But sometimes he did.

ELLA HELD ON TO THE IDEA OF THE PARTY AT THE ZOO UNTIL A FEW WEEKS BEFORE Michael's birthday, when she finally told him that it could not happen. She explained that she had not lied to him, that she really had believed he would be able to have a zoo party when he turned seven, and that by then it would all have been over. And she said that she was sorry she had let him down.

Michael, sitting next to her on the couch as he fiddled with a Koosh ball, was obviously disappointed. But he did not cry. He asked if he could have a hug and Ella said, "Of course, honey," and then, with carefully modulated composure, he said, "Sometimes a hug really does help when things aren't great."

Instead of going to the zoo, they planned a party outside on the sidewalk in front of their building. Although it was the end of

September—and just after the High Holidays—the weather had not yet broken. It was a searingly hot afternoon the day of the party, and the city was shimmering and volcanic, capturing the heat and making it dance in waves. Days earlier, a group of militants had entered the park from the east and set fire to a patch of the Northlands adjacent to the Pale, blanketing the eastern part of the neighborhood in ash. The fires were still not entirely under control and when Ella lifted her eyes from the children and looked east, she saw gray-and-yellow clouds of smoke rising up behind the buildings. She could smell burnt wood and rubber and also the metallic tang of the water in the street.

They had received permission to close the street and to open the fire hydrant. Ethan was able to get some colored chalk from some smugglers north of the Pale. And Joel did his best to bake a cake in the shape of a lemur, which was recognizable until it began to melt in the sun.

Michael and his friends wore bathing suits as they played in the water. It seemed quite an extravagance to flood the streets while less than half a mile away the park was burning, but they had petitioned both the neighborhood council and the manager of the checkpoints for permission weeks ago and—though they expected a visit from a guard in the hours leading up to the party informing them that it would no longer be possible—the permission was not rescinded. For this Ella was profoundly grateful and she thought, *Well, we all do what we can to celebrate.*

Michael, despite his disappointment about the zoo, seemed genuinely excited about the party. He had made a number of friends over the summer and during the first weeks of school—mostly children who lived in their building or in one of the other buildings on the street, and this was a new and wonderful experience for him. He had been quite shy in daycare and Ella was pleased to see him opening up. And yet, watching Michael run with his friends, his laughter cool and bright like water, she found herself on the verge of tears.

"What is it?" Ethan said, rubbing her back. Behind them, her father was standing at a fold-out table cutting pieces of cake and talking with some of the other parents.

"Tell me," Ethan said.

Ella flinched and moved away from him. "I wish we could have gone to the zoo."

"I know."

"I just wanted to give him something to look forward to." She looked at Ethan reproachfully. "Don't say anything."

"I wasn't going to say anything, Ella."

"He has nothing," Ella said. "His life has been emptied out."

"It's okay," he said. "Look how happy he is."

"He shouldn't be."

"Maybe not," he said. "But he is anyway."

Just then Michael looked back. He smiled through waves of heat—through a spray of water and rainbows—and he called out something that they could not hear. Then he waved and turned and ran away from them down the street, chasing a boy who was a little older and a little faster, shining and blurred by mist, as if his whole body was made of light. Watching him, Ella forgot about the fires in the trees and she thought, *Here is the creation of the world.*

IX

IT TURNED OUT THAT ETHAN RATHER ENJOYED LIVING WITH ELLA'S FATHER. DURING their first year in the Pale, they would often spend time together in the afternoons, before Ethan had to leave for evening meetings or to schlep contraband up from the underground. They would sit near the window in the living room, playing chess and drinking a bitter green tea that Joel loved and of which he seemed to have an endless supply. He would brew it in a small ceramic pot and when it was ready he would reach up along the windowsill where Ella's jasmine vines continued to thrive, pick a few flowers, and drop them into the bottom of each cup. This always reminded Ethan of his first afternoon with Ella and he realized that she was very much her father's daughter, possessed of a precision and economy of motion—the grace with which, for instance, they both plucked the flowers and poured the tea—that seemed to reflect concomitant habits of mind, a hard, bracing kind of intelligence. Ethan did not really care much for Joel's tea. But he learned to tolerate it because he enjoyed sharing it with him.

On some afternoons Michael would join them as well and, over the course of several weeks, his grandfather taught him how to play chess. Michael did not particularly like chess. But he liked sitting with Ethan and with his grandfather and he liked trying the tea (though, like Ethan, he did not really enjoy it) and he liked flipping through his grandfather's books, which Joel brought with him in two large suitcases on the day after Miriam died and the planes fell.

Some of them were tracts on philosophy and some of them were hollowed out to conceal bullion, but most of them were books about art, music, and literature, which had belonged to Miriam. Joel stacked them in a corner of the living room and eventually they comprised a kind of ever-changing wall that divided the room and they created for Joel a little office and Michael called it the castle and soon enough they all did.

Late at night, after everyone else had gone to bed, Ethan would sit alone in the castle. The room was heavy with the smell of old books and the fragrance of jasmine flowers and he would often sense the spectral presence of Michael and Joel and Ella, as if they had vanished into the air. Sometimes their absence would become so acute that he would get up and tiptoe into the bedrooms, first into Joel's and then into the bedroom that he shared with Ella and Michael. He would watch until he saw the rise and fall of their chests and he would lean over and kiss Ella and Michael softly, a charm against disappearing. Then he would return to the castle, where he would stare blankly at his laptop.

ONE EVENING, AS ETHAN SAT AMONG THE BOOKS AND JASMINE FLOWERS, THE MANager lingered in her office at the southern checkpoint. The breadlines had unwound and the warehouse had been vacated and all the petitions and paperwork and irregularities had run their course for the day. In three minutes, the last guards on shift would clock out and the iron dogs would clatter off into the late light. Soon enough, she thought, she would follow them.

But thirty minutes later, when the last of the light had faded and the curfew went into effect, she was still in her office, standing at her window and looking out over the southern reaches of the Pale. The apartment buildings on the far side loomed like enormous sentries—guardians of an ancient and long-silent civilization. Most of their windows remained dark, but the ones that held light appeared gilded. She would watch them as they winked on, five, ten, twenty stories up, a scattered caravan carrying torches traveling up by night. A depth of quiet settled over the streets and she cherished and savored it like a rare delicacy, not peace, she knew, but maybe a close cousin to peace.

The manager lived with her husband and two daughters in the suburbs north of the city, in a small bedroom community along the river. They had moved there several years earlier, even before they had children, because she and her husband wanted a life that was quieter and removed from the convulsions of the city. And it was quieter, for a time. But the concentration of anomalies in that part of the country—five inside the state's three-hundred-square-mile border—was the highest anywhere in the world and in the past several months the struggle for control over them had become increasingly intense. Activists gave way to militias and militias gave way to armies and armies became more activist and activism became more militaristic and on and on in a kind of frenzied spiral, unintelligible to the manager and even to her superiors in the city government. *Let's wait and see*, her boss had told her at the beginning of her rotations. Meanwhile the children's school ran drills. They learned by sunlight when the power failed. They fired air pistols and sang anthems she did not recognize. There were a few Jews living in a tent community in the woods along the river, moving each day to avoid authorities, though who the authorities were and what they might do was not always clear. Sometimes they would come into town like deer, trying to beg or steal food, only to be stunned by lights, cars, words, laughter, grenades. Other times they would come in with guns and rocket launchers. Or perhaps those were different Jews. Or perhaps they were not Jews at all. Often the manager felt that it would be an act of mercy to bring them to the Pale, where they could find a measure of quiet before whatever was to come. But the Jews along the river were beyond her jurisdiction and she was a person who valued process and procedure, the handmaidens of tranquility. Three days earlier a tank, of uncertain provenance, had rolled past their house and her daughter said, "Mommy, Mommy, come see!"

Unlike her children, all of whom had been born after the Second Event, she did not believe that she bore the Jews any real animus. She grew up in a heavily Jewish suburb of a city seven hundred miles to the west and she'd attended around thirty bar or bat mitzvahs when she was in seventh grade. She remembered enjoying and being somewhat overawed by the parties, many of which were lavish, and which, she became increasingly aware, would have been far beyond her parents' means. As it happened, the glitzy chain of Saturday nights at this or that restaurant coincided with a period of upheaval in her own family. Her father, whose presence in their lives was peripatetic and unstable, finally succumbed, that September, to whatever demons haunted him. After he vanished, drifting off somewhere into the drunken north (or so she understood), her mother had a string of men, none of them good. Then, toward the end of that school year, the First Event. Her mother's boyfriend at the time was a preacher, already given to violent flights of reverie, and he believed the world was ending and so together they set out across the country, founding churches and then abandoning them to apathy, insolvency, or fire. Until her mother finally put an end to it, during her senior year of high school, she experienced her life as an endless, senseless, grinding scramble, and she knew that something precious had been taken from her even though she could hardly remember what it was. For this she knew that she should blame her mother and the preacher. And she did blame them. But she also blamed the Jews, whose lavish celebrations ushered in a world of chaos. After graduating from high school, she went to college at a research university in the west, thousands of miles from the small coastal town where they were living when her mother, at last, had forced the preacher from their lives. There, she hoped to restore order and tranquility to her life. She studied urban development and she met the man who would become her husband. The university had a large Jewish population, which happened to include a girl she knew from middle school, Sarah Greenfield. She remembered Sarah only vaguely. But she felt guilty about how the mess of her adolescence was tied, in her imagination, to the excesses of the Jews, and she tried to be friends with her, which was easy enough because Sarah was kind and bright and they shared a lot of interests. But when the Second Event happened at the beginning of their junior year, the campus was suddenly roiled by conflict, a pitched battle the contours of which were beyond her. It all seemed forthrightly crazy—the new regulations and restrictions, the Jews protesting in front of the president's mansion, the counterprotests, the water cannons and stun grenades—and she said so to Sarah one night when they were sitting together in her dorm room. She was startled when her friend became suddenly guarded and then indignant and Sarah said that she was privileged and oblivious to the world around her.

Outside she heard car alarms and sirens and through a small window she saw the orange glow of a bonfire in the center of the quad. As her friend left, she felt herself returned to chaos. She did not make or seek out any Jewish friends after that. They were, she decided, a restive and troublesome people. Wherever you had Jews, there you had conflict, struggle, tension, perhaps through no fault of their own. And although she tried, now and then, to rid herself of this notion, it remained, like an unhealing wound. She married and moved east. She worked for the city. She rose.

As the manager made her way to her car, which was in the parking lot adjacent to the warehouse, she heard one of the iron dogs discharge its primary weapon several streets away—a shattering, grotesque sound, followed by the crystalline chimes of falling glass, followed by a dull *thwack*. She was only a minute's walk from her office and she wondered if she should go back to call it in. But she decided that the neighborhood council or the dogs themselves could take care of it. She thought of her children, of her daughter, who just recently, on a dare, snuck out of the house to throw a bag of dogshit at one of the forest Jews. She did not approve of that kind of behavior and she promised herself that she would talk to her daughter again. But as she pulled into her driveway, thirty minutes later, she saw through the window that her husband was sitting with their children on the couch in the living room, reading them a book or perhaps helping them with the last of their homework. The promise she had made to herself faded. She did not think of the pitiful forest Jew or her daughter's prank or the sound of the iron dog. *For peace*, she thought, *it is worth paying a very great price.*

AFTER BAKING THE LEMUR CAKE, JOEL BAKED A LOT MORE CAKES. HE HAD NEVER been particularly interested in baking and he offered no explanation for this new hobby. But in a week and a half following the birthday party he went through their entire monthly allotment of flour and sugar and thereafter Ethan took it upon himself to secure extra from smugglers whenever he could. It was not terribly difficult, Ethan assured him, but it required a little bit of negotiation with Noah and Alice, who had become regular contacts. Ella was touched that Ethan made this effort for her father and she was impressed that he accomplished it with such consistency.

One afternoon, as Joel sifted together flour, baking powder, and salt, he said to Ethan, "Did you hear about the woman from yesterday?"

It was about two months after the party and, after some initial fits and starts, the school year was humming along in a fashion that was strangely normal. The refrigerator was covered with worksheets and drawings and calendars and when a cool breeze came in through the kitchen window they rippled and settled like plumage. And one of the drawings, a blue monkey, wafted down onto the floor.

"Yes," Ethan said, kneeling to pick up the drawing.

"What do you think?"

Joel turned on the electric mixer and creamed together the butter and sugar. Ethan watched the beaters spin and then he put the monkey back on the fridge. He thought about a few different ways of interpreting Joel's question and then settled on one of them.

"Maybe it will be a low point," Ethan said. "I heard that the city is going to have hearings. And the current manager at the southern checkpoint seems reasonable. The guard will be arrested."

"Is that what your friend Kyle says?" Joel laughed. "Don't look so shocked. I don't stay in this apartment all the time, you know. I hear some things."

"Kyle is not a friend."

"No, of course not. And I'm sure you don't really believe that that guard from the checkpoint is going to be arrested."

"I don't know."

"But I know. You're not like my daughter."

"What do you mean?"

"She thinks everything will be fine."

"You know, when we first met, we were kind of reversed. She had this sense of everything that was going on and I was sort of the opposite." He was quiet for a few seconds and then he added, "I almost never thought about myself as a Jew."

Joel smiled. "Well, you do now."

"Yes. But maybe Ella's right about things."

"You don't act like you think so."

"What do you mean?"

"Well, with all of your nighttime excursions and your involvement with Moti's Crew. I appreciate your getting the sugar and flour, by the way."

"Of course. Anyway, sometimes I wish I could see things more from Ella's perspective. I admire her a lot."

"I know you do. But you're not like her. And it's good that you're not." Joel added the eggs one at a time, scraping down the sides of the bowl after incorporating each. "Mimi approved of you."

"She didn't really know me."

"She would have, if she did."

"How do you know?"

"Did Ella ever tell you that her mother was raised by her grandparents?"

"I don't think so, no."

"Mimi's parents died in an accident when she was a child."

"That must have been very hard."

"Her grandparents were refugees—they both came here when they were about ten years old. They loved her but they were pretty unstable. So Mimi always really valued people that weren't like them."

"Did you meet them?"

"I visited her grandmother once in Florida."

"What was she like?"

He added the sifted flour to the wet ingredients. "She came to the door in a heavy down coat. And she was scared of everything. Dogs, the cold, cars, the internet, the ocean."

"I can relate to that lately."

Joel nodded. "Yes, but you don't show it. And there might be a time not so long from now when that will become very important. When that time comes you will need to make some decisions. And you will need to move very fast, maybe faster than some other people who are around you." He paused. "Do you understand what I mean by that?"

"Yes, Joel."

"Don't forget it."

"I won't."

"You'll be okay."

"Do you really think so?"

"Yes," he said. "My daughter is lucky."

"I don't know if she feels that way."

"She will. One day soon."

"God forbid."

"Yes," he said, pouring the batter into a round cake pan. "God forbid."

Then, as he slid the cake into the oven, he said, "It seems that I'm an old man now. I think it happened very recently. I hardly noticed."

• • •

LATER ON, ETHAN FOUND JOEL SITTING IN A PLASTIC CHAIR ON THE ROOF AS THE SUN was going down. It was a cool evening and the trees in the park had lost most of their leaves. Joel was smoking a joint, which Ethan had never seen him do before, and, coughing as he exhaled, he offered it to Ethan. They shared it quietly and watched drones flit around above the park. There were more of them over the past few weeks, and, though it went uncommented upon, it worried them both. To the south they heard a burst of gunfire.

"It feels like the fighting is getting more intense," Ethan said. "The other night there were flashes in the sky to the south. Michael woke up."

"Yes."

"I feel like we should do something about it, but I don't know what. It all seems kind of impossible."

Joel said, "Do you know what the ancient rabbis said about people who ignore danger? They said, 'God protects the simple.' " He shrugged. "There are a lot of things from yeshiva I don't remember, but I've always remembered that."

"I'm not sure I like it."

"I'm not sure I do either."

Another burst of gunfire, then a siren, then quiet.

Ethan said, "You were involved in the early research, right?"

"Yes, I was. I mean, I didn't really have much to offer. I was just on one of the interdisciplinary delegations." He paused and then he smiled. "I don't know why everyone feels like it's a sensitive subject. You should feel free to ask me anything you want about that time. We're family."

"I don't know what to ask."

"Sure you do."

"How was it?"

"Strange." Joel passed the joint to Ethan. "But it was also stimulating. I guess it was exciting to be a part of something. I know it's hard to imagine now, but it felt like there was a lot of goodwill back then. Like, even with the tragedy of it, maybe we were on the cusp of something. A lifting of a veil. I remember feeling terribly guilty about that. Both Miriam and I were really involved in Jewish community at that point and it really was a horrible time. So much loss and all of it inexplicable. But it was only a few weeks after the First Event that someone from the government contacted me and after that I found myself carried away by the work. And it really was people from all over on our team. There was this brief and wonderful sense of shared striving. We had a physicist from Chile, an engineer from Scotland. There was an ecologist from Russia. The other philosopher was from a university in Australia. We produced this interdisciplinary report six months after we visited. It was over eight hundred pages. I'm not sure who ended up reading it. Anyway, we really didn't say too much."

"I'm sure you said more than you think."

"No. And truthfully I don't know how much there was to say. You know, a few months before the planes went down there was an article in the paper about how the state of research today really isn't that much different from how it was in the beginning. Did you see that?"

"I don't think so," Ethan said.

"The writer actually called me for a quote. They didn't end up using it."

"What did you tell them?"

"Well, she asked me if I had anticipated more progress. I told her no. I decided pretty quickly that we were asking the wrong kind of questions. Or trying to provide the wrong kind of answers. We were trying to be constructive—to offer the world something. But the thing in the desert is opposite of all that. It's an undoing. It's where things come apart and fall silent. There is nothing to say. It's a wound, ancient and endless. That was clear to me almost immediately."

"What about the distortions?"

"Those were mostly subtle things. It was hard to keep time. On the last day I saw a bird flying upside down."

"You got pretty close."

"Maybe twenty feet? They let some of the actual scientists get closer."

"They who?"

"The military people. Like the assholes who work the checkpoints. It seems like whenever anything remarkable happens in life the same kind of assholes appear soon afterward to contain it and tell you what you can and cannot do."

"And you felt the urge?"

"Yes," he said. "I did."

"Stronger than here?"

"Much stronger. But I only went there after it expanded. You know," he said, taking another hit from the joint, "I've seen the one here also. Just after it opened the city put together a little group to go down to take a look and because I went over in the beginning they invited me to come along. Miriam didn't want me to, but I went. The one down there is beautiful, Ethan, like a dark, polished gemstone, perfectly black, which is just how the hole in Jerusalem looked, at least according to most of the early descriptions of it. I don't know why but it reminded me of this other thing I remember from yeshiva, this old story from the rabbis about how when the Israelites were crossing the sea a mother could reach through the walls of water to pick pomegranates for her crying child. I thought about that when I was down there in the subway station near the

Northlands. It felt like I could reach through and grab hold of something. The one over there is different. Maybe it was once the same, but it isn't anymore. I don't think it's just a question of size. The darkness of it is terrible. And the pull of it was so strong. There was another Jew on my delegation, a geologist named Cohen. They let him get up close to take samples. But then they had to restrain him." Joel paused. "Of course the pull of the first anomaly is even stronger now. It's been building over the years. Did you know that after only a few years it became impossible for Jews to speak once they got within a certain range of it? Some kind of cognitive linguistic malfunction. That was always unsettling to me. How can you have Jews without a language? And there were some things written about that at the time, but they never really got much attention. Anyway, it's been building here as well. You feel it too, don't you? At least we can still talk about it."

Joel flicked away the last of the joint. They were both a little high and the question hung between them for some time before being reabsorbed, unanswered, into the quiet of the evening. The last of the light had faded. Four fighter planes raced across the sky in formation, heavy, hard, and fast, first the jets and then the sound of them, closer and lower than either of them could remember. Ethan jumped and fell from his chair and when he looked over he saw that Joel's hands were shaking.

"Here," said Ethan, "let me help you inside. Michael is still up. We can all have a piece of your latest cake."

"You didn't answer my question," Joel said, rising from his chair.

"I'm not with the Rabbits," Ethan said.

"Oh, I know. That's not what I was implying."

"I guess I think we all probably feel it building," Ethan said.

"Yes, I think so too," Joel said. "Anyway, let's go down. Cake is a good idea."

• • •

BUT WHEN THEY GOT DOWNSTAIRS THE CAKE WAS ALREADY HALF GONE AND ELLA AND Michael were not alone. Only Ella was facing toward the hallway, but Ethan recognized Kyle from the back, large and cumbersome, his left arm draped heavily over the shoulder of a younger woman with curly red hair, his pistol resting on his thigh. Next to the red-haired woman (Ethan assumed this was Abby) there was another couple, a man and a woman. And in the living room, huddled around a book, Ethan saw Michael with a child. They were laughing, a bright and beautiful sound. But when Ella saw Ethan and Joel standing at the mouth of the hallway her face was drawn.

She smiled a tense, angry smile and said, "Noah and Alice Rosenfeld have decided to try life on the inside. Kyle, who I guess knows where we live, thought maybe we could help them get situated."

Kyle turned, his face perfectly relaxed, guileless, and amused. "I think she's mad at me, Ethan. Didn't you tell her that we're friends?"

X

THAT SAME EVENING, IN A CITY TWENTY-FIVE HUNDRED MILES WEST, THE GREENBAUM family approached the anomaly at the central station.

The parents, both doctors at the largest hospital in the city, had been talking about going through for over a year. But they were always forestalled by their sense of obligation to their patients, which remained in full force, even as the women with deteriorating cataracts and old men coming in for chemo increasingly refused treatment from clinicians named Greenbaum. Their older son, Asher, who was seventeen, could not understand their loyalty to people who hated them and over the past several months had threatened many times to simply go through the anomaly on his own or head east to join up with one of the Jewish militias. Perhaps he would have, but for his younger brother, Nathaniel, who begged him not to. Their father, a quiet and gentle man, was concerned about his older son's radicalism, but as restrictions tightened he found that he was not really able to counter Asher's arguments. And when at last the doctors Greenbaum were dismissed by the hospital, they found that they had little reason to stay. Surely, they said, there were Jews in the underground in need of medical care.

They made their preparations. From their uncle, who had contacts in the east, they secured MetroCards. They acquired bullion and tents and, in an uncharacteristic act of rebellion that elicited a "Fuck yeah!" from Asher, following their final shifts at the hospital they stole several suitcases of medical supplies—syringes, bandages, medications, scalpels, a portable EKG machine, a defibrillator. Their house, located in a beautiful suburb on the edge of the desert, was desirable and easy to sell, though a new injunction prevented Jews from profiting on real estate investments so they were forced to take an offer well below market rate. They put the proceeds from the sale into an overseas bank account. Asher said they should buy more gold.

Just before leaving their house, as the sun was setting over the mountains, Nathaniel and Asher went out into the backyard to admire their mother's cactus garden, which blended almost seamlessly with the wild desert. The cactuses—saguaro and prickly pear—were planted by a landscaper soon after they moved into the house and over the years they had begun to list toward their wild cousins beyond the property line, blurring and finally eroding the distinction between the yard and the wilderness.

As the light faded the sky's haze yielded to a dazzling expanse of stars. The boys heard the rattle of a diamondback, the scream of a coyote.

"We should go in," Nathaniel said.

"Are you afraid?" Asher asked.

"No," Nathaniel said quickly, "of course not. There are always snakes."

"That's not what I mean," Asher said. "Listen, bro. We might have to really kick some ass down there. Are you ready for that?"

Nathaniel held his mother's hand as they stood in front of the anomaly and for the first time in his life it was not for his sake but for hers. Asher had assured him, earlier that evening as they listened to the snakes, that through the anomaly there would be a station very much like the one from which they departed and that because they had their tickets they would definitely get seats on the subway below the subway. Nathaniel, for his part, was fairly skeptical of his brother's prophecy. Asher knew a lot of things but how could he really know that? He knew that his brother was trying to take care of him. And he did feel cared for. But as they stepped forward into the gluey, viscous dark, he was pretty sure that Asher was full of shit.

XI

NOAH AND ALICE FOUND AN APARTMENT IN A BUILDING THAT WAS ALL BUT ABANdoned. It was a block south of Ethan and Ella's and at night Ethan and Ella could see their window illuminated on the fifth floor, the only one. Jacob and Michael made a game of signaling to one another in the dark. Their parents worried that the flashing lights would attract the attention of the drones or the iron dogs, but they seemed not to. And none of them had the heart to tell the boys to stop. Meanwhile violence in the neighborhood would spasm and subside. Meanwhile the food available at the warehouse would dwindle to almost nothing, only to be replaced by sudden plenty and no one inside the Pale knew why and the guards could not or would not say. Meanwhile the days and weeks and months rolled on, flowing almost imperceptibly, like water.

Throughout the second winter snow fell steadily and was rarely cleared away. Salt was delivered to the neighborhood council by the city, but without consistent access to trucks it was difficult to distribute. The roads and sidewalks were icy and perilous and the only things that moved with confidence were the iron dogs that patrolled the city overnight, enforcing a curfew from midnight until five a.m. The horse-like clatter of their feet broke through the quiet, leaving behind eerie fissures that glinted like diamonds in the morning.

At the beginning of December, Joel fell on the ice. He likely broke his kneecap, but he was unable to get much care because, earlier in the fall, the Pale's last remaining orthopedic surgeon had tried and failed to get across the river in an inflatable inner tube. In the days after the injury, Joel limped around the apartment, smoking weed and baking and, when he felt up to it, playing and reading with Michael. Though still in significant pain, by Hanukkah he was able to stand long enough to help Ella make latkes.

Movement through checkpoints slowed precipitously. Cell phone service ceased entirely and internet access became more severely restricted. The warehouse of goods at the southern checkpoint was replenished with less frequency and with second-rate products—produce that would barely last the day, outdated electronics, commemorative T-shirts featuring World Series victories that never happened. Only a handful of external websites loaded reliably and Ethan and Ella suspected that even these were heavily censored. According to one of them—a news website that was accessible only intermittently—sustained fighting had reached the suburbs and would soon enter the city. But the Jews in the Pale could not tell who was fighting who or what it might mean. They waited. They thought, *Let's see what will happen in the spring.*

One evening in the middle of February, Ethan surprised Ella with a new tablet, smuggled up from the underground, onto which the latest season of one of her favorite shows from before had been downloaded. Her birthday had passed two months earlier with very little celebration, and the gift, which was not so easy to acquire, did not accompany any particular occasion. But as their isolation together stretched on, the romance between them began to dwindle and Ethan hoped that the gesture would rekindle something. In the beginning, after the initial shock of the Third Event subsided, they had settled into cozy rhythms of domesticity, a kind of life which neither had ever specifically imagined for themselves but which turned out to be welcome and deeply comforting. Their disagreement about the nature of their situation receded into the background. It was a low-level hum, discernible only in those moments when they chose to pay attention, and then it would erupt into violent and burning conflagrations of mutual recrimination. But usually it did not and so they moved with relative ease through those first two years, packing lunch, getting Michael to school, taking Joel to doctors' appointments, taking meetings, packing lunch, taking meetings, taking Michael to doctors' appointments, making dinner, brushing teeth, doing bedtime, arranging playdates, taking meetings, doing bedtime, taking meetings, packing lunch, getting Michael off to school, taking meetings, arranging playdates, brushing teeth. And in the evenings they would smoke a joint on the roof or look through one of Ella's photography books or share a piece of Joel's latest cake or have sex.

But over the last several months, their time together in the evenings had degraded. Ethan began teaching expository writing classes at the high school, at first on a temporary basis to cover for a teacher who, so it was said, escaped across the river, and then permanently when no replacement could be found. He was good at it and he discovered that he enjoyed it much more than he ever enjoyed journalism and he wondered why he had never thought of doing it before. He devoted hours each evening to lesson planning, reading student work, and communicating with parents, which, given the restrictions, often meant going to students' homes. This allowed Ella to sink further into her own work—a series on workers at the checkpoint warehouse, a series on new religious trends in the Pale, a series on malnutrition among second graders, a portrait series depicting the leaders of the various neighborhood committees and organizations that reported, directly or indirectly, to the neighborhood council. She still sent photographs to the magazine but with much less frequency and always under the watchful eye of a censor. Nonetheless, she worked, and she found that depicting the harshness of the world to some extent inoculated her against it. She would sit cross-legged on the couch, editing photographs, while Ethan did his grading at the kitchen table. Aside from their daily conversations about logistics, their time together passed in collegial silence. Ella, for her part, rather enjoyed the quiet (though she knew that it worried Ethan) and she appreciated the fact that he allowed it to continue and did not muddle up those nights with a lot of nervous chatter. But eventually, after a tense evening that culminated in both of them saying they felt invisible to the other, Ethan suggested that they see a couple's counselor—an old, sparrowlike therapist who had worked out of the same home office for forty years. She urged them to address their malaise concretely. So Ethan surprised her with the gift of the tablet, the first gift he had given her in quite a while.

Ella was touched. But she was also disturbed by how excited she was to watch the show. It seemed a great luxury and it made their world seem pitifully small. All of this passed across her face like a shadow as Ethan pressed the tablet into her hand, and at first Ethan thought that she did not like the present.

"How did you get it?" she asked.

"Through Kyle."

"I still don't like him."

"Me neither," he said. "But that's not the point."

“Thank you,” she said, quietly.

“I’m sorry,” he said. “I’ll think of something else. I guess I thought it would mean something to you.”

“It does. No, it really does, Ethan. You’re sweet. I love you.”

“I love you too,” he said.

But when they sat down to watch they quickly fell asleep. And the following afternoon, when Ella took Michael to his piano lesson, they found that the teacher was gone.

OUTSIDE, THE IRON DOGS WERE LUSTERLESS BENEATH THE MOON, GUN GRAY, AND the winter stretched on into the spring.

The miracles seemed to come with more regularity, a product, perhaps, of the increasing distortions around the anomaly. They were not miracles of great consequence. There was a car that never seemed to run out of gas. There was a baker who baked bread that tasted different to everyone who ate it. There was an oak tree near the northern checkpoint that did not lose its leaves for the entire winter. There was a tune of unknown origin that traveled around the Pale and the tune had power—to bring sunshine, to enchant a border guard, to ensure an easy death.

Inside the Pale the Jews prayed, each in their own fashion. The larger synagogues still functioned, but there was a widespread suspicion that they were being monitored by the city and the rabbis were circumspect in how they spoke. A rabbinical council met weekly with a representative from the city, but the content of these meetings was not released widely. After each meeting the rabbis fretted and talked in circles about how they should proceed, about whether or not the city officials could be trusted, about whether or not the hole in the Northlands was expanding, about why the pull of it was growing stronger.

Smaller communities grew up all around, minyanim in buildings and on rooftops, study groups organized around special interests—food, ethics, dance, combat, activism, meditation, virtual reality, mushrooms, old movies, new movies, jokes, raising kids, music, mysticism. Some of these had rabbis of their own and some of them had other kinds of leaders but most of them were leaderless. And Ethan and Ella drifted between these communities, without really finding a home.

Ella found herself increasingly nostalgic for the Jewish community of her childhood, the large Modern Orthodox synagogue where her parents were married. As their isolation stretched on, her father had begun praying again each morning, something he had not done in several years, and she would sometimes watch him from the kitchen as he stood by the window, his tallis hanging loosely over his shoulders, his body reedlike in the early light, and she would remember sitting next to him during services when she was a very little girl, hiding herself beneath the wings of his prayer shawl and watching with wonder as sunlight filtered through the soft, thin wool, throwing shadows and brightness all around.

Ethan had no such memories. At the very beginning he felt lost and mute among the Jews and then, as he became more involved in the politics and the social dynamics of the Pale, he came to feel as though he was playing a version of himself onstage. He was engaged in various projects and he believed that they were important, but he never felt connected to them in the way that he thought he should and over time, as the novelty of them wore off, Ethan was left feeling as though he was a fraud. He confided this to Joel one night while they played chess and Joel nodded and told him not to worry, that it was a common experience. "That's tragic," Ethan said, and Joel said, "Yes, it really is."

As the second winter lingered, the meetings and committees

that once held Ethan's attention began to seem small and useless. He remained devoted to his teaching at the high school and he remained devoted to Michael, Ella, and Joel, but other things started to slip away from him. In the evenings he still trained with Moti and with some of the others, or he would go to Isaacson's to drink and eat the miracle tomatoes and listen to the zealots go on about one thing or another. Often there was talk of an uprising, if they could secure enough weapons, but it was unclear to Ethan what they were trying to accomplish. Increasingly, at night, he had trouble sleeping, and when he did he would go up onto the roof and watch the iron dogs patrol the street, their locomotion smooth and impossibly lifelike.

Once, early in the spring when the ground was white with snow, one of them looked up, the black, metallic eye watchful and unmoving like the eye of a god. Ethan stood near the ledge and tried not to move. Being on the roof should not have registered as a violation, but after a few seconds he saw that one of the guns mounted above the shoulder extended. He held his breath. Earlier in the week he saw a woman bleeding out in the street. He thought of the woman now and he wondered what it would feel like to get shot and then he wondered if it would feel like anything at all. He hoped that Michael would not see his body.

Ethan waited. There was no use trying to make sense of it. He knew with certainty that he was going to die there, in the Pale, and he could not understand why. And he knew it even after the dog turned away, running easily through the snow and disappearing into the night.

THE DOG HURRIED ON. IN THE UPPER QUADRANT THE BUILDINGS WERE FRACTURED and multiplied. Three buildings became nine, twenty-four windows became two hundred and sixteen. Their lights flickered. The lenses focused and refocused. The upper quadrant merged with the lower. The eye in the front, between the gun barrels, merged with the eye on either flank and then with the eye above the tail, each eye breaking the world into little shards, triangles, squares, more buildings, more windows, winking like stars. The quadrants shifted and shimmered. The images blurred, broke, and reassembled into a single sphere. An approximation of the world. The feet clattered on the ice. The dog moved along through the dark, hunting.

At the corner, the street opened out onto a broad square, bright and disorienting. The upper quadrant, suddenly flooded with light, went black. The images broke again—not one but four, not four but twelve—and a mechanism between the ears whirred into action. The aperture closed. The dog moved again, throwing shadows on the ice, climbing the great dome at the center of that square where the streets converged and disappeared into one another as if drawn beneath the earth. The quadrants merged and broke and merged again. The squares and triangles fused. Then, a twinge of motion. The dog leapt from the top of the dome and the quadrants shook and the sphere shifted and whirled and the moon shone on the ice. Everything was too slow.

Whir, click, rattle. A diagnostic report ran and was sent. Feet planted, toes sinking down into the snow. The guns extended and retracted and extended. A wheel spun. A light winked, red, green, red, solid red, solid red.

The laser eye settled onto the chest of a man, who stood there shivering, his head bowed and his arms folded in front of his body as though carrying something heavy, a book or a bag of groceries. His hands were empty. He had come from beneath the dome. He swayed in the wind and the wind carried the smell of hot metal, rubber, smoke, and snow. He looked down and touched the red spot between his ribs, watched the laser jump from finger to finger. Then he raised his hand, unafraid, and said, "Nice dog."

The man spent that night in the empty square. And in the morning, a Monday, the square came to life. Vendors, buskers, children running—their voices rising up around him like a great wave, cresting and crashing down. He lay on the bench and allowed the sounds of the square to wash over him, warming and wonderful. Then he stood up, walked to the center of the square, and, adding his voice to the din, proclaimed himself the messiah.

XII

WHILE THE MESSIAH WAS INTRODUCING HIMSELF TO THE PEOPLE OUTSIDE THE SUB-way station, Ella and Michael were eating breakfast. As they ate, Michael played a game on her tablet and Ella edited a photograph on her laptop. In the photograph a woman was standing in front of a line of guards at the northern checkpoint. In her gloved hands she held a framed picture of her husband, who died a few days earlier when a dog malfunctioned and fired thirty rounds through the window of their apartment. Ella was always quiet and rather remote when she was working and Michael had to say "Mommy" three times, with increasing urgency, before she lifted her eyes over the rim of her computer and said, "What is it, honey?"

Michael looked at her with exasperation. "Can I ask you something?"

"Of course."

"Why are the goyim so afraid of the holes?"

"Well, no one really knows how they work."

"Are they really getting bigger?"

"A little."

"Is that what scares them?"

"Do you remember what happened during the First Event? We've talked about that a little."

Michael nodded.

"I think some of the goyim are just afraid that the holes will hurt them," Ella said. "Or that one day they will get bigger and bigger until they cover the whole world."

"Is that true?"

"I don't think so."

"Maybe they're jealous," Michael said.

Ella blinked. "Why would they be jealous?"

"Because we can feel the holes and they can't. Maybe what's on the other side is only for us."

Ella watched Michael. She tried to decide on a response. But before she could say anything he asked, "Why did we stop having people over on Friday nights?"

The question caught Ella off guard. "Do you remember when we did that?" she asked.

"Yes. Only a little bit, but I do. We don't have any fun. It's like we're not really alive anymore."

"Did you hear someone say that?" Ella asked, frightened.

"I don't know. Was that a bad thing to say? I'm sorry, Mommy."

"Do you really feel that way?" Ella asked.

"Not really. Only sometimes. When can we leave again?"

"I don't know, honey. Soon." Then she said, "Would you like to invite people over this week? It's just hard, you know, because the warehouse where we get food isn't like a supermarket where you can get as much as you want. It's not as easy to make food for other people. But maybe Ethan can get some extra vegetables and sugar and flour. You can ask Zeyde if he wants to make a cake."

Michael's face lit up. "Really?"

Ella smiled. "Yes, absolutely. Is there anyone you would like to invite?"

"Can we invite Jacob and his family?"

"You and Jacob Rosenfeld have really become friends this year, huh?"

"We have a secret handshake. And he's really into primates too."

"I think inviting him for Shabbat sounds like a great idea. I'll ask his mom at drop-off today."

Later in the day, when she told Ethan about their conversation, he told her that it would be difficult to find anything extra for the meal. He said that he and some of the other members of Moti's Crew were meeting with some smugglers in the Northlands early the next morning—three men with black hats and sidelocks who had replaced Alice and Noah as the main representatives from the underground—but that they were likely bringing crates of soap, batteries, and school supplies, rather than food. As he spoke he became increasingly frustrated. It seemed to him that the birthday party incident was repeating itself and that Ella still did not appreciate the reality of their situation. What was worse, Michael would be disappointed again because she had offered something they could not provide. But he did not say any of this. And by the middle of the week, he had indeed managed to secure some extra items, having taken them from the apartment of a man who tried to swim across the river and was shot by dogs. This in itself was something of a risk and he resented Ella for forcing him to take it. Members of Moti's Crew, along with a few other neighborhood organizations, were generally responsible for redistributing the property of people who disappeared for one reason or another. According to their shared protocol, all items were supposed to be deposited in a central storage facility that had once been a karate dojo. But because Ethan arrived at the man's apartment before anyone else he decided that he would simply take what he wanted, and though he thought he would feel guilty about it, he found he did not. He was only nervous that he would get caught. And he arrived home on Wednesday evening with almonds, frozen spinach, little containers of applesauce, garlic, onions, frozen chicken thighs, apricot jam, eggs, flour, and sugar.

Ella did not ask how he acquired these things and Ethan did not volunteer the information, which Ella decided was just as well. She thanked him and kissed him and said that it meant a lot to Michael.

"Maybe it can mean a lot to all of us," he said.

"Yes," she said, "maybe it can."

ON FRIDAY AFTERNOON, ETHAN AND MICHAEL WALKED HOME FROM SCHOOL AND SAT in the living room, reading and playing board games while Joel and Ella cooked. Ella roasted the chicken with the garlic, onions, and apricot jam and Joel made a sponge cake. When the food was ready, shortly before sundown, Joel plugged in the hot plate and filled up an electric urn. These observances—the traditional prohibitions against cooking and heating food on Shabbat—had been a fixture in their lives since Joel moved in. They persisted despite all the things that did not. For Joel they ached and pulsed like a phantom limb as the four of them stood near the window while Ella lit candles, their reflection soft and bright like a child's night-light. Then they bundled up and went around the block to a minyan, a prayer quorum, that met every Friday in what had once been a bodega called the Sunshine Marketplace.

Ethan, Ella, and Michael attended the minyan only sporadically, but Joel went regularly. The leader of the minyan, David Blom, was also the proprietor of the store, having taken over from a Sudanese man who fled the Pale in the early days. A retired accountant, he maintained the bodega mostly as a service to the neighborhood—an attempt to preserve something from before—and for nearly a year, to his wife's consternation, he ran the market dutifully and treated it like a real business. He said that it was important for a neighborhood to have a place where people could buy a Coke or a bag of chips. He worked long hours until his knees and back ached and he developed a stoop. He tried to keep the shelves stocked with supplies from the warehouse at the southern checkpoint and with products that were smuggled in by Moti's Crew and by others. Mornings, when the ingredients were available, he would make egg-and-cheese sandwiches and omelets and pancakes on a small griddle behind the counter.

Eventually, as access became more and more erratic, he gave up on actively maintaining the inventory and now the shelves held only a small and motley assortment of items—canned ravioli, fish food, mineral oil, bubblegum-flavored toothpaste, bug spray—and the space had taken on an eerie, tomb-like quality. No one could really understand why David still opened up each morning at six a.m., but he did, without fail. And on Friday afternoons he would string colored lights above the windows and make coffee and people would come to pray, not so many, really, but enough that the room felt warm and full and cheerful.

The Sunshine Marketplace was more crowded than usual on that night. All of the seats inside were taken and there were people standing along the walls and overflowing onto the sidewalk. Among them, standing near the counter, was the man who called himself the messiah.

When Ella, Ethan, and Michael arrived, Michael found Jacob and the two of them went into the stockroom at the back of the store, where Blom kept some toys and where there were already a few other kids congregating. The room was lit by a single lightbulb dangling from a black cord, which made the small space dusky and dreamlike. Michael knew most of the other children by face, if not by name, because they all went to the same school in the southern district of the Pale. Most of them were a little older and Michael was excited and nervous about being alone with them.

They were already in the midst of a game when he and Jacob arrived. One of the oldest children, a thirteen-year-old girl who was beginning to experiment with the bossy pleasures of adulthood, had organized a game of radioman, a version of "killer" known to all children in the Pale above a certain age. Michael had never played before and he watched as the other kids, eight in all, milled around the room in silence, shaking hands and periodically falling onto the ground. When there were four players still standing, one of the kids, a boy who was a few years older than Michael, pointed to a little girl in a white dress and said, "It's you! You're the radioman!" and the little girl laughed and said, "*Shema, yisrael, Adonai, eloheinu, Adonai echad*," confirming the boy's suspicion. Then everyone stood up and got ready for the next round.

When the older girl saw Michael and Jacob, she went over to them and said, "Hi. I'm Dafna. Do you two want to play?"

"How does it work?" Michael asked.

"You've never played radioman?" she asked.

"No," Michael said. "I think I've heard of it."

She explained that in just a moment everyone would close their eyes and then she would walk around the room and tap one of them on the shoulder. That person would be the Jew.

"But we're all Jews," Michael said.

"Not in this game," said one of the other children.

"The Jew," Dafna continued, "is radioactive and their goal is to cause the Second Event. Do you both know what that is?"

Michael and Jacob nodded.

"So you do that by walking around the room shaking hands. If someone offers to shake your hand you must shake, but if someone scratches your wrist then you know that's the Jew and they gave you a dose of radiation. You have to wait thirty seconds before you die. The goyim win if they identify the Jew. The Jew wins if they radiate everyone. Do you understand?"

"My daddy says the radiation in Canada was a hoax," Jacob said. "He says that when the holes opened up during the Second Event there was never any radiation anywhere. He says that wasn't real."

"It doesn't matter," said Dafna.

"But why isn't the Jew hurt by radiation?" Michael asked.

"Because Jews are immune," said the girl in the white dress. "Everyone knows that. That's why they put us in here. Because we have powers."

"Even though it wasn't real?" asked Jacob.

"Yes," said the girl in the white dress, nodding sagely. "Even so. But that's not the only reason we're here. One day they're going to feed us to the hole. I saw it on a video made by a man on an island."

"There are no new videos in the Pale," said another child, a small boy only a little older than Michael.

"It was old-fashioned. From before."

"That's not real either."

"It is!"

"Okay, never mind that," said Dafna, cutting in authoritatively. She looked at Michael and Jacob. "So you're both in?"

"Yeah, okay," Michael said.

"Good," she said. "Just close your eyes."

"Are we going to be done by the time the singing starts?" Michael asked.

"Why do you want to sing?" asked the boy who identified the Jew in the first round. "It's stupid."

"Shabbat isn't stupid," Michael said, alarmed.

"Of course it's stupid," said the other boy. "It's just a day when we don't do anything. But what do we need that for? That's every day here. I guess you're too young to remember what it used to be like."

"I'm not!" Michael said.

"Then tell me one thing you remember."

Michael looked at Jacob and then at the older girl. He chewed his lower lip. He thought about going back into the main room. Ethan would kiss his forehead and he could sit on his lap and feel the great thickness of his arms around his stomach. But something held him there.

"Let's just start the game," he said.

WHILE THE CHILDREN WERE PLAYING, ELLA AND JOEL FOUND SEATS NEXT TO JACOB'S parents on the far side of the room; Ethan felt restless and so for a while he remained standing at the front of the store near the cash register. And while he waited for the service to begin, he spoke with the messiah.

He was a small man, with a short beard, dark hair, and watery blue eyes. He spoke English fairly well, but his accent was hard to place. Ethan did not recognize him.

"I haven't seen you here before," Ethan said. "Do you live in the southeastern quadrant?" Ethan leaned forward against the counter and took a piece of gum. The bodega had an apparently limitless supply (some said it should be counted among the miracles) and Blom gave it away for free.

"What is meant by this, the quadrant?" said the messiah.

"This part of the Pale, you know, the neighborhood right around here."

"I am sleeping for the last few nights near the dome that is covered with paper."

"You mean the subway station?"

The messiah raised his hands and shook his head. "Subways I have not seen."

Ethan nodded. "Are you one of the sellers?"

"No."

"Did you come up from across the park?"

"I don't know." The man blinked. He was older than Ethan, perhaps sixty-five. His face was blank and gray and he looked searchingly across the room. Ethan was reminded of his great-grandfather, who spent the last four years of his life living in a memory care facility. Then the man lost his balance and stumbled, slamming his face against the counter.

"Are you okay?" Ethan asked, touching the man's forearm. "Here, let me help you." Again the messiah spoke, a muffled sound, like far-off waves. His lip was bleeding. "What?" Ethan said. "I'm sorry, I didn't catch what you said."

The man touched his lip gently and looked down at blood on his fingers.

"Maybe you live in the Jewish Home," Ethan said. "I can take you there."

"I have been for a long time in the dark," he said.

"What do you mean?"

The messiah did not answer.

"Do you know why you came here tonight?"

"Yes," he said, his eyes watery, "I am going to show you what it means truly to be a Jew."

Before Ethan could say anything further, Blom banged on the counter. He started singing a wordless melody in a minor key and the messiah, who seemed to know the tune well, sang a harmony.

When the service was over the families walked home together. They walked quickly so as not to violate the curfew, which began two and a half hours after sunset and thirty minutes before the dogs came out. Before they left, Blom gave the children chocolates wrapped in silver paper. Neither Michael nor Jacob could ever remember having seen such things and they were delighted and a little bit fearful. Somewhere to the north they heard an explosion. It rattled the windows.

But it was far enough away. It did not touch them. And they carried the chocolates with great care, as if they were jewels.

THEY SANG TOGETHER. THE PARENTS BLESSED THE CHILDREN, THE WINE, THE BREAD. They ate. Ella told a joke about a Jewish man who had gone to live in a monastery in the Himalayas—the first joke Ethan had heard her tell in quite a while. She was not a natural joke-teller and she botched the punchline, but she still laughed her easy, startling laugh and soon they were all laughing. The children fidgeted and pecked at their food and then disappeared down the hall, while the adults remained, talking and laughing and trying not to think too hard about any of it.

Ethan and Ella enjoyed the Rosenfeld family, though they did not become friends until after the boys became close. In the beginning, after they first came into the Pale, Ethan assisted them in getting situated, a fact of their relationship that at times, when they were together, led to an awkward cordiality that they had to work to transcend.

There were not many refugees coming across the park or down from the suburbs—two or three each month—and although there were rumors about why, nobody really knew. When they did arrive there were no systems in place to help them get acclimated. Officially, relocation into the Pale was illegal, a piece of legislation that the neighborhood council tried and failed to topple toward the end of the first summer, when the emergency injunctions following the Third Event still seemed pliable and somewhat unreal. But in practice the city officials were content to turn a blind eye, so long as residents could produce a record of entry with a date preceding the legislation, and these were easily forged. And, besides, if a few Jews wanted to sneak into prison, why stop them? Ethan helped the Rosenfelds secure papers and he also helped them find their apartment, one of the many that had been abandoned in the very early days when the checkpoints were still quite porous. When it became clear that they were still lost, Ethan took it upon himself to help them navigate school enrollment and signed them up for the dollar-a-day health coverage that one of the urgent-care clinics began offering after leaving the Pale for medical care became mostly infeasible. None of these tasks was particularly difficult and Ethan could not quite grasp why the Rosenfelds struggled with them as much as they did. When he was a teenager, just before the First Event, his parents joined a community group that helped resettle a family of refugees from a war in the Middle East—a mother and two children. The kids went to Ethan's school and the mother took English lessons at a nearby community center and sometimes, in the afternoon, one of Ethan's parents would give them all a ride home. These rides were always characterized by a deep, reflective quiet—a quiet somehow amplified by the chatter of public radio—and, despite the other kids' kindness, self-possession, and obvious gratitude, Ethan was struck by how remote they seemed, as though they were wearing spacesuits. And the Rosenfelds, at first, reminded Ethan very much of that family and he had trouble understanding it. But when he mentioned it to Ella, she shrugged and said, "Well, they aren't from here." "Yes," he said, "but they both grew up in the city, just like you." "That was a different time," Ella said. "Besides, who knows what happened to them over the last year," and Ethan understood, immediately, that she was right. And although the Rosenfelds were not necessarily the companions that they would have chosen for themselves, they did not really interrogate it and they were happy that Michael had a friend.

"Should we call them back?" Ella said, nodding toward the children.

"No," said Ethan. "Just let them play."

They listened to the children, their voices a balm. Joel, who no longer had the patience to sit in a chair for long periods of time, retreated to his bedroom to read.

Meanwhile, Ethan, Ella, Noah, and Alice remained at the table, picking through the ruins of dinner. Through the window Ella saw a helicopter hovering just beyond the southern checkpoint, most likely scanning the neighborhood for someone who was trying to make it to the river dock a mile south of the Pale. There was, according to rumors, a boat that would take Jews north under the cover of night.

"I hope they make it," Ella said, to no one in particular.

"There is nowhere to go," Alice said. "Not that way."

"You don't think so?" Ethan said.

"We never heard of anyone making it north," Alice said. "It doesn't make sense."

"What makes sense?" Ella asked.

Ethan's hand was draped over the back of Ella's chair. He squeezed her shoulder gently and she smiled, a slight tightening of her lips, so fast that he missed it. Then, once more not addressing anyone specifically, Ella said, "Do you find it surprising that we don't talk more about it?"

"About what?" Noah said.

She gestured toward the window. "About all of it. About what's going on out there. And about what's going on in here. The forest Jews in the rivertowns? The Jewish militias in the south?"

"I heard one of them is led by an ex–Israeli commando," Noah said. "Nimrod Yovel."

"Yes, but what do we really know about any of it?" Ella said. "It's like everywhere there is a dense fog."

"One of the checkpoint guards told me that there was a measurable increase last week," Alice said. "In the size of the anomaly."

"You believe that?" Ella asked.

"Can't you feel it?"

"I don't know," Ella said quietly.

"The Rabbits are organizing another descent in a few weeks," Alice said. Then, after a short pause, she said, "They say the subway below the subway is going to make a stop sometime soon."

"Is that why you came here?" Ella asked.

"No," Noah said quickly. "We came here because a bomb went off right near us. And we had a close call with a dog. It didn't seem worth it to stay outside any longer."

"But it did before?"

"Someone made us an offer. From the city. We had some protection."

Ella glanced quickly at Ethan. "I see," she said. "In exchange for what?"

"It doesn't matter anymore, does it?"

"I guess not."

"Right," Noah said.

"But there are bombs and dogs up here," Ella said.

"Exactly," he said. "So it's all the same."

Ella rolled her eyes in exasperation. "It's like I'm living inside some old Jewish joke," she said. "And that's another thing. Where did the dogs come from all of a sudden anyway?"

"The police have been using them for a few years now," Noah said.

"I don't remember that."

"Of course they have," he said. "They were developed by that robotics company out west. I forgot the name of it. After the Second Event."

"I guess so," Ella said.

Noah shifted in his chair and leaned forward. "What are you getting at, Ella?"

"Nothing. I don't know." Then, "The world used to be so small. Or it used to feel that way. But then we got caught in here and it was like the world out there expanded so much that it became unknowable. It's strange."

The table was quiet. Ella listened to the sound of the boys laughing in the next room and she looked south through the window and watched as the helicopter rose up and away. Finally, she said, "I do hope they made it."

"Who?" Noah asked.

"Whoever was trying for the river docks. And if they didn't I hope it wasn't the dogs."

Everyone nodded. Noah said, *"Baruch hashem."*

Then Ella smiled and said, "You know, earlier tonight Ethan met the messiah. He doesn't seem to have very many followers, though."

• • •

BUT LATER ON, WHEN THEY WERE ALONE ON THE ROOF, ETHAN SAID, "YOU'RE RIGHT. It is strange."

"Why didn't you say so earlier?"

"I don't know. I don't know what to say about it."

"Me neither."

Ella rubbed her hands together. Ethan blew warm air into his fists. "Have you noticed that the neighborhood seems emptier?" he asked.

"Yes."

"My classes are smaller also."

"Where is everyone?"

"You know where they are, Ella. There are more going down every day."

They watched the dogs and the drones and the lights of the skyscrapers winking on and off in the distance. Finally, Ethan said, "It's been a while since we've come up here."

"Yes, it has."

"I don't know why we stopped."

"It's been cold," she said. "Do you miss it?"

"Miss what? Coming up here?"

"All of it."

"Yes," he said, turning to face her. "Of course I do."

Ella looked out over the city and Ethan looked at Ella. She was wearing the yellow coat that she wore on the first day they met on the balcony of their office building. It was not warm enough for the weather, and when she shivered he moved to put his arm around her. She looked older than she did when they first met. Her hair, which she had not cut since the previous winter, had a streak of gray running from the left side of her forehead to the base of her neck and there were small, almost imperceptible creases around her eyes. She shifted her weight against his chest, looking up at him briefly.

He thought she was about to say something, but instead she looked away, her face placid and distant. He could not imagine what she might have said. In many ways, she was still a stranger to him. But as he felt her body move against his, he tried to remember his life before they met, tried to envision a life without her, and he found that he could not or that he would not, which he decided were about the same.

Then he surprised both of them and said, "Do you think we would have stayed together if it wasn't for all of this?"

"Does it matter?"

"Yes," he said. "I think it matters quite a lot."

Ella touched his arm gently. Then she reached into the inside pocket of her coat and took out a piece of white paper, which was folded in half.

"It has been too long since we've been up here," she said.

"What about the dogs?" he asked, taking the paper.

"Fuck the dogs."

He knelt down. He tried to fold it but his hands were too cold. "Here," she said, kneeling next to him, "let me do it."

When the plane was finished, Ella handed it back to Ethan. She smiled and said, "Go ahead."

"You should fly it," he said.

Ella nodded and rose to her feet. Pinching the fuselage between her thumb and forefinger, she carefully adjusted the orientation of the wings. She was still for a few seconds and she drew a breath. She smiled and winked and to Ethan she seemed, in that moment, strangely girlish, as if she had altered time. She was free. Then she moved, stepping forward, one-two-three, her shoulder pitched high like an archer's and the white dart of plane drawn back behind her ear, pausing as a light wind swept east from the river, holding, holding, and finally accelerating forward in a perfect arc, her right arm a blur and the plane moving silently up into the sky, gliding easily across the street and then catching an updraft and rising higher, above the apartment complex opposite theirs and then racing south toward the checkpoint—one block, two blocks, three, four, five—its ascent steady and unbroken, and Ethan and Ella watching from the rooftop, their eyes wide, their mouths parted slightly, as it continued to gain speed and altitude, moving on, rising up, and disappearing.

"Did it fall?" Ella asked, a little breathless.

"I don't think so."

"I've never seen one fly like that."

"Me neither," Ethan said.

They continued looking south. The helicopter had returned, lower now and with a searchlight.

"I hope there really is a boat," Ella said.

"Me too," Ethan said.

Then they held hands and watched as the helicopter dropped a black rope and a few officers slid down to the ground, disappearing below a line of apartment buildings like dark seeds planted in the earth.

THE FOLLOWING AFTERNOON, THEY WENT OUT FOR A WALK WITH MICHAEL. ELLA AND Ethan were shy with one another, unsure of what to make of their conversation on the roof, and around them the Pale was gray and sullen. It was late March, still chilly, though no longer quite as cold as it was the night before, and the sidewalks were wet with slush and slick with decomposing leaves, which had not been cleared away at the end of the previous fall.

Michael was still excited about having spent the previous evening with Jacob and he thanked Ethan and Ella over and over as they made their way east toward the old express stop. Ella was on his right and Ethan was on his left and they held hands as they walked.

"You're great parents," Michael said, with a wide smile. "I think I just really missed that kind of thing, you know? Can we have Jacob's family over again?"

"Sure," Ella said, somewhat saddened by how self-aware Michael had become.

"When?"

"Sometime soon," she said. "We'll see."

She tried to make eye contact with Ethan. But she missed and they went on and even though Michael was getting a little too heavy for it, every few feet they would swing him up into the cold, clear air.

They were on their way to a playground a few blocks west of their apartment. To get there they had to pass through the large square. A week earlier, the neighborhood council had ordered all of the flyers removed and now, once again, the dome of the station rose above the square like a cut gem. Ethan, feeling the faint vibrations of the subway passing beneath his feet, lifted his eyes and saw the station, stark and beautiful. Without the flyers it looked the same as it did on the day when he first came to Ella's apartment, a miracle of glass, hard and eternal. He imagined that they were all walking to catch a train and, swinging Michael once more into the air, he allowed himself to be carried away by the fantasy. Then Ethan slipped and landed on his side and, though he was not hurt, he was very wet. Ella quickly bent down and helped him up.

"Do you want to go back to change?" she asked.

"No," he said. "It's okay."

"You'll be cold," she said.

"I'll be fine," he said. "Let's keep moving."

"What were you thinking about?"

"I don't know," he said. "I was looking at the train station. And I was thinking about the first time I left your apartment."

She smiled and touched his back gently. "I remember that day," she said, and when she said it he had the distinct impression that she was recalling a dream. "I'm glad I invited you over. I almost didn't."

"Why not?"

"I was afraid you'd never leave."

WHEN THEY REACHED THE SQUARE, THEY FOUND A FEW VENDORS SELLING CHARGING cables, earmuffs, and roasted nuts. But for the most part the market tents—which unfurled each weekday morning across the square like a flock of enormous white birds—were closed, folded and stacked in a pile just inside the station. There were no official religious restrictions on doing business during Shabbat. To the extent that the Pale's rabbinic council had any formal authority, they were uninterested in mandating religious practice. But nonetheless a kind of piety had become commonplace throughout the neighborhood. Time seemed increasingly plastic, a contrivance. Who could say? Perhaps a day of rest might save them. And, in any case, there was not much business to do.

But although there were not many vendors, on that afternoon the area around the station was crowded with people. There were several guards stationed at the perimeter of the square, heavy with Kevlar and ammunition, their rifles slung over their shoulders and protruding from their stomachs. Congregated in the center, there were men wearing prayer shawls, men and women carrying home-printed sidearms, women with children, older children keeping watch over their brothers and sisters. All of them encircled the old station.

The frame of the dome was dull and black against the sky and the windows shone gray against the clouds and at the apex was the man who called himself the messiah. His eyes were closed and he swayed like a weather vane. They all waited. Michael tugged on Ethan's hand and said, "That's the man you talked to last night. I think he's going to do something."

Then he opened his mouth. But instead of speaking he stumbled, steadied himself, stumbled, and fell. The assembly gasped and several men rushed in. They formed a messy semicircle, crouching low. Overhead, the messiah flailed wildly and screamed something in a language that nobody knew. But it was not until several seconds later that they realized he was falling up. Soon after that, a few others joined him in his ascent, lifting off the ground and tumbling up before veering east toward the park—a woman with two children, a man in a wheelchair, a group of high school students holding hands. Michael watched them rise and then he pointed up.

"Ethan," he said, "isn't that your friend?"

Ethan lifted his eyes and saw Moti's face, full of elation, as he went up.

"Where is he going?" Michael asked.

"I don't know," Ethan said.

Ethan watched as Moti drifted away. And because his eyes were fixed on the sky he did not notice that Michael was growing light upon the earth. Michael rolled back onto his heels and then forward so that he was standing on his toes.

"Mom," he said. "What's happening?"

But Ella, like Ethan, was still looking up. "I don't know, honey," she said, without looking down. "It's okay."

She rested her hand on his shoulder. Her fingers were light, barely touching him, his body young and soft and, it seemed to Ella, impossibly fragile. She thought about the iron dogs standing next to the guards. She thought about how easily his body would break if they found themselves in the wrong place at the wrong time, how he could be taken from her or carried away by a crush of people if there was a riot. When was the last time there was a riot? She tried to remember. Everything around her suddenly seemed blurred and impressionistic as if the world had been poorly rendered. She tightened her grip. Michael said, "Mom, that hurts a little," but she did not hear him. Still the people were flying east after the messiah. They seemed to move very slowly, as if carried by a light wind. Then, suddenly, the world snapped into focus and rushed ahead with crushing, breathless speed. When Ella looked down, Michael was already two feet off of the ground and rising. She tried to hang on but his legs pitched up and the pressure was too great and he slipped through her fingers and she screamed, "Ethan! Ethan!" and Ethan leapt into the sky with a savage energy and grabbed Michael's forearm. "Ella, help me," Ethan said. "I can't hold him." "You're hurting me!" Michael screamed. "Stop it!" But Ethan did not stop. He pulled and pulled, his heart racing, until once again Ella was holding on as well, and then they both dragged Michael from the sky with all of the force they could muster, their fingernails digging deep gashes into his arms. They did not let go until, at last, they saw the messiah and his followers plunge down into the Northlands and disappear beneath the tree line, racing on toward the hole in the world. At last the sky's gravity relaxed and Michael's body was again soft and limp beneath their weight. He was crying and there was blood on his arms and they knelt together on the ground and showered him with kisses.

Ella rose to look around the square. The iron dogs were gone. The guards on the perimeter stood motionless in their Kevlar vests, their bodies swollen with death. In the little cages around the little trees she saw little flowers blooming, purple and white crocuses with small flames of orange in the center. One never knows what will arrive in a moment of crisis. Looking out on the crocuses and the still guards, Ella thought, *Soon it will be Pesach.* She wondered if matzah would come through the checkpoints, as it had last year, and she wondered how some thirty Jews could fall into the sky while still the guards remained, watching, ready. She gathered Michael up in her arms and held him as she had when he was very young, his legs wrapped around her waist and his chin pressing into her shoulder. The smell of his body was sweet and overwhelming. Then she leaned her face very close to Ethan's, her lower lip brushing against his earlobe as she whispered, "We need to get out of here."

LATER ON THEY SAT IN THE LIVING ROOM, LISTENING TO FRIGHTENING SOUNDS OUTside. A boom in the distance. The voices of drones. The clatter of the dogs' feet as they patrolled the streets. Ella lay against Ethan, her head pressed to his shoulder and her left hand resting on his stomach. She watched his chest rise and fall as he breathed, his skin pale beneath the reflected light from the streetlamps. Finally, Ella said, "I want you to tell me again."

"We did the right thing, Ella."

"Do you really think so?"

"Yes."

"I guess I always assumed we could run if we had to."

"We can."

"What if the city closes off access to the anomaly entirely?"

"They wouldn't do that."

"But what if they did?"

"They won't."

"Promise me that if it happens again . . ."

"It's not going to happen again."

"Promise me that if it happens again we'll let him go."

THEY WERE UNABLE TO SLEEP. AFTER LYING AWAKE FOR QUITE SOME TIME THEY PUT on spring jackets and went up onto the roof, where they stood quietly for quite a while, looking south toward the twinkling, silent city that had once been their home. Finally she said, "I want you to find out about the subway."

"The subway doesn't stop here," Ethan said. "You know that."

"The other one."

Ethan waited to see if she would say anything further. When she did not, he said, "I have MetroCards."

"What? What do you mean?"

"I mean I have MetroCards."

"How do you have them? There are hardly any circulating. Last week I heard about a woman a few blocks away who traded her apartment for two MetroCards."

"I got them a while ago from Alice. It was before, when they were still living across the park. It was the first time I met them, actually. They had the MetroCards and they were selling them for only a few hundred dollars each. It's amazing how valuable they've become."

"It's something to hope for."

"I only have three, Ella."

She put her hands to his face and kissed him.

He laughed. "So you're some kind of Rabbit now?"

"I don't know what I am. Why didn't you tell me?"

"Until today you'd been so set on staying. I guess I didn't think you would want to know."

"You're probably right."

"What changed?"

"I guess it was something Michael said. He said he thought we weren't really alive."

They were quiet for a few seconds. Then Ethan said, "Ella, it's only three."

"I heard you the first time," she said. "My father wouldn't be able to go anyway."

"He could try. You shouldn't break up your family for me."

"You're my family, Ethan."

"I asked you if you thought we could have been together if none of this had happened."

"I know. I don't know what you want me to tell you."

"I guess I want you to tell me, 'Yes.'"

Ethan stepped away from her and sat down on one of the plastic chairs that had been on the roof since the summer. It had become brittle over the winter and as he sat down he wondered if it might crack beneath his weight. But it did not crack. It wobbled and held and then he leaned his head back and looked up, his eyes tearing as a cold wind came in from the west.

Ella studied his face. It was thinner than when they met, strained. *He is so kind*, she thought. Even now he was trying to understand and forgive her. But beneath his facade of self-possession, she saw that he was angry and hurt. When cast out on endless waters there are some who thrash and kick. Others surrender. He looked like a man drowning and it enraged her and filled her with compassion.

"Ethan," she said, "let's get married."

"What?"

She kissed him gently on the mouth and then she pressed her palm into his chest. "Let's get married and then we'll go."

• • •

THAT YEAR PESACH BEGAN ON A SATURDAY NIGHT. THROUGH HIS CONNECTION WITH what remained of Moti's Crew, Ethan was able to acquire a few boxes of matzah that had been left behind two years earlier at an apartment overlooking the river, and he gave one box to the Rosenfelds and kept two for themselves. The acquisition of the matzah coincided with the partial restoration of the internet for a few days at the beginning of the month of Nisan. For the first time in a long while it was possible to stream videos and read news from abroad, which the Jews in the Pale did with ravenous enthusiasm, like starving men, gorging themselves but unable to fully assimilate the nourishment, their machinery slowed and atrophied. The metro anomaly in Paris had grown significantly, sending France into turmoil. The border with Germany closed. Baguettes were rationed. Militants operated from a base in Versailles. A physicist in the Netherlands believed that he had re-created an anomaly in his lab. A lab in Denmark failed to reproduce the results. A marine biologist from Australia claimed to have discovered a hole at the center of the Great Barrier Reef. He posted a photo of dead fish, of bleached and broken coral, another of pickled herring, another of Jews dancing at a wedding. A video went up online that appeared to show a Jewish family entering an anomaly in London and emerging three months later from an anomaly in Istanbul. No one knew where it came from and experts disagreed on what it could mean. At first it caused a great stir in the Pale. But over a period of forty-eight hours worldwide opinion began to coalesce around it being a fake and much of the excitement inside the Pale subsided. Then the internet slowed to a trickle once more. Opinions became retrenched. Life returned to its rhythms. Ethan and Ella prepared for Pesach.

A week before the seder, eggs became abundantly available at the warehouse adjacent to the southern checkpoint. This was surprising and it lightened the mood once again and it gave rise to rumors that perhaps things were changing on the city council and in the country as a whole. Jews came with wire pushcarts and loaded them high with flats of eggs and the sidewalks around the warehouse were yellowed with yolks and when Ella took Michael along to get their eggs he pointed down at a broken egg near his feet and said, "It looks like a little sunrise." In the synagogues the rabbis gave sermons about leaving Egypt and about how every generation is redeemed anew. They spoke about the mitzvah of "recognizing the good," which was a matter of grave importance. For the most part they did not render opinions about the Istanbul video, except for the ones who did and then they were lauded for courage or castigated for intemperance.

In the days immediately preceding the holiday there were several curfew violations. They were discovered on successive mornings—a dead man with a shredded face, a family of four bobbing near the bank of the river, pieces of flesh splattered on a mailbox. The number of iron dogs increased noticeably throughout the week and they began patrolling during the daytime as well as at night. They accompanied children on their way to school. By the night of the first seder the mood in the Pale had once again turned dark and fearful and the Jews who were left huddled at home with their eggs and their matzah and felt the pull of the hole in the earth. It was an unhealing wound, a deeper darkness within the night.

BEFORE THE FIRST SEDER BEGAN, JOEL SAT WITH MICHAEL AND TOGETHER THEY read through the Haggadah. In the second year of the restrictions, the public schools in the Pale added a component of Jewish literacy to the curriculum so Michael knew more about the seder than he used to and he was proud and excited to tell his grandfather what he had learned.

Just before Ethan and Ella called them to the table, Joel flipped back to the beginning of the Haggadah and said, "Look at this—it's a picture of hunters and dogs trying to catch a rabbit. Did your teachers ever mention that?"

"I don't remember."

"Have you ever heard of Bugs Bunny?"

"No. Who's that?"

"He was a Jewish rabbit in a cartoon that was made before I was born. Maybe if the internet starts working again we can watch it together."

"What does he do?"

"Plays tricks on people and then runs away." Joel laughed. "Anyway, this picture is important for years like this one when the seder falls on Saturday night. It reminds us about the order of things."

"How does it do that?"

"Well, in Yiddish—do you know what Yiddish is?"

Michael shook his head.

"It's a language that Jews used to speak a long time ago," said Joel.

"Like when you were little?"

"Before that. You know how you call me 'Zeyde'? That's a Yiddish word."

Michael nodded and Joel said, "So in Yiddish the words *jag den has* mean 'hunt the hare.' But they also sound like the word *yaknehaz*, which is a Hebrew abbreviation that reminds us about the special order for tonight. You see, the picture reminds us of some words and the words remind us of some other words. Do you understand?"

"Not really."

Joel smiled. "That's okay. Look"—he tapped on the page with his forefinger—"in the picture the rabbit is getting away."

"What happens when the hunters catch him?"

"They never catch him," Joel said. "Not in the Haggadah."

"But what happens if they do?"

"I guess they eat him."

"What about Bugs Bunny? Do they ever catch him?"

"Never."

"How did he get away?"

"Well, lots of different ways. Sometimes he would dive down into a hole in the ground."

"Just like Jews today," Michael said, and his grandfather nodded and said, "Yes, I guess that's right."

WHEN THE SEDER WAS OVER, ETHAN PUT MICHAEL TO BED AND ELLA SAT WITH HER father at the table. Joel always liked the after-dinner songs and Ella listened as he sang them quietly to himself, joining in here and there when she knew the words. When he sang the song about the little goat, he started laughing. He asked Ella if she remembered how, when she and her sister were small children, her mother would place a new toy or object on the table for each verse—a cat to bite the sheep, a dog to bite the cat, a stick to hit the dog, and so on until the verse about the Angel of Death, for which her mother would use a dried flower. When God slaughters the Angel of Death, she would quickly remove the dried flower from the table and replace it with a fresh one.

"Yes," Ella said, "I remember."

"I miss your mother, Ella. She would have helped us through all of this."

"I know, Dad."

He sang through the song once more, slowly, and without words. "Listen," Joel said. "I'm not going to be able to leave with you."

"Dad, we haven't—"

"You're right, you need to go."

"You'll come with us," she said. "Ethan will find a way to get one more ticket."

"No," he said. "I'm going to take my chances here. Besides"—he smiled an impish philosopher's smile—"from Egypt all of the people went free. But only the children entered the Promised Land."

Outside they heard voices and at Joel's insistence Ella helped him over to the window in the living room. Some of the Rabbits, having secured a dispensation from the city to violate the curfew, had organized a seder-night exodus and, from above, Joel and Ella watched them move along the street on their way to the park, their faces illuminated by the light of their cell phones, most of which had not received service in months. After they disappeared around the corner, Ella helped her father walk to bed. He could hardly put any weight on his hip and so Ella very nearly carried him. She found that she was able to do so easily, that he seemed almost weightless.

XIII

AT THE BEGINNING OF MAY THEY WERE STILL ABOVEGROUND. ETHAN HAD DECIDED that he wanted to finish out the school year—that he owed it to his remaining students not to abandon them—and he suggested that they wait until summer to see where things stood. He said that they could let Michael have this time with his friends and with his grandfather, because who could say when he would have time with them again? This worried Ella—not his concern for Michael but his willingness to wait. And whenever she dwelled on it she came to the conclusion that she and Ethan were bound to one another but mismatched, like puzzle pieces forced together.

In any case, she agreed that they could stay a while longer. And soon enough the acuteness of whatever she felt earlier in the spring dissipated. For weeks after the messiah's distortion, Ella had watched Michael's feet as he walked to see if they would rise from the ground. But they never did and eventually she stopped watching. Meanwhile, Ethan continued his teaching. And Ella, following the surprising success of a new photo essay about women who had given birth in the Pale, received a special invitation from her magazine to travel through the southern checkpoint in order to attend a brokered meeting with members of the city council, one of only a handful of such dispensations that had been awarded over the previous six months.

They argued for several days about whether or not she should go. Both Ethan and Joel thought it was too risky. The last Jew to leave—a lawyer and former alderman who was selected to appear before the city council—was captured and beaten almost to death in the subway station near city hall. It was irresponsible, they said, and she should consider Michael. But Ella argued that it was the lawyer's decision to take the subway that had been foolish, a silly symbolic gesture, and she reminded them that the city council was sending a car, which would meet her just beyond the checkpoint. She would be careful, she said, and she would not take any chances. And, even more to the point, she was considering Michael. She wanted to remind him that there was still a world beyond the Pale.

On the morning of the meeting, two border guards came to their door to hand-deliver the papers, a boy and a girl who could not have been much older than eighteen or nineteen years old. It was just before sunrise and the landing outside their apartment, which had only a single southern-facing window and a dim fluorescent light fixture, was still mostly dark. The guards held assault rifles with black straps slung over their shoulders, and their faces were contemptuous and monstrously calm. Michael was afraid of them and he hid behind Joel when he saw them standing in the doorway. The girl laughed.

"How old is he?" she asked, as she handed Ella a white envelope.

"He's seven," Ella said.

"Isn't he a little old to be hiding like that?"

Ella tried to smile. "He just doesn't meet very many new people. Michael," she said, turning back, "it's okay. Would you like to come say hello to the guards?"

But Michael ran away down the hall, where Ethan was waiting. As she opened the envelope, Ella could hear him crying softly. "Thank you," she said, looking up.

"You should leave soon," said the boy. "Sometimes it takes a while to get through. Though you should wait until sunrise, of course. Unless you want to meet the dogs."

"Yes," Ella said. "Okay. Of course."

The boy whispered something to the girl and she laughed again. Then he leaned in close so that his face was only a few inches from Ella's. "You should take that kid out more," he said. "You don't want him to be a pussy."

Ella remained in the doorway, shaking. She listened as they descended, their boots squeaking against the marble staircase. Behind her she could hear Michael saying, "I really don't want Mommy to go. Why does she have to go?"

"Your mommy takes amazing pictures," Ethan said. "She's letting everyone know what's going on in here. That's why the goyim outside want to talk to her. They want to see how special she really is."

"They won't hurt her?"

"No chance. Your mommy is too tough."

"What about the dogs?"

"You know the dogs turn off during the day."

"Not anymore. Sometimes they don't."

"You're right, Michael. There are some risks. But it's going to be okay. Mommy is smart and careful and really strong."

"What is she going to do in the city?"

"She's going to talk to the city council. That's the government, the people who run the city."

"I know what the city council is. Maybe she can ask them to let us out," he said, and when Ethan did not answer right away, he continued, "Or maybe she can ask them if we can go to the zoo once before we leave."

Ethan bent down and kissed him on the cheek and forehead.

"Come on," he said. "Let's get your shoes on. We'll walk Mommy to the checkpoint before going to school. We can wait in line with her."

But when they arrived at the checkpoint there was no one in the building apart from a few guards. One of them, a woman about Ella's age, examined her papers quickly and waved her along without speaking. Ella hugged Ethan and Michael. Then she snaked her way along an empty queue made from chain-link fencing. Ethan and Michael, standing in a small vestibule that opened back out into the Pale, watched her go back and forth, her gray messenger bag bobbing against her hip. With each switchback, her body was crisscrossed with more and more wiring so that she appeared to blur as she made her way along. They had expected a lengthy process. But she was through in a matter of minutes.

THAT DAY MICHAEL HAD TROUBLE FOCUSING AT SCHOOL. AT FIRST HE THOUGHT ABOUT his mother, the image of her body flickering as she walked back and forth between the fences. He tried to imagine where she had gone and to remember what it used to be like when they would go downtown together, to see a movie or to get a treat at one of the bakeries where they let Jews get treats. He knew that he had done these things because she told him so, often with great swells of emotion that he did not entirely understand. But he could remember only a single time, standing with her outside a tall building and looking up at the sky, clear and quiet.

Throughout the morning, the warplanes and helicopters flew over the Pale every fifteen minutes, much more frequently than he could ever remember. Ms. Kaplan assured them that they were safe, that the goyim were fighting far away. Mr. Handelman would make an announcement through the intercom if there was anything to worry about, she said, and an alarm would sound and they would have plenty of time to get someplace safe. For the most part, despite the disturbances, the day progressed normally through the morning. The class was in the middle of a science unit and, though it was controversial among the students' parents, they were studying some of the basic properties of the anomalies. Ms. Kaplan reminded them that most of the holes were not very big, about the size of a small car, and that nice people called engineers built large structures around them to make sure that nobody would fall in.

"But they're getting bigger," one student said.

"Very slowly," Ms. Kaplan said.

"What about the one in the Northlands?" another student asked. "Isn't that why they locked us in here?"

"It is a very hard situation," said Ms. Kaplan. "That's why we are all learning about science. Maybe one day you will grow up to be real scientists and help make the world better."

But later, during reading groups, a formation of planes flew low and the windows rattled in their frames and Leah, the girl sitting across from Michael, started to cry. She was new to the reading group, having only recently moved up from another, and she was already nervous.

Michael wanted to help her feel better but he did not know what to say, so instead he read his paragraph aloud, just like Ms. Kaplan said, trying to make his voice carry over the sound of a siren outside, the sound of someone yelling in an adjacent room, the sound of five hundred Jews marching down the street in front of the school, chanting something that Michael could not make out. He focused on the page. He wanted to make his teacher happy and he understood, not consciously but with a child's intuition, that Ms. Kaplan was working very hard to make sure they knew that all was well. And she needed their help to maintain the illusion.

The book they were reading was called *Uncle Kitty* and it was about a family of cats. The cats lived in a big city, like theirs, but in the summer they would go to visit their uncle in the country and they would have all kinds of adventures. It was divided into chapters and after each chapter they had to answer comprehension questions. How did Julian feel about going to visit his uncle? A.) Excited; B.) Scared; C.) Happy; D.) Sad.

Leah was supposed to read the next paragraph, but when Michael finished she was still crying.

Michael said, "Leah, it's your turn, okay? You'll do a good job if you try," but she looked away and started fiddling with a paperclip.

Across the room, Jacob folded a paper airplane. It was not well-made. Michael could see that before he threw it and when he did, it drifted limply to the floor. Ms. Kaplan saw but said nothing. Why did she say nothing? She remained behind her desk, checking over math worksheets from earlier in the morning and now, when the warplanes flew over once again, she twitched. Leah, still crying, slipped off her chair. She went underneath the table, like they had practiced, and drew her knees close to her chest.

"Ms. Kaplan," someone said, "Leah is under the desk," and some other students laughed nervously.

Ms. Kaplan stood up and looked out over the classroom. She was wearing a loose-fitting green dress and red glasses and Michael thought she looked very beautiful and very scared and because the teacher was scared he was scared and outside the voices were getting louder. Ms. Kaplan walked over to their reading group and knelt down next to Leah. She rubbed her back gently.

"Why don't you go get a drink of water?" she said.

"I want to go home," Leah said.

Ms. Kaplan smiled. "It's going to be okay, Leah. Those weren't bombs; they were just planes. They're flying far away from here. And besides, this is a big, strong building, and we've done our drills. See, you're doing it just right. You were paying attention."

More screaming from outside, two competing sirens, the screech of a bullhorn, the metallic clatter of dogs, the sound of an explosion. She went over to the window and looked out. A brick came through. Then another. Something tore at Ms. Kaplan's face and she turned around and stumbled forward. Blood dripped onto the floor, onto the table. She said, "I'm okay. Kids, I'm okay." A gunshot. The sound of broken glass. A voice crackled over the speaker system. "Teachers, barricade all doors." Then static. Then silence. Michael got under the desk.

From afar he willed the door shut. But the door remained open. Most of his classmates tried to keep quiet, their bodies shaking. Two of them ran over into the closet where they had been told to hide if they could get there. Three fled down the hall. Two more squeezed their bodies into the pine cubbies, wiggling their arms and legs and then remaining very still. Another gunshot. An older boy ran down the hall. Ms. Kaplan, dazed and distant, mumbled something, and then she closed her eyes and fell forward, her face landing near Michael's feet.

Again Michael turned his head toward the door. He saw men walking the halls in heavy boots and the boots were old and worn like the ones he had seen in some of his mother's old photography books. They had dogs on chains, not metal dogs but dogs made of fur and flesh and they barked and growled as they moved along, straining against the chains, their teeth flashing white. The men who held the chains seemed to waver. Their faces were blank and indistinguishable, like in a dream, and they spoke a language Michael could not understand.

Michael looked for Jacob across the room but Jacob had already fled down the hall. The two girls were still in the closet. The two boys were still in their pine cubbies, motionless now and with holes in them. Michael wanted to go home. But he did not know how to get home. He remembered once again that his mom had gone through the checkpoint and that she would not be at their apartment, even if he made it back, and maybe that was related, somehow, to the men with the dogs and the boots. After creeping out from beneath the desk, he crawled over to the window, the glass blurred and grayed by soot, smoke, ash, but the world outside snapping into focus where the brick had gone through. The street was empty and there was a fire burning. It blackened the ground. He blinked and saw carriages, helmets, tanks, vehicles he did not recognize, a piece of a horse. And at the far end of the block he saw a man running. The man jumped over what remained of a car, fell, seared his arm on a piece of burning metal, cursed and screamed but got up quickly and continued running, faster than before until he reached the school and stopped short and looked up, shielding his eyes from the sun.

"Michael!" Ethan said. "Stay right there. I'm coming to you."

Michael crawled back under the desk and remained very still until he saw Ethan standing in the doorway. Ethan said, "I'm here," and Michael ran over to hug him and then together they made their way along the hallway and down the stairs leading to the lobby, stepping around backpacks, broken glass, bullet casings, bodies, none of whom Michael could recognize. To the left of the security desk there were several large bulletin boards featuring student work—short essays about Pesach, book projects, self-portraits done in pastels—most of it now hanging in shreds.

Michael said, "I used to have something hanging up there," but Ethan only said, "Come on, we need to walk quickly, Michael," and he dragged Michael along, wrenching his arm.

"Ouch," he said, "you're hurting me, Ethan," and Ethan turned back and said, "I'm sorry, I didn't mean to. It's just, we really have to go fast. Can you do that for me?"

Michael nodded. Then said, "I guess school is over—"

Ethan did not respond but only hurried ahead, pushing through the crash bar on the front door with his shoulder. He held the door for Michael and the light streamed in along with dust and ash. Coughing, Michael stepped outside. His eyes stung. As they descended the front steps, he heard something behind him inside the building, a voice calling out.

"Someone needs help," Michael said, but Ethan said nothing as he guided him down the street and Michael, looking back for just a moment through black smoke, thought, *It isn't a school anymore. It's something else now.*

Several minutes later, as they turned onto their street, they could still taste the stinging, bitter tang of smoke. Ethan, pulling Michael along, was startled when his phone buzzed against his thigh. He stopped and Michael said, "What is it?" and, blinking and rubbing his eyes, Ethan read the text from Ella: *trying to get there, you should pack.* Ethan coughed. His eyes burned and the screen blurred and at first he almost could not understand what he was reading. Although Ethan did not realize it, it was a small miracle that the text came through. There were many on that day.

• • •

LATER IN THE AFTERNOON, ETHAN STOOD OVER THE BED THROWING CLOTHES INTO A green duffel bag. Michael watched him from a chair in the corner of the room. Ethan's movements were jerky and syncopated and he reminded Michael of the malfunctioning iron dog they had seen once when they were walking home from the Sunshine Market.

After stuffing the outer pocket of the bag with socks and underwear, Ethan turned to Michael and said, "Honey, I want you to go get your backpack and go into your room and find a few books and toys that you want to take with you."

"I want to take all of them."

"We can't take all of them. You should pick your favorites."

"What will happen to the rest?"

"I don't know."

"When is Mommy getting back?"

"Soon. I think soon." Then, glancing up at the shelf in the closet where the MetroCards were still hidden inside a pair of Ella's shoes, Ethan said, "Do you understand what's happening, Michael?"

"We're getting ready to go through. Like the Rabbits."

"That's right."

"I saw the text Mommy sent."

"She wants us to be safe."

"When are we going?"

"I don't know for sure."

"All of the rest I don't understand completely."

"Me neither," Ethan said. "Sometimes we have to do things even if we don't understand them."

Throughout the afternoon and early evening, Ethan and Joel did their best to present a calm and united front. Ella would be home soon, they said, and when she arrived they would all talk about what to do next and make a decision together. There were fires burning in the north, but, after the initial spasm, the southern checkpoint held and, for the most part, the neighborhood immediately surrounding their apartment remained quiet. Outside they could hear birds, someone playing music, gentle wind. But as the sun faded and the hour of the curfew drew near, Michael became more and more agitated and the charade became increasingly difficult to keep up.

Eventually, after a tearful hour, Michael fell asleep in the living room with Ethan's tablet resting on his forehead and when he did, Ethan carried him into the bedroom and placed him carefully in the center of the bed. Then he returned to the living room and joined Joel in the castle of books. The jasmine flowers were in bloom and Ethan suggested he make tea, but Joel shook his head and suggested they wait until Ella got back.

"Yes," Ethan said, "absolutely."

Meanwhile the hole widened, like the sudden rupture of a valve in the heart.

ETHAN JERKED AWAKE. HE LOOKED UP AT ELLA'S FACE, BLOODY BUT INTACT.

"What happened?" he said. "Where is Michael?"

Ella was sitting next to him on the couch, her fingers resting gently on his thigh. She was backlit by the light from the kitchen and her face was shadowy and indistinct, as if she had been painted with quick brushstrokes. But when she leaned forward and touched the side of his neck, he could see that her lip was crusted with blood and that her left eye was swollen.

"He's asleep," she said. "Right where you left him. And thanks for asking but I'm fine also."

"I'm sorry."

She smiled. "It's okay. I know that being with Michael has always been among the most appealing parts of being with me."

"That's not true."

"I think it is. And it's okay. I understand."

"What time is it?" Ethan asked.

"I don't know. Around eleven o'clock, maybe. The clocks aren't working."

"They've always been wonky around the anomalies."

"No, I mean they've stopped. Or they're spinning out of control."

He struggled to process what she was telling him. "You mean the one in the kitchen?"

"I mean all the clocks in the city, Ethan."

"What are you talking about?"

"I don't know, something's happened. There are riots everywhere. Somewhere in the south one of the militias is entering the city. They're marching for the Pale. The hole in the Northlands is getting bigger."

"How do you know?"

"Can't you feel it?"

His eyes were bright with desire. "Yes," he said. "I can feel it."

"Apparently they can too," Ella said.

"Who?"

"The goyim."

"That's not possible."

"They think it's finally going to happen, just like in Jerusalem. I heard it at city hall."

"You made it there?"

"Yes, and I made it back. Like I said I would."

"How?"

"Kyle helped me."

"What? Why?"

"He found me in midtown. I don't know how, but there he

was, coming out of the crowd. He led me back through the subway tunnels."

"Why would he do that?"

"He just said he wanted to help." Then she said, "You don't believe me."

"Of course I do," he said. "When have you ever lied to me?"

"No you don't," she said. "I can tell."

THEY FELL ASLEEP NEXT TO ONE ANOTHER ON THE COUCH AND WHEN THEY DID THEY shared a dream. In the dream there was the distant whirr of a drill; voices in the dark; the clang of the doorknob of their apartment as it lurched off and fell; a sharp beam of light streaming from the stairwell; the sound of footsteps, soft and precise; breathing; somewhere a heartbeat; somewhere the luster of an eye. Something tumbled and fell. A light went on and then burst into darkness as the glass from the lightbulb rained down. There was a scream as Joel lurched forward from the shadows, yelling in pain with his crutch held high. He brought it down. He brought it down again. Again. The crack of a gunshot.

And when they woke up the dream remained. Ella's pulse jumped in her throat and she said, "Ethan, someone is here."

They made their way quickly down the hall and found Joel, half-naked, standing in the doorway of their bedroom. In front of him, on the floor, was Alice Rosenfeld, bleeding from a gash above her eye. Joel stood over her, looking down. With his left hand he held the wall for support. With his right hand he held the gun that Ethan had brought with him on the day he made it back.

Joel was shaking. He pointed toward the pile of boxes, shoes, and tote bags that had fallen from the top shelf of Ella's closet. "The gun went off when everything came down," he said.

Gently, Ethan took the pistol from Joel. His hands were steady as he chambered another round and Ella noticed it and she frowned as she thought of Moti and his goons, how over the winter, before Moti went up with the messiah, they built a makeshift shooting range in the basement of one of the abandoned schools.

Ethan, passing into shadow, stepped into the room and stood over Alice. She was crying and dabbing her lip with her finger.

"Where are the MetroCards?" he said.

"I don't have them," she said.

"But that's why you're here."

"Yes," she managed to say. "That's why we're here."

Still holding the pistol, Ethan dug through the pile of fallen objects and took the three MetroCards out of Ella's boat shoes, where he had left them. He walked over to Ella and kissed her on the forehead. "It's going to be okay," he said. "Everything is okay."

Standing in the half-darkened room, they all tried to make sense of what was happening to them. Alice stayed down on the floor, in pain. Ethan and Ella held on to one another. They slipped over the edge of something they could not see and fell into a frightened, dreamlike paralysis. From the stairwell they heard Noah call out, "Alice, what's happening?" But it was not until they heard Michael—first his feet along the old floorboards and then his soft, high voice—that they were restored to the present and to themselves.

He was standing in the hall and he said, "Why is Jacob's mommy here?"

Ethan crouched down so that they were on the same level. "Jacob is here also," he said. "Isn't that right, Alice?"

"Yes," she said. "He's down the hall with Noah."

"They heard that we're leaving," Ella said quickly. "They came to say goodbye. Isn't that nice? Why don't you go give Jacob a hug?"

"How did they get here? Aren't there dogs outside?"

"Something happened in the city," Ella said. "I guess the rules are a little different now." Sleepily, Michael made his way down the hallway. After the boys said their goodbyes, Ella helped Alice to her feet and together they walked out into the stairwell. For some time none of the adults spoke. Then, looking away, Noah said, "Can you just leave the gun? Please. We will come back for it tomorrow."

"Why would we do that?" Ethan asked.

"If you find the subway you aren't going to need it."

"How do you know?"

"I'm begging you," he said, "as a fellow Jew."

"We'll see," Ethan said.

THE RABBI WAS AWAKE. SHE ALWAYS ROSE EARLY, EVER SINCE SHE WAS A LITTLE girl, and when she was older she discovered that the most important code of Jewish law began with the statement, "A person should rise in the morning like a lion to serve their creator," and she applied the line to herself and it became an organizing feature of her life, which had now reached the tail end of its eighth decade. Her husband, who was a few years younger, did not get up so early and so every day she had several quiet hours alone, to read or write or study or, more recently, to scroll through photographs on her phone and daydream about when her children were young. Her sons had moved overseas in their early twenties, first to Europe and then to Israel. They had both become more traditionally observant than their parents, an occupational hazard of her work in a congregation, and they settled in a religious community in the Galilee, where they led sunstruck and windswept lives. The rabbi and her husband did not see them as much as they would have liked, but her sons dutifully texted photographs of their five grandchildren, young and thin and tan. In one set of photographs that she particularly liked they were all hiking together—pictures of her grandchildren on a rock slide, followed by a photograph of the boys themselves, their arms around one another's shoulders, their faces strong and beautiful, only three days before the First Event. Each morning she would begin there and scroll back, watching as the grandchildren got smaller, as she and her husband aged backward, as her children returned finally to her womb, an inversion of life.

When the doorbell rang, just before sunrise, she looked up from her phone and wiped the past from her eyes. When she opened the door she saw a young couple—a man and a woman.

His face was thin and tired and her face was bruised and quite pretty and then she saw a little bit of gray hair around his ears and she realized that they were not really so young but then again neither was she. She did not recognize them right away and, intuitively, she tried to decide if she should know them from somewhere, if perhaps they were congregants or parents from the Hebrew school, when there was a Hebrew school. She had only retired altogether five years earlier and she still knew most of the families at the shul, though it was harder and harder for her to remember the younger ones. And since the checkpoints went up, she seldom went to her office, a small room adjacent to the sanctuary that had long been the domain of the rabbis emeritus. To the extent that the synagogue still functioned, the rabbi was not well acquainted with who remained, and she thought, *No, I do not know them.*

"Can I help you?" she asked.

"We're so sorry," said the woman. "Did we wake you?"

"No," said the rabbi. "I'm an old woman."

"Are you the rabbi?" asked the man.

"I'm a rabbi," said the rabbi. "I'm Rabbi Shapiro."

"We want to get married," said the woman.

"You know," said the rabbi, "it's not really possible to register the marriage with the city."

"We don't care," said the man.

"Okay," said the rabbi. "Maybe we can find a time to meet later in the week to talk about it?"

"No," said the woman. "We're leaving today. It has to be now."

"Oh," said the rabbi. "I see. Well, why don't you come in? We just need to be quiet so as not to wake my husband."

The rabbi led them into her living room and then left them there while she went to the kitchen to boil water for coffee. She could hear them talking quietly but she could not make out what they were saying. She took a breath. She thought of a teaching from the Talmud about travelers in the desert who lose track of the days and no longer know when to observe Shabbat. On the day they realize that they have lost track they are supposed to start counting and on the seventh day they are supposed to rest. At one time she believed this was a beautiful and wise sentiment. But now it struck her as entirely unreal. Here were the things that were real: The day before yesterday a child was beaten for smuggling phone chargers through a checkpoint. A week earlier her husband confessed that he had not felt hungry in weeks. A week before that an iron dog shot a man in the leg as he was walking his daughter to school. Day followed day in fear and in confusion and in malaise. The trains raced through the stations but would not stop. A person lost in an unforgiving wilderness cannot observe the Sabbath.

She brought the coffee and sat down across from the couple. She said, "I need to copy down the ketubah. Do you know what that is?"

The woman nodded.

"I would just print it out, of course, but, you know—"

"Yes," said the man. "Of course. We understand."

"Is there anybody you would like to be there besides us?"

"My father and son," said the woman. "They're at our house. My father doesn't walk so, well, so we were hoping you could come there."

The rabbi nodded. "In just a bit we can wake my husband. He can serve as one of the witnesses. The second we'll have to find down on the street, but that shouldn't be a problem. It's all Jews down there." She paused and in her mind she tried to sift through all the couples whom she had married. Was it thirty? Forty? She could not say. "Do you have any questions?" she asked.

"No," said the woman. "Thank you for doing this."

"Of course," said the rabbi. "Mazel tov." But as she raised her cup of coffee she felt the tug of the anomaly and she thought, *Why on earth would anyone want to get married now?*

JOEL GAVE MIRIAM'S WEDDING RING TO ETHAN, PLACING IT IN THE CENTER OF HIS palm and folding his fingers over the top. He kissed him on both cheeks and then he nodded, his eyes shining. "Come on, Michael," he said, limping across the room with his grandson. "It's time."

In the living room, near the window, stood the rabbi—her small frame cast in silhouette by the rising sun—along with the witnesses as required by Jewish law: the rabbi's husband, Leonard, and a man named Joseph, whom they met on the street. Leonard was small, just like his wife, with a poorly kept beard and a sleepy, distant demeanor, like an ancient mystic. Joseph was a very tall man, young but with hair prematurely gray and eyes that looked wildly around the room. He frightened Michael and Joel said, "It's okay, honey. This will be quick," and a minute later Ella came in from the other room wearing a floral sundress and high heels, a bright and unexpected apparition, as if transmigrating from another world. They all laughed at the strangeness of the scene and Ethan said, "You look beautiful, Ella," and Ella smiled and rolled her eyes, stumbling in her heels as the rabbi chanted, "Blessed are those who come in the name of Adonai." She went through the liturgy quickly, without flourish. When Ethan broke the glass, nobody stooped to gather the shards.

The rabbi and the witnesses left when it was over. Joel, through great physical exertion, had baked a small cake for the celebration and Michael cried when it was gone because that meant it was time to say goodbye. Joel embraced his grandson and said, "When it's safe you come back and tell me what's down there," and Michael asked, "What if that isn't how it works?" and Joel said gently, "That's okay too, honey. Don't worry about that."

Ella, Ethan, and Michael left shortly thereafter, waiting out a swift and fierce cloudburst, and then stepping into the bright morning. Joel watched them from the window as they maneuvered around the mangled remains of a motorcycle. When he could no longer see them he limped into the kitchen, where he took a paring knife from the butcher block on the counter and carved an inscription into one of the subway tiles behind the range:

כאן גרה משפחה יהודית שמחה בין התחנה הקודמת לתחנה הבאה

Exhausted, he slumped into a chair at the dining room table. In the apartment there was food for a month, one working cell phone, the printed gun, the generous sunlight, the rain-freshened air. Alone, Joel wandered the world in his mind. But his body would not take him farther than the bedroom and there he lay down and slept.

• • •

THEY STOPPED ON A STREET CORNER A FEW BLOCKS EAST OF THEIR APARTMENT. ELLA knelt in front of Michael and asked him to extend his arm. She took out a red Sharpie and, holding his arm firmly, she printed, between his elbow and wrist, her name and Ethan's name, her father's name, their address in the Pale, and all of their phone numbers. Then she reached into her duffel bag, took out a box of plastic wrap, and wrapped his arm.

"It feels weird," he said.

"It's so it doesn't get wet and smear."

"But I know your names. If anyone asks me I'll just tell them."

Ella looked at Michael and then she looked up at Ethan. They had discussed it just before sunrise, while Michael was still asleep. They had decided that it was a good idea to write the names and numbers in case they were separated and Michael was found by someone who did not speak English. And then, without saying it, they also decided that it was a good idea in case, when he was found, he could no longer talk.

"It's just to be safe," she said, pulling his sleeve down over the plastic wrap. "There might be a lot of people on the other side of the anomaly and we want you to be able to find us if we get separated."

"Okay."

"Don't tell anyone about it unless you have to."

"Not even other Jews?"

"You never know."

He ran his fingers over his forearm. "It tickles a little," he said.

"I know," Ella said. "Look, Michael, I want you to listen to me very carefully. If something happens—if you see me or Ethan get hurt or if we can't go any further and we tell you to keep going, you keep going."

"What?"

"You don't stop once we say run, do you understand me?"

"I don't want to be without you."

"I know, and it won't happen, but if it does you keep going. You do exactly what we say and you don't worry about us."

"What if I can't keep going? Will you leave me?"

"Never."

"But I should leave you?"

"That's right. I want you to promise me."

"Mommy, please—" He started to cry.

"You promise me right now, Michael."

"Okay," he said. "I promise."

THEY CARRIED WHAT THEY COULD CARRY: TWO SMALLISH DUFFEL BAGS FILLED WITH clothes and toiletries; a messenger bag filled with charging cables, their laptops, cell phones, and other electronics; another messenger bag filled with tools and first aid, a flashlight, a box of Allen wrenches, a screwdriver, a utility knife, two boxes of bandages, antibiotic ointment, painkillers, a bottle of vodka, a travel sewing kit; a backpack filled with canned food, bottled water, and their IDs; a smaller backpack filled with the toys and books that Michael had chosen, his monkey stuffie, two of his primate books, paper and colored pencils, a little bag of Magna-Tiles; a fanny pack filled with gold bullion. The MetroCards they carried in their pockets.

Kyle was waiting at the entrance to the Northlands, and he asked for the bullion in exchange for letting them pass through. Ethan thought he was joking.

"You're a fascist," Ethan said, but he was smiling when he said it and he punched Kyle gently on the shoulder. "Come on," he said, "let's get going. I don't want to wait for what's happening in the south to make its way here."

Kyle said, "All you fucking Jews do is run. You ever think maybe that's why we can't stand you? You disgusting fucking rats. Just bringing disease everywhere. You know they burned my apartment building three nights ago?"

"Who did?" Ethan asked.

"I don't know, some fucking militia. I heard they did it because there were some Jews inside, some rats who managed to stay out of the Pale all this time. So I guess that's a saving grace."

"Come on, Kyle," Ella said. "It's not funny in front of Michael. I can't imagine your bosses care about who enters the park today."

"My bosses?" Kyle laughed. Then he moved quickly, grabbing Ella by the shoulder and forcing her onto the ground until she was flat on her back. He took his billy club from his belt and raised it high above his head. His fingers were white and his eyes were feral. Ella looked up at him and started to cry.

"I guess I gave you a mistaken impression," he said. "Just because I like the feel of a Jewish asshole you think we're friends?"

"Why are you doing this?" Ella asked.

"You want to know why they're coming? It's because of that fucking hole. Just like that guy on the island says, just like everyone says. There was a scientist on TV. Those holes will eat you or they'll eat the world."

"That's not true," Michael said, looking up. "Right, Mommy, that's not real?"

"They're gonna push all of you inside," Kyle said. "Or maybe just into the river."

"We're already going," Ethan said. "Just let us through."

"I'll do that my way," Kyle said.

"You saved my life," Ella said.

Kyle grabbed her crotch. "And I didn't take what was coming to me then." He adjusted his sidearm. "Maybe I'll take it right here instead of the gold." He looked at Ethan and smiled. "What do you think, brother?" He slapped Ella on the hip.

She winced and Michael started to cry. "Stop it," he said, "you're hurting her."

Kyle dragged Ella to her feet and said, "Look, just give me the gold and get going. I would stick to the woods if I were you. I don't know what's going on with the drones."

To their surprise, Kyle said that he would walk with them as they entered the park. "Michael and I will lead the way," he said, taking Michael's hand. "Isn't that right?" Michael tried to pull away but Kyle held his grip.

Ella said, "It's okay. Kyle's a friend. He was joking just now. Look, I'm fine." She smiled and then said, "Ethan and I are right here."

As they walked, Ethan did not take his eyes from Michael. He wondered what would happen if he went for Kyle's gun. He was frightened and ashamed of himself and when he touched Ella's hand her body stiffened. But fifteen minutes later Kyle was gone and they were still together, the three of them walking down the stairs and then walking on through the old turnstile, blind until their eyes adjusted and then blind again when they approached the anomaly, waded into the dark, and passed through.

PART III

METRO

XIV

LIKE A MUSEUM OF NATURAL HISTORY—THAT WAS HOW IT SEEMED TO ELLA SEVERAL months later as she made her way slowly along a narrow tunnel, damp and cool and cave-like, past camping tents with their front flaps open, or black tarps supported by metal poles, or small rooms constructed from heavy cardboard or corrugated metal. Everywhere the smell of mold and unlaundered clothes, here and there perfume, kitty litter, grilled meat, urine, shit, something dead. The tunnel itself—like all the tunnels down there—was paved with tracks and haphazardly illuminated by caged lightbulbs. Most of the individual encampments had their own light sources as well, battery-powered lanterns or lamps plugged into small generators, and these combined to give the little villages—because what should she call them if not villages?—a dreamlike, chiaroscuro quality, like dioramas of Neanderthals and Denisovans, their bodies strung with leather and bone, their faces fixed and timeless and without life.

But Ella saw Jews. They had entered from everywhere. From

their city and from others. From Berlin and from Melbourne and from Toronto and from Buenos Aires. From many other cities as well, together or alone, with many things or few things or with nothing, with dogs and cats that children could not bear to leave behind, with toys and weapons and drugs, with shoes or with bare feet, blistered and bleeding, passing through every anomaly but the first, the great hole in the Middle East, or so it seemed. Why this was the case was the subject of debate and speculation among the Jews and their opinions generated the incandescent fervor of those who grasp in the dark. The Israelis were hidden among them or they had gone on ahead lighting lamps for those who would follow or the first hole led elsewhere or it opened to the primordial deep or it led nowhere at all. Meanwhile, the tunnels seemed endless. Who could fathom their farther reaches? In the beginning the Jews worried about what might come down the tracks and they moved along, two by two, in a state of constant tension, like small animals. But the trains did not come and this they attributed to signal malfunctions or to investigations at unseen stations or to sin.

Like many others, during their first days underground Ethan and Ella went to one of the many kiosks, which were covered with notes and images of missing people, some on paper and some glowing on little screens. The kiosks were staffed by harried officials in blue vests who spoke through a filter that allowed them to communicate in a variety of languages. They wore visors embroidered with Stars of David and they were somehow connected to the big Jews with crowbars and to the various councils and assemblies that sprouted from the disorder. But the connection between them was unclear and, like the turbid speculation about the fate of the Israelis, perhaps imaginary. It was very rare to find anyone this way. Still, the officials in the blue vests took down every name with gentle forbearance, pasted notes or uploaded images or forwarded messages to their colleagues in adjacent tunnels or to other kiosks halfway around the world. Then they would write out a little receipt, which included names and a case number, and slide it beneath the glass that separated them from the desperate Jews in line and the lines moved along and cycled through and every day, it seemed, there were more kiosks and more officials in blue vests, all of them kind but none of them helpful. Ethan gave up after only a week, but Ella continued going most every day to search for any trace of her sister.

On that day she wandered further afield. She visited other kiosks, tunnels where the accents were different, where the music was foreign to her. She saw Jews from other places and other times. Jews from every land. Jews speaking dead languages and Jews speaking their language and Jews speaking languages not yet created. Jews of every size and shape and color. Jews from little towns hidden away in misty hills. Jews wearing turbans and smoking hookah. Jews preaching. Jews building bombs. Jews hammering leather and cutting fabric. Jews baking bricks. Jews selling wine. Jews festooned with henna. Jews slaughtering chickens, their clothes cracked with dried blood. Jews making medicines. Jews drinking schnapps. Jews collecting alms. Jews shining shoes and getting their shoes shined. Jews begging. Jews pickling fish. Jews swinging half-moon blades. Jews hammering away on keyboards. Jews playing chess, backgammon, violin. Jews dancing. Jews working miracles. Jews writing code. Jews standing up and telling jokes. Jews composing funeral dirges. Jews flagging down droshkies that did not come. Jews talking baseball. Jews grinding organs. Jews discussing the anomalies. Jews arguing over politics. Jews remembering life in the city. Jews singing "The Internationale." Jews deciding when and where to run. Jews going up in smoke. Jews with MetroCards and Jews without. Jews lingering around the station. Jews looking for the subway below the subway, just like they were. Their darkened faces assailed her with blunt, savage strength, like the sword of an ancient king. And from the wound the old questions rose like winged creatures—Ella watched them fly.

Somewhere in the dark Ella could hear the sound of a prayer quorum. Men and women were talking and singing and then, rising above the chaotic chatter of the unseen congregation, she heard the rich voice of the cantor. He was singing a tune she had not heard for quite a while but which she recognized at once as the melody for the first night of Rosh HaShanah, stately and magnificent and very much at odds with the squalor of the underground. Ella could not understand why he was singing it and she continued wondering about it long after his voice faded away into the distance, after she turned again and then again. And she was still wondering about it when suddenly she saw a ten-by-nine orange tent, jumping from the dark like a jack-o'-lantern at the base of a staircase. The staircase, long abandoned, was stacked with empty glass bottles, pearlescent in the half-light like small teeth. The flap of the tent hung open. Inside she saw duffel bags, scattered clothing and wires, some dirty stuffed monkeys (useless now), a small black safe, a little table on which Ethan and Michael were playing cards beneath the pale white light of a battery-powered lantern. Absently, she began to hum the Rosh HaShanah melody. When she did she realized that through all of their aimless revolutions underground, the world above, blessed by time and light, had raced ahead. Already the year was turning over. And when she stepped inside the tent she felt a strange mixture of revulsion and relief and she thought, as if for the first time, *I'm home now.*

Michael looked up from the game and handed her a few pieces of dried apple. "Look what Ethan got!" he said. "One was a little moldy, but most of them are still sweet." Then he said, "*Shanah tovah*, Mommy. That's what we say, right?"

"Yes, honey, that's what we say."

She kissed both Michael and Ethan and then sat down cross-legged on the floor. They stayed in their tent because there was nowhere to go and nothing to do. As the evening stretched on, the crying of the children in the surrounding tents and structures became louder and louder as they grew hungrier, as the older ones realized that their parents were lying when they said, "Tonight we will find noodles, tonight you can eat until you're full." Eventually, Ethan and Ella zipped the flap of their tent in a vain effort to keep out the smell of shit and urine and unwashed bodies and through the diaphanous velum they watched forms move along in silhouette—parents taking their children to defecate at the end of the tunnel, men ambling drunkenly through the tunnel, women carrying children who whimpered softly or did not make any sounds at all.

Earlier in the day, Ethan had visited one of the distribution centers where the big Jews with crowbars sometimes gave out canned food or grain or bottles of water. All day long Jews came through the anomaly and when they had food, water, medicine, or electronics, the big Jews would confiscate a portion of their supplies for public distribution, and in exchange they would help their brothers and sisters find suitable places to pitch their tents. Then they would take them to the kiosks to find their living or their dead, depending on what they believed and depending on the shape of their hopes. This had once seemed unjust to Ethan but he learned to see the wisdom in it and he only wondered how long it could last. How long before the stream of Jews dried up? How long before the big Jews used their crowbars for something other than prying open crates? And it was there, at the distribution center not far from their anomaly, that he bartered for the apples, along with two bottles of water, a can of mushrooms, and a small can of tuna.

After eating, Michael was still hungry, but he went to sleep quickly because Ella said that he would feel better if he slept, though she did not know if that was true. Ethan set the empty cans onto the floor and sat down next to Ella. With care, they took turns filling their cupped hands with a few drops of the bottled water, which they then used to wash their faces. They did so quietly, like a ritual, just as they had the night before and the night before that, their silent lustrations an attempt to wash away some residue of their journey through, something of the anomaly that had seeped inside and taken root—a great, yawning absence. But, their washings notwithstanding, it remained, or so they feared.

When their ablutions were complete, Ethan leaned his head on Ella's shoulder. As Michael slept, Ethan retraced the phone numbers and contact information on Michael's arm. Somewhere below them, deep in the earth, they heard the growl of a train. The rumble traveled up through rock and steel and hummed in their chests. It did not happen every day nor even every week, just as headlight sightings were invariably brief and insubstantial. And yet always, when these things did occur, their hearts would race. They would be momentarily breathless, stirred by frissons of joy.

It had been four months since they had seen the sun.

THE FOLLOWING DAY ETHAN FOUND SOME JEWS WHO WERE CELEBRATING THE NEW Year. Having entered through the anomaly in Moscow, they spoke Russian among themselves, but their prayer books were in Hebrew and French. This was not so uncommon in the underground, where everything was mixed and nothing was straightforward or easy. Ethan could not read Hebrew well enough to follow along consistently and what help was offered was offered in Russian, so for the most part he was lost, only occasionally finding his place before inevitably losing it once more. The voice of the prayer leader, a tenor, was rich and suggestive, but the words were meaningless to him, as they had been for as long as he could remember. Perhaps in another time or place their mysteries would have stirred him, but on that morning they did not. He was simultaneously bored and frightened, as he was almost all of the time.

His mind wandered. He thought about the man who called himself the messiah. He had gathered his followers not far from where they had pitched their tent and he seemed robust and clear-eyed, so different from the person who had smashed his face on the counter at the Sunshine Marketplace and then fell up into the sky. Ethan decided that whoever he was and whatever he was trying to accomplish, life in the underground suited him, and in the days just after they passed through Ethan spent some time lingering around his camp, talking with his followers or watching them dance or listening to them argue among themselves about something their leader had said. Moti was among them. But Moti was changed and they both realized quickly that whatever had bound them to one another in the Pale had loosened and fallen away.

When the cantor reached his climax, Ethan thought about Ella and about Michael and, as ever, he wondered how and if they would survive the week. Ella was increasingly distant from him, but it did not anger or frustrate him as it once did. He remembered what the messiah said in the Sunshine Marketplace about why he had come and it occurred to him, as they schlepped along, that he had indeed discovered something of what it means to be a Jew.

WHILE ETHAN PRAYED, ELLA AND MICHAEL READ AND PLAYED CARDS AND COOKED ON a panini press that they borrowed from one of their neighbors. That morning, in honor of the holiday, there were hot dogs available at a nearby distribution center, along with diet root beers, which were a wonderful treat. The carbonation of the root beers was a surprise to Michael and made him laugh and Ella said, "You'll have to try one when they're cold. Or with ice cream."

"That sounds amazing," Michael said. "What's it like?"

"Like this but better," she said.

"When will I get to have one?" he asked.

"Someday," she said, wiping her eyes.

AFTER THE HOLIDAYS, ETHAN AND ELLA ENROLLED MICHAEL IN A SCHOOL, OF SORTS, that met in the train station adjacent to the anomaly. Michael recognized a few of the other students, some from the neighborhood and some from the back room of the Sunshine Marketplace, and among them was Dafna, the older girl who had explained the rules of radioman. He did not have particularly fond memories of that evening but he found himself delighted to see her nonetheless.

The teacher, happily, was also a woman Michael knew. She had been the middle-school science teacher at his school in the Pale and, even though he was too young to have been in her class before, he was very excited when she recognized him and he gave her a hug. Four mornings a week—in exchange for canned goods, toiletries, or Jewbucks—she prepared lessons for about forty students, covering basic reading and math. The old subway station was the largest and most well-lit space in the immediate vicinity of their tent, a raised platform that bulged toward the center and narrowed considerably as the subway tracks curved along the tunnel and disappeared into the dark. And in the center of the platform, just beyond the turnstiles, was the anomaly.

On days when there was not very much to do, which was true of many days, the class would pause in the early afternoon to watch

Jews coming through. They would look on as the other Jews came slowly into view, their bodies gradually becoming solid again, as if reconstituted from smoke. And one morning, a few weeks after he started attending the class, Michael spotted Jacob and his family.

He swelled with excitement when he saw them and he laughed and called out, tugging urgently on his teacher's wrist. "Ms. Wasserman," he said, "I know him! Do we have room for another student?"

But as the family emerged fully from the anomaly, their bodies coming into view as if rising slowly from black water, Jacob did not look up. Michael called his name again and still he did not look up and when finally they made their way through the turnstiles and then along the platform of the station, having surrendered a portion of their belongings, Michael saw that it was not Jacob at all. Their faces—the mother, the father, the child—were entirely foreign to him and he was ashamed of his excitement and he realized how much he had missed his friend.

When they returned to the corner of the station that they used as a classroom, Ms. Wasserman started teaching a lesson about the different denominations of Palemarks, one of several currencies that was in circulation. On a stained whiteboard she drew crude pictures of the prutah, the quarter, the half-buckmark, and the bills in denominations of one, ten, and twenty. But, although he usually enjoyed all of the math-related lessons, Michael found that he was unable to concentrate. He thought about Jacob and about the boy who was not Jacob and he became very anxious and then distraught. Leaning against a large steel girder, he cried.

"Oh, honey," Ms. Wasserman said. She stepped out from behind a raised dolly that had been repurposed as a desk and walked over to Michael. Standing over him, she placed her hand on his shoulder. "Can you tell me with words what's wrong?"

As she rubbed his back, his body remained tense and he

continued to cry, pressing his face against one of the girder's rivets until there was a red mark on his cheek. This alarmed Ms. Wasserman. She had always known him as an even-keeled and steady child—both over the course of the past several weeks and also from before, when they saw one another in the Pale—and she was frustrated by the fact that she was unable to comfort him. Finally, she asked one of the older students to walk Michael back to his tent.

"Your mother is usually there during the day," she said. "Is that right?"

When Michael nodded, Ms. Wasserman turned to a boy sitting toward the back of the class and said, "Nathaniel, would you take Michael back to his mom?"

"Do you know how to get there?" he asked Michael.

"I think so," Michael said.

"Okay," said Nathaniel. "I'm sure we'll find it," and then, with the stilted but earnest tenderness of a child who had prematurely adopted an adult bearing, he took Michael by the hand and led him away.

MONTHS EARLIER, NATHANIEL HAD WIPED THE DARKNESS FROM HIS EYES AND SEEN nothing familiar whatsoever. The gentle pressure of his mother's fingers remained, but there was no one next to him. And although a hive of activity buzzed around him, he knew at once that he was alone. After he wandered around the station for half an hour a woman approached him and, in a recognizably northeastern accent, asked him if she could help him. Did he know where he was staying that night and was anyone with him? Ms. Wasserman herself had only come through a few days earlier, but she was able to help him get situated. She found him a tent and eventually—with the help of one of the kiosks—managed to connect him with his cousin, who had lived in the suburbs to the north of the city and who Nathaniel remembered vaguely from Asher's bar mitzvah. Before long they started sharing a tent, even though Nathaniel did not care much for the cousin. He did, however, like Ms. Wasserman. He was grateful to her and he began to feel oddly protective of her. He had the sense that she had been alone for a long time, even before coming through, and when she decided to start her little school Nathaniel was one of her first students. At twelve, he was older than most of the others and he became a kind of teacher's aide as the class grew. Because of his age, he had well-formed memories of life before the harshest restrictions, and this made him the subject of some curiosity and admiration among the other students, particularly among the younger ones. It was a distinction that began to suit him and he thought that Asher would have been proud. He was, in a fashion, really kicking some ass.

THE DISTANCE FROM THE STATION TO MICHAEL'S TENT WAS NOT TERRIBLY GREAT, but their progress was slow. They were not lost. Michael discovered that he did indeed know his way home. But there was no journey in the underground that was entirely straightforward.

They passed kiosks and tents and small huts constructed out of corrugated steel. They wandered through a small market where men and women were haggling over cans of condensed milk, nail polish, live rabbits, bags stitched together from old clothing, stuffed animals. Here was a row of latrines. Here were some musicians playing for Palemarks. Here was a man selling socks, another selling broken electronics, two women selling meat from mysterious animals. Some tunnels that seemed to lead away from the subway station in fact led back. Others crossed at strange angles or switched floor for ceiling. Still others, once entered, seemed enclosed inside of themselves like impossible staircases.

They also had to negotiate a variety of obstacles as they made their way—a disturbance at one of the kiosks when a woman, distraught over the kiosk worker's perceived indifference, swung at him with a wrench; a circle of men and women dancing; a large group congregating nervously around a malfunctioning iron dog that had somehow made its way underground, the first of its kind, an evil omen. They scavenged it for parts—wires, pistons, metal, and bullets.

But as they walked, meandering unnoticed between the adults, Michael gradually became calmer. He enjoyed being with the older boy and although Michael had only spoken with Nathaniel a handful of times he liked him and felt safe with him, and his face, which was somewhat pale, reminded him of Ethan's. Just after circumnavigating the dog, which rattled and twitched and sent up sparks as it died, they passed a rusted folding table and behind the table was a man whom Michael recognized from the Pale. His table was illuminated by small tea lights and he was selling little trinkets that he had folded out of aluminum cans, along with small packets of raisins and sunflower seeds. His face was almost unrecognizable—a red beard, wet with perspiration, and his skin scaled with eczema, and his green eyes sunken into thick, fleshy lids. Hanging from the edge of the table was a tattered piece of posterboard that read, LONG LIVE OUR MASTER, KING MESSIAH, FOREVER AND EVER. His shirt was mostly open and Michael could see that the entire left side of his body was inflamed and infected and when he noticed Michael looking in his direction his eyes became fervent and wild and he said something that Michael could not understand.

"You should try not to stare," Nathaniel said, leading Michael away.

"I know him," Michael said. "He used to work with Ethan. His name is Moti."

"Who is Ethan?"

"Ethan is my best friend."

"He's not in our class."

"He's my mommy's boyfriend. We lived all together in the Pale in a big apartment building. For my birthday last year we opened a fire hydrant and flooded the streets."

"That sounds fun," said the older boy absently.

"Did you ever do that on your street?"

"No," said Nathaniel. "Where I'm from we weren't allowed to waste water. It was too hot."

"You lived outside the Pale? I've heard about the Jews who live in the forests north of the city."

"No. I lived farther away than that. In a city to the west."

"Where there are cactuses and lizards and things?"

Nathaniel smiled. "Yes, there were some of those. There were rattlesnakes in our backyard."

"Really?"

"Really."

"How did you come here?"

Nathaniel shrugged. "We all went through over there. We had our tickets and everything. But only I came out in this place."

"Are you by yourself now?"

"Sort of."

"I'm sorry."

"I live near Ms. Wasserman. Sometimes my cousin and I share a tent, but he's older and he spends a lot of time hanging around the hole trying to get in with the big Jews who tax people as they're coming through."

"Why does he do that?" Michael asked.

"He's an asshole," Nathaniel said, and Michael nodded and they walked on.

• • •

JUST BEFORE MICHAEL'S TENT CAME INTO VIEW THEY REACHED THE PLACE WHERE the man who called himself the messiah gathered his followers. There was a great deal of commotion and, though they tried to push their way through, before long they were forced to stop. They sat down next to one another on a narrow staircase leading up to a locked door. The door was covered in decals and symbols that neither of them recognized, remnants of the Jews who built the staircase but who could not penetrate the door, the same Jews who spun an endless web of tunnels beneath the earth.

Eventually the messiah climbed on top of an overturned oil drum and began to speak in his strange, vacillating accent. Nathaniel had seen the messiah a few times before—on those occasions when he brought his followers to the station to welcome Jews as they emerged—but he never heard him say anything. Men and women and a few children swayed around him. They wore head coverings made of woven electrical cords, and glow sticks around their necks and wrists, and these became lurid smears of color as they cheered and clapped and danced and called out. Drawing on the energy of the crowd, the messiah's voice vibrated with the intensity of a great fantasist. He told the Jews that they would always outpace the iron dogs and that just as they ran, so also the world turned, spinning beneath their feet. He said that their pious ancestors, in their wisdom, sank the tunnels deep. He said that they could run forever and that the tracks were endless. He promised that he would show them how to be at home again in the dark.

When the speech wound down, he turned to one of his attendants, a young man only a few years older than Nathaniel's brother. Nathaniel, getting to his feet, stood at the base of the staircase and watched the attendant push a metal trash can forward until it was even with the messiah's oil drum. Once it was in place, the young man took a matchbook from his pocket and, on the messiah's signal, struck a match. When he dropped it inside there was a whoosh and the fire jumped and cracked and rose up. As the messiah took a MetroCard from his pocket, the tunnels all around them seemed to groan and expand and from somewhere beneath their feet came the shriek of wheels against metal. The people jumped and cheered. They clawed frantically at their pockets, confirming that their MetroCards were just where they had left them or discovering, to their horror, that they were not. And those unfortunates screamed and tore at their clothes and at one another.

The commotion lasted for a minute. Two minutes. Then the messiah stepped into the crowd and came up alongside a woman whose MetroCard had been lost or stolen. She had fallen onto her knees and her fingertips were bloody from clawing at the ground. The messiah lifted her back onto her feet. Her body shook as she pressed her face against his chest.

"Don't worry," he said. "We must become, all of us, like you."

The woman looked up at him, uncomprehending, as he pressed his MetroCard into her palm and then, for just a moment, her face blossomed with delirious, childlike joy. With his hands on her shoulders, he pushed her gently toward the fire. Their bodies threw shadows onto the wall—huge, indefinite forms like cave drawings—and Michael, who had climbed to the top of the staircase, watched as the messiah continued to guide her, as he whispered into her ear, as she hesitated, as his voice echoed along the tunnel: "Show them," he said, "that you are a daughter of Israel." She dropped her new MetroCard into the fire. The fire crackled and hissed. The followers of the messiah gasped and screamed and fell quiet. The smoke darkened. They lined up. *"Am yisrael chai,"* said the messiah. "The people of Israel live."

Bursting with anger, Nathaniel pushed his way through the crowd to where the fire burned and grabbed the man who called himself the messiah by the forearm.

"You can't take them all," Nathaniel said.

The man looked momentarily startled. But he smiled as he said, "There can be, for you, a place here, *shayne punim.* You have maybe a MetroCard?"

"You know that I do."

"I can see how heavy it is. Let me take it from you."

Smoke from the trash can fire swirled around them. It clouded their faces and stung their eyes. The children who were lined up with their parents coughed and their parents rubbed their backs and covered their little faces with sleeves or socks or crumpled face masks. The man's voice rang out again—"It is revealed and known that this fire will burn for a thousand years and still the subway below the subway will not have come"—but Nathaniel had already turned and he did not look back. They were still burning MetroCards when he reached Michael. He wrapped his arm around him and gently pulled him along.

"I didn't understand what he was saying," Michael said.

"He was saying that he can save all of us," Nathaniel said. "But only if we stay down here forever. He thinks we're only really safe on this side of the holes."

"Why would he think that?"

"I guess there have been Jews down here for a long time, building these tunnels."

"But what does that have to do with the messiah?"

"I don't know," Nathaniel said. "Maybe this is where he came from."

• • •

WHEN MICHAEL AND NATHANIEL APPROACHED THE TENT, ELLA WAS INSIDE BOILING water on an electric burner. She saw Michael through the open flap and she rushed outside, knocking the pot to the ground and scalding the back of her leg.

"What happened?" she asked. She pulled him close and looked at the older boy with suspicion.

"He was just a little bit upset," Nathaniel said. "He thought he saw one of his friends coming through the hole, but it wasn't him."

"Who are you?" Ella asked.

"My name is Nathaniel. I'm in the class. Ms. Wasserman asked me to walk with him. I brought him here as quickly as I could."

"Is that true, Michael?" she asked.

Michael nodded. Shaken and confused, he glanced over his right shoulder and saw that the MetroCard fire was still faintly visible at the far end of the tunnel, just below the horizon, had there been a horizon.

"Honey, what happened in class?"

"He told you."

"Was it just that you're missing Jacob?"

"I don't know."

"Michael, I want you to look at me," Ella said.

Michael did not lift his eyes. She kissed his head and neck and smelled fire. "Where were you?" she asked.

Michael's voice was pinched. He spoke as though each word was frightened of the last. "We saw people burning their MetroCards," he said.

"What?"

"Would you and Ethan ever do that?"

"Absolutely not," Ella said. "Why would you think that?"

"Are you sure? You really wouldn't?"

"Of course we wouldn't," she said. She turned to Nathaniel. "Where did you take him?"

"But what if he told you that you should?" Michael insisted.

"Who?" Ella asked.

"They listened to him. You really wouldn't listen?"

"No."

"You promise?"

"Yes, I promise."

"It wouldn't matter who he is?"

Ella was frightened. "It wouldn't matter," she said. "Michael, what are you talking about?"

"Promise me again."

"I promise."

"It was the man we saw in the Pale," Michael said. "The one who fell up into the sky."

XV

MICHAEL BECAME INCREASINGLY WITHDRAWN IN THE DAYS AND WEEKS THAT FOL-lowed. The fire, which continued to gather fuel, was faintly visible from their tent, and its smoke traveled the length of the tunnel and turned the air acrid. One night Michael had a nightmare in which the smoke consumed all that it touched and when he woke up his heart was racing and he gasped for air. He refused to be comforted for several days. He would not agree to lie down in his sleeping bag or to shut off the electric lamp and when he was with Ella and Ethan he would hide his face in their chests, unable to meet their eyes. He would remain awake long into the night before eventually falling asleep upright in their arms, at which point they would carefully zip him into his sleeping bag, where he generally slept, fitfully, until early in the morning when the citizens of the underground started to rattle awake around them, opening cans and boiling water and surveying the damage of their dreams. This worried Ethan and Ella, of course, but they comforted themselves by reminding one another that he was still alive and that he was less hungry than some and that children were resilient. Plus, he always seemed to perk up when they took him to his class. As they approached the platform he would run up ahead, disappearing into a crowd of children by the time they reached the station. The class was growing. And for this they were very grateful. It allowed them to go on, in a fashion, with their lives.

They settled into a fragile rhythm. Mornings, after sharing a breakfast of rice or canned fruit, they would take him to the station and drop him off at school. Then, for about thirty minutes, they would walk together through the cool, damp tunnels, sometimes stopping at a distribution center to collect canned goods or painkillers or antibiotics or rat poison. As they made their way back to their tent, they would pretend that they were walking elsewhere—along a beach, or along Garden Boulevard at the southern reaches of the city, or through deep woods. And after that they would part and would not come together again until much later in the day.

Ella spent most of her time walking the tunnels and trying to map them in her mind. When she was able to charge her camera she took photographs, though she had no real way of storing or editing them. At night, after viewing them quickly on the small screen on the back of her camera, she would delete them and start fresh the following day. She deleted photographs of dying iron dogs, photographs of Jews warming their hands on giant samovars, photographs of men with unspeakable injuries, photographs of young couples kissing and undressing one another, oblivious to the world around them. She repeated the ritual day after day in an effort to make sense of their situation but, cumulatively, it had the opposite effect. Every afternoon she was concerned that she would not be able to find her way back. She felt increasingly unmoored. But simultaneously, and with an incongruity that she did not interrogate, she began to feel more and more like the person she remembered. When she was much younger, just before she met Tucker and when her career was in its very early stages, she took an assignment photographing what remained of a small suburban community that had been lost to a wildfire in the west. The fires died out so there was no real danger, only the gray-black skeletons of homes and the insect-like drone of generators that supplied power to demolition crews and to the trailers of those residents who chose to remain or who had nowhere else to go. And there was Ella, having come in from afar, disturbed but ultimately free of their misfortune, thrilled by the fantasy that she would document what came next. Many nights, when Ethan and Michael were asleep, she would sit outside of their tent and watch the small light from the messiah's fire, like the white eye of an approaching train. It filled her with dread. But the smell of the smoke reminded her of the town in the west and now and then, in spite of herself, she felt the old thrill rise in her chest, the sense of a road opening, and, recalling her father, she would say in an undertone, "Blessed are you, LORD our God, King of the Universe, who has kept us alive and sustained us and brought us to this moment."

Ethan, meanwhile, would spend his days mending their tent in the places where it was torn or walking from market to market trying to gather food or news from afar. Sometimes he would hear a rumor about a headlight sighting and then he would investigate it with great fervor or he would perch on a platform adjacent to one of the locked doors, an exit sign glowing above him like an apparition, and squint out into the darkness trying to catch of glimpse of something himself. But he never saw anything.

Once, he met a man who claimed that he had entered the underground years ago through the great hole in the Middle East, the "OG," as he said. Ethan assumed he was full of shit and after talking with him for several minutes he recognized him as Kramnik, the man who took over Isaacson's after Isaacson fled, purveyor of the miracle pickled tomatoes. He looked older and he had grown a long beard, but Ethan was sure it was him.

He confronted him about it when he saw him again, a few days later, and in response Kramnik took him surreptitiously back to his tent where he cleared away a pile of mildewed newspaper, empty soap bottles, and tangled charging cables, to reveal a single jar of tomatoes, which he caressed like a lover.

"It still works," Kramnik whispered. "Just don't tell anyone and you can have some whenever you want."

"I'll remember that," Ethan said.

ONE EVENING, SEVERAL WEEKS LATER, ELLA ANNOUNCED THAT SHE WANTED TO travel on. Michael had fallen asleep and as she spoke she watched his chest rise and fall. She said that she saw no advantage in remaining tethered to the anomaly when there were tunnels fanning out in every direction. Though she could not articulate why, she wanted to be in motion.

"What about the food," Ethan asked, "and the distribution centers?"

"There are Jews in every direction," she said. "They're managing somehow."

"But we have tickets," he said.

"Have you seen any trains down here?"

"You've seen what I've seen," he said.

"When was the last time anyone saw headlights?"

"But it could come at any time. We don't know."

"That's right," she said, "we don't. And there is no reason why the train would stop here as opposed to anywhere else."

"Where is this coming from all of a sudden?"

Instead of answering, Ella opened the flap of the tent and stepped outside. Ethan joined her and they stood side by side. After a few seconds her hand found his. They shuddered at the sudden warmth. The fire burned in the distance.

"There is more smoke today," she said.

"It doesn't seem much different to me."

"I keep thinking about Michael's nightmare."

"I had a dream like that when I was young. One I couldn't forget, I mean. It'll be okay."

"I don't want to be here anymore," she said, her voice cracking like a child's. "I hate this place."

"I know. I wish I could say something."

"Will you make a joke?"

"I'm not sure you've ever found me particularly funny."

"Try."

He thought for a moment.

"A man loses his brother and at the shiva there is this other guy there from his synagogue. He doesn't know him very well and he is nonplussed by his presence. The guy stays later than a lot of the others also. Finally as he gets up to leave but before he goes he walks over to the man who lost his brother and says, 'I'm so sorry for your loss. I just have one word for you.' 'Okay,' says the mourner. The visitor waits and then says, 'Plethora.' The mourner nods his head and says, 'Thanks, that means a lot.'"

"That's funny," Ella said, without laughing. "See, you're funny. Tell me another one."

"That's all I've got."

"Please."

Ethan thought again and then said, "You know that photo series you did of the families getting ready to go through? I looked at the photographs for a long time and I remember thinking not so much about the photographs but about you. Which is weird because I didn't know you, of course. But I wanted to. It was like an ache. And I thought to myself, *Here is someone who wants to document the end of the world.* Now maybe you'll get your chance."

She had never told him about her experience photographing the dead town and she was unsettled that he had so accurately guessed something that she had trouble understanding herself. "Is that a joke?" she asked.

"I guess not," he said.

They were both quiet. When they turned to go back inside they saw Michael, sitting upright in his sleeping bag, his eyes wide and alert.

"Ms. Wasserman stopped teaching the class a few days ago," he said, quietly, as if disclosing a secret. "I'm sorry I didn't tell you. Are you mad at me?"

Ella was confused, shaken. "What? What are you talking about?"

"She went to join up with the messiah. Nathaniel said it's happening more and more and that's why all the lines are shorter."

"Who is Nathaniel?" Ethan asked.

"He walked Michael home the other week," Ella said. "I told you about him."

"He's the boy who sort of helps her," Michael said. "He's teaching the class now. He's going to save us."

"From what?" Ella asked.

"From whatever happens."

"We don't know what's going to happen," Ella said. "Neither does he."

"I don't want you to leave me," Michael said. "I would never want that, okay?"

"Michael, we are not going to leave you," Ethan said. "Why would you even think about that?"

"Nathaniel says you will have to. Is that real?"

"No," Ethan said. "Absolutely not. That's just a scary thought. It can't hurt you."

"Like my dream?"

"Yes, just like that."

Michael looked up at him. "Mommy was right, though. Maybe we should run away."

"But I'm not sure there is anywhere for us to go," Ethan said. "You're old enough to understand that."

XVI

THEN IT WAS NISAN ONCE AGAIN. ETHAN AND ELLA, FOLLOWING A BRIEF NEGOTIATION, acquired a small tin hut from an older Jew who had managed to fix an abandoned railcar and who decided to head off east in search of the Istanbul exit. Ethan knew the man from one of the market stalls and he liked him and he tried to tell him that he was crazy, that the reports about the Istanbul exit had been debunked long ago and, besides, who could say which way was east. But the man only embraced him and said that he was not going to wait around for a miracle. "I never had a MetroCard anyway," he said. "I just came down here. The truth is, even before all this, I had my doubts about everything up above." Just before leaving—and upon receiving five hundred Palemarks in exchange for the hut—the man invited Ethan, Ella, and Michael to join him on the railcar. And when they declined he shrugged and wished them well and said that he hoped they would be happier in the hut than he had been.

The new tunnel was wider and more well-lit than the one in

which they had pitched the tent for the past year and Ella thought they would be less vulnerable to the muggings that had become commonplace. In the days that followed they argued about whether or not they should have accepted the man's offer, their conversation repeating itself nightly, beat for beat, like a dance. Ella hung string lights from the ceiling and some of Michael's drawings on the walls. She covered the floor with pillows and blankets and she and Ethan, utterly exhausted, found themselves sleeping frequently during the days. Michael worried over them and he was frightened for them and of them, but for these things he did not have words. They decided that he could walk to class alone.

There were only a handful of transits through the anomaly each week—harried, desperate people who had made their way south from the forests or who had been living in the half-empty apartment buildings of the Pale. One morning, while Michael was at school, Ethan and Ella invited one of these newcomers to have tea and they peppered her with questions about the neighborhood. Was there still a minyan in the Sunshine Marketplace? Did Jews still try to make it across the river by night? Was there a new manager at the warehouse? What was going on at the level of city government? Did they still carry the dead away through the checkpoint? The woman, who had only recently arrived from the west, could answer none of these questions. In fact, she only slept a single night in the Pale before passing through. But Ethan and Ella found it comforting that there were still Jews up there and that wherever the anomaly had taken them they were still tied, in some fashion, to the city in which they had lived most of their lives.

Meanwhile, the tunnels around them seemed to shift and change daily, as if rewoven from concrete and rock and steel. The messiah continued to gain followers and there was an influx of

Jews from farther out. There was a group from Great Britain that brought along hundreds of unclaimed MetroCards that they had collected along the way from those who no longer needed them and they sold them or traded them for batteries, canned goods, tents. Some of these were cherished like heirlooms. Some of them found their way into the messiah's fire. There was another group that had entered the underground in Madrid. They had been traveling for months, they said, and they told stories about communities they had encountered along the way: Jews who had refurbished and reprogrammed an entire pack of iron dogs and who were now planning an assault on the anomaly in Stockholm; Jews living in darkened tunnels who spoke a language no one could recognize; a community of old women who went up in smoke; a community of children living alone in the anomaly beneath Amsterdam Centraal. This, they said, was not so uncommon.

AS PESACH APPROACHED THE MAN WHO CALLED HIMSELF THE MESSIAH SAID HE would demonstrate his power on the final day of the holiday. They would celebrate what they had accomplished by surviving in the underground and then he would show them how to descend to an even lower level. Though he made this promise only to members of his inner circle, rumors spread, feathers from a torn pillowcase.

The rumors reached Ethan and Ella independently. Ella heard about the upcoming miracle from a woman who had a market stall in the tunnel adjacent to theirs. She was tough and flinty and she reminded Ella of her mother and, though Ella did not really need anything that she was selling that day, they talked for a while as she sold batteries and T-shirts and winter hats and individual packages of fruit snacks that she acquired from who knows where. She told Ella about the miracle just as Ella was leaving and then she gave Ella three unopened toothbrushes. Ella refused to take them and told her that she should sell them instead, but the woman said that she did not anticipate being in business much longer anyway and that she had more where those came from. And as Ella left the woman said that perhaps she would see her when the miracle happened. Ethan, meanwhile, heard about it while he was standing near one of the kiosks that was still in operation. The woman at the window was asking the man in the blue vest if the kiosks would remain staffed even after the miracle and the man said that he didn't see why not and that as far as he was concerned the kiosks could remain open until they were no longer necessary. For some reason the woman did not like this response and she became increasingly upset and she started yelling and eventually the man asked her to step aside so that he could help others.

That night Michael was particularly agitated and it took him quite a while to fall asleep and by the time he did, Ethan and Ella were exhausted. But as they lay next to one another in their sleeping bags, Ethan said, "Listen, I heard something today."

"About the messiah's demonstration? I heard about it too."

"What do you think?"

"I'm too tired," she said. "Let's talk about it tomorrow."

"Yes," he said. "That's a good idea."

Michael was between them, his face like a still pond, his breathing slow and even. The warmth they shared was startling when they folded him in their arms. But in the morning neither of them knew what to say.

ON THE AFTERNOON LEADING UP TO THE SEDER, JUST BEFORE MICHAEL GOT HOME from class and in a moment of urgency that startled them both, Ella said, "I want you inside of me." When they were finished, Ethan's lip slightly bloody from where she had bitten him, they sat naked and breathless with their backs against the wall.

"Listen," he said, "I want us to go hear whatever the messiah has to say."

Ella did not respond. She searched his face and found something there that she had never seen before. It twisted her up.

"After that we'll do whatever you think is best," he said. "We'll move on, if that's what you want."

"We'll keep going for as long as we can?"

"Yes," he said. "What else is there to do?"

BUT WHEN MICHAEL RETURNED, FIFTEEN MINUTES AFTER THAT, HE BEGGED THEM not to go. Under the influence of Nathaniel's warnings, he had become terribly afraid of the messiah and he said that if they went they might burn their MetroCards, like so many of the others had already, and maybe they would not return at all and then he would be all alone and he would not know what to do.

They did not answer immediately. Ethan was arranging what they had on a paper plate—a chicken bone and an egg that he had acquired from a man who lived with some chickens at a small station toward the end of a mostly empty tunnel, a piece of matzah that Ella received after waiting on line for several hours, a little scoop of apple jam, two chocolate-covered jelly rings. While Ethan was carefully arranging these meager things inside of the circles that Michael had drawn on the plate, Ella leaned back against one of the floor pillows and marveled at how much older Michael seemed. He was slightly taller than he had been only a few months earlier and, like all of them, he was thinner. But it was not how he looked that disturbed her and, briefly, brought tears to her eyes. It was some other, harder-to-define aspect of his expression—something disquieting and adult, as if the lingering residue of his childhood was vanishing at that exact moment. Michael was quiet, struggling for words that remained just beyond his grasp, and Ella understood, with a sudden, silent clarity, that she would never again be able to dispel his fears entirely.

"I really don't want you to go there," he said again. "Please."

Finally Ella said, "Well, Ethan thinks we should."

Ella immediately regretted having said it. She was shocked by her own betrayal. She tried to make eye contact with Ethan in order to apologize, if only silently, and she decided that later on she would apologize again, maybe with her hands and with her mouth. And when she imagined it she felt, in spite of herself, a stirring between her legs. But she was unable to catch his attention. He remained focused on the seder plate, his hands shaking slightly, perhaps from anger or perhaps from something else.

Setting the seder plate onto the ground, he gathered Michael into his arms, which was a much more cumbersome task than when they first met. As Ella had only moments ago, Ethan measured the unmistakable inscription of time on Michael's still-small body. He was by no means tall. But he was taller and harder and somehow heavier, despite his skinniness. He had a boy's half-wild strength. As Michael wrapped his arms around Ethan's waist, Ella sang all the words that she could remember. Ethan held Michael through the entire seder, such as it was, his eyes closed and his breathing slow. For seven days he tried not to let him go. And one night, as they were sleeping side by side, Ethan dreamt that their bones and flesh had fused, like the healing of an ancient wound.

THE MORNING OF THE DEMONSTRATION, NATHANIEL, DAFNA, AND A FEW OF THE other older children went up and down the tunnels trying to find as many students as they could to let them know that they could go to the platform for a class-wide game of radioman while their parents were watching the man who called himself the messiah. Radioman was unknown in the western part of the country, where Nathaniel had entered the underground, but he learned it early on from the children who had come down from the Pale and he used it often when he could not think of anything else to do.

When Nathaniel reached Michael, he and Ethan were standing thirty feet from their shelter, warming their hands above a woodfire that was burning inside a large steel drum. Michael was excited to see him and he ran over and gave him a hug. They talked for about a minute, after which Nathaniel asked Michael to go inside while he spoke with Ethan.

Michael was unsure how to respond. He looked from Ethan to Nathaniel, and then Ethan nodded and said, "Why don't you go inside and see if we have any jam left. I bet your friend hasn't had jam in a long time."

As they waited for Michael to return, Nathaniel explained why he had come. He assured Ethan that everything would be completely safe, and that he just wanted the children to have a place to go that night. His manner was very calm, simultaneously adult and childlike, and Ethan did not know entirely what to make of him.

"What's in it for you?" Ethan asked.

Before he could answer Michael returned with a little bit of apple jam on a plastic spoon.

"Here," Michael said, smiling and extending his arm, "it's really sweet. I've never had anything like it. Not that I can remember, anyway."

"It's for you, buddy," Nathaniel said. "Enjoy it. Listen, I've got to go talk to some of the others. But I'll see you later, okay?" Then, turning to Ethan and speaking in an undertone, he said, "You should really let him go."

"I love him," Ethan said.

"Then you've already decided," said Nathaniel.

That night, before they headed over to the demonstration, Michael asked Ethan and Ella to write their phone numbers and address in the Pale on his arm, just as they had before going underground. They had continued to do this with some regularity, like a kind of runic inscription, even after it became clear to Ethan and Ella that those numbers would likely mean very little to them in the future. It seemed to calm Michael and it certainly calmed them. But in more recent months they had allowed the practice to lapse, and they were surprised when Michael asked. Ella inscribed Michael's arm with great care.

Then they both accompanied him to the station. Michael's mood brightened, somewhat, when they left the tent and for a while they walked side by side holding hands, Ethan on the left and Ella on the right and Michael in the center. Michael asked Ella to tell him about how it was when she was a child and Jews lived all over the city and went to the parks and the zoos whenever they wanted. This had become a frequent request in the last few months and, as she often did, Ella told him the story about the time she and Sophie went up to an observatory on the top floor of the tallest building in the city and watched as a skywriter wrote a message that she could no longer remember—birthday wishes, perhaps, or an advertisement or a declaration of love. Michael never tired of hearing this story and he always said, "That must have been amazing," and Ella always replied, "Yes it was."

Then, after a brief silence, Michael said, "Hey, Ethan, what is Albuquerque?"

"It's a city on the other side of the country."

"Is it still there?"

"I think so. Why are you thinking about that?"

"Zeyde used to say that Bugs Bunny always got into trouble because he should have taken a left turn at Albuquerque."

"I remember that, yeah."

"Why does he always make the same mistake?"

"I don't know, honey. It's a good question."

"But Albuquerque isn't near us, right?"

"No," Ethan said.

"And if it was, we'd turn left?"

But before Ethan could answer Michael spotted one of his friends and, laughing, ran on ahead.

FOR THE DEMONSTRATION, THE MAN WHO CALLED HIMSELF THE MESSIAH GATHERED his followers together along a length of track that was disconnected from the larger web, as if it had once been part of an expansion project that was hastily abandoned. Toward the end of the tunnel, where the tracks ran up against a large bollard, was a rusted-out maintenance car onto which the messiah's followers had moved the MetroCard fire. It was from there that the messiah would perform marvels.

The tunnel, which came to a dead end about thirty feet beyond the bollard, was mostly dark, apart from firelight and the blue glow from a handful of working cell phones. Amplifiers and instruments were plugged into generators set up along the rails, their cords stretching out in every direction, and when Ethan stepped forward into the tunnel he thought of a tentacled fish, glowing in the deep ocean.

Ella, standing next to Ethan against the wall, touched his shoulder. "What is all this?" she asked.

“I don’t know,” Ethan said.

“It looks like there is going to be a concert.”

“I guess there is music everywhere,” he said. Then, after a pause, he said, “It hurt me last week when you told him that we were only going because of me.”

“I know,” she said. “I shouldn’t have said that.”

“Was it true?”

“No,” she said. “Not entirely.”

“Do you think it’s okay that we let him go to the station?”

“Yes,” she said. “I know that it was.” Then she said, “Thank you, Ethan.”

“For what?”

“For getting us this far.”

“I wish he was with us,” Ethan said and Ella squeezed his hand and said, “We’ll see him later.”

The band was still in the process of setting up. A drummer was adjusting the height of the cymbals. A bass player was checking to ensure that the microphones and amps were set to the appropriate levels. Two Jews from Australia were unfurling a long piece of white cloth, inside of which were a pair of didgeridoos. Ethan watched them work, their legs mostly hidden by fog from a fog machine. Ethan and Ella found seats on a platform beneath a steel door. Ella rested against his shoulder. Then she hopped down onto the tracks and started taking pictures.

“Come back and sit with me,” Ethan said. But Ella only reached up and brushed his leg with her fingertips and kept on shooting.

Folding his hands across his lap, Ethan looked out at the dimly lit faces. A few of them he recognized, but all of them seemed very remote, like pictures in the hall of a grand museum, their features popping from shadows as if rendered by an old master. Beautiful faces and frightened. It occurred to him that they could easily slip away. The vast majority of people in the area had come to see the messiah work his wonders, and the tunnels would be passable. If they left now they could make good progress before resting for the night. They could run. But instead he remained on the platform, while above the door an exit sign glowed red.

Fifteen minutes later, when the setup was complete, one of the messiah's followers called out, "In accordance with the wishes of the King Messiah we will now hear, for the first time in history, the music of all the Jews in all the lands!"

The didgeridoos figured prominently in the opening song (which was the only song), a lengthy ballad sung in a combination of English and Hebrew. It included several wild, polytonal guitar riffs, a minute of silence broken by a tape of children laughing, and a section toward the end that featured the elemental drone of a didgeridoo duet played underneath a distorted recording of "Jerusalem of Gold." Ethan, in spite of himself, found the music extremely affecting and by the end he was moved almost to tears.

When the band was finished the messiah stepped up onto the old maintenance car. The people surrounding the car jumped and cheered and jumped and sang. They formed a wreath around him, circling and dancing, screaming for water, for happiness, for luck, rushing forward and rushing back, like the beating of a great heart. Eventually, when they were exhausted, he raised his hands for quiet. He prepared himself to speak. But when he opened his mouth it filled with sounds rather than words—the hum of acceleration, the screech of wheels, a distant voice asking all the Jews to mind the gap. The head of the man who called himself the messiah tilted back as the Jews looked on. His body spun and twitched and then where he once stood there was only the black pupil of an eye, a tunnel going down, an anomaly within an anomaly, lovely and irresistible.

Ella, still standing beneath the platform, struggled to make sense of what she was seeing. She watched with fascination as the Jews followed their messiah, some moving slowly, some wearing finery, some wearing nothing but their glow sticks, some ragged, some with broken and battered faces, some with ears and noses spurting blood, some whispering incantations, some ancient, some limping, some running, some dancing once again—on the walls, on the ceiling, along the endless railways, their MetroCards flashing as they dropped them into the fire, as what remained of their messiah pulled them on into the dark.

The band was playing again, a reprisal but with variations. Ella moved along with the others, slowly at first and then with great convulsing speed. Her MetroCard shone in the firelight, the holograms changing as her arms twisted in time to the music, her hands held high, her face tilted back. Dimly she thought, *They must only know one song.* As she danced she recalled their lives in the Pale, small but somehow rounded off inside of themselves. She remembered her father walking them to the subway after the seder two years earlier, not in spite of the danger, as he told Miriam with a mischievous wink, but because of it. She remembered how Ethan carried Michael to the subway. She thought of Michael. His face was a telescope, through which the unpromised future was momentarily visible. She imagined all that he would do in the world that was coming. But she could no longer hold the images in her mind. And when she extended her hand she felt a terrible, searing heat. She screamed. She held on tight. She lurched forward.

It was Ethan who restrained her. She twisted and jerked, but his grip was firm and at last, when he extracted her from the crowd, her body relaxed. The burns on her were white and shining and her fingers were numb.

Ethan looked at her, his eyes shining. "It happened to my hands too," he said.

"But you didn't let go?"

"No," he said, holding it out in front of his face, "I didn't."

"I would have if it wasn't for you."

"Maybe. It doesn't matter."

"It does," she said.

"Maybe it does."

Ethan hugged her. Her voice broke. "You had two of them."

"No," he said, "only one. Michael has the third."

"You're lying to me."

"I put it into his back pocket, just before he ran off to join his friends." Ethan helped her onto her feet. "Here," he said, "let me carry it for you."

Their MetroCards were black with soot.

WHERE YOU FIND JEWS, THERE YOU FIND DOGS, THIS ONE A STRAY, HAVING TUMBLED through an anomaly on the far side of the world. The lenses aimed at the upper quadrant were badly damaged in transit and the gun barrel was distended and warped, half-concealing the front eye. The apertures were locked in place. They twitched and struggled to open. Triangles and squares would not merge. The world, broken into patches of light and shadow, remained scrambled, unintelligible. The grind of gears, the hiss of hydraulics. A diagnostic report. The dog limped along the tracks. It stumbled and fell and righted itself. Its hind leg, slick with axle grease, erupted with wires. It hunted, according to its nature.

Meanwhile the Jews carried on. In the minutes after the messiah demonstrated his power, those who remained searched for their tents and for their children. Half blind from smoke, they did not see or hear anything until it clattered drunkenly from the deep shadows and out into a thin pool of light, as if landing on the moon.

But by then the wheel was already spinning. The red light trembled and held. Just before the bullet ripped through its broken body, a woman screamed, "Dog!" It would have torn into her throat as well. But instead the man she was with fell on top of the animal. There was heat and pressure and everything was wet. Things were coming out of him. But he held on until the whirring stopped and the red light winked out.

AFTER FIVE ROUNDS OF RADIOMAN, THE CHILDREN GATHERED AROUND NATHANIEL IN concentric rings as he read a picture book about a train station in the center of a large city. In the story the city was situated between soaring mountains and a great expanse of water. The artist, working in watercolors that bled and bloomed across the page, had covered the city in a heavy mist and for reasons that were unstated in the story the city was vacant of cars and people. The buildings loomed black, like unhealing bruises from an ancient war. But the train station, like an alien form descended on the landscape, was burning with a dazzling light. Perhaps it was on fire, but it was hard to say. Many of the children could not remember having seen such a marvelous book and they did not know where it had come from. Maybe, they thought, their teacher Nathaniel had conjured it. He was known to do such things, from time to time, or so they believed. And he pointed to the station in the picture and said, "Tell me what you see."

Michael, who was sitting in one of the rings near the center, thought of himself as too old for picture books but he was nonetheless transfixed by the image of the station—its impossible arches and buttresses, its windows and lintels outlined in gold, the single figure, little more than a blur of paint, looking on from the empty streets. As Nathaniel spoke about the calamity that must have befallen the citizens of that city, the image of the station seemed to glow and expand. But it was not the picture, it was his voice. And it was not his voice but the half-dark platform beneath them unfolding, piece by piece, shaking off its decay, shuddering, and then cracking open like a gilded egg. Michael squinted and shielded his eyes, so bright were the lights when the new station revealed its wonders—monitors alive with news of the world, fine mosaics, posters on the walls advertising movies that no one had ever seen, plays that no one had ever heard of, free concerts, lectures, TV premieres.

Michael watched as floor-to-ceiling turnstiles sprouted and burst like spring flowers. Then Nathaniel closed the book and led them through. The children tapped their MetroCards and the screens flashed blue and the doors spun easily on their axes.

Unlike many of the others who had been there for the messiah's demonstration, Ethan and Ella saw it with their own eyes, just as a smooth, disembodied voice said, "THE TRAIN WILL BE ARRIVING SHORTLY, PLEASE EXERCISE CAUTION." Ethan was pale and he had trouble walking and there was blood in his mouth. He stumbled. His fingers were red and black. He felt Ella's body against his, small but strong, pulling him up as he went down and he heard her say, "Ethan, stay on your feet," but he could not see her and then the light from the station blinded him and there was metal against his face and he held his stomach to keep everything inside.

"THE TRAIN WILL BE ARRIVING SHORTLY, PLEASE EXERCISE CAUTION."

Ella positioned Ethan's head between two of the bars and took out her MetroCard. She tapped. "We'll get through," she said. "Just hang on." She tapped again. Again. She slammed a fist against the screen and called out in pain. She tapped again.

Cursing, she ran over to the wall opposite the turnstile and mashed her fingers against the screen of the ticket dispenser. It was unlike any she had ever seen. The symbols were strange and she could not figure out where to put in money or where to tap her phone and, in any case, she had no money and she had no phone. "THE TRAIN WILL BE ARRIVING SHORTLY, PLEASE EXERCISE CAUTION." Turning quickly, she saw that Ethan was slouched over with his face against the ground and she ran back to him, tripping over the Jews who remained, some of them fighting with the ticket dispensers, some of them trying to force the doors, some of them still tapping their MetroCards. She sat down next to Ethan and lifted his head. His ear was sticky and black.

Michael, standing among a throng of children on the far side, saw them through the glare, their faces partially obscured by iron. His eyes were not fully adjusted to the light and for just a moment he was unsure that it was them. But then he ran, spinning and dodging past the other children, moving with startling grace, like a dancer. He reached his arm through and Ella took his hand.

"I'm sorry," Michael said, his voice breaking. "I wasn't careful enough. We were playing and someone had a water gun. The numbers got smeared."

She brushed a curl off of his forehead. "That's okay, Michael."

"Mommy," he said, "you hurt your hands."

"I'm okay."

He looked down at Ethan, his body slumped against the iron fence that separated them.

"He's tired," Ella said. "He was so excited to come back to see you. He loves you so much, Michael."

"Ethan, open your eyes," Michael said, and so he did and looked up into the new lights of the world.

"THE TRAIN WILL BE ARRIVING SHORTLY, PLEASE EXERCISE CAUTION."

"Come on," Michael said. "You need to hurry."

"Michael, listen to me," Ella said. "We can't get through. Something happened to our tickets."

"What happened?"

"It's hard to explain. When you're older maybe you'll be able to understand."

He looked at her questioningly but he could see that she did not have an answer. "Okay," he said. "I'll just come over to you. It spins the other way." He started to enter the turnstile.

"No," Ella said, her voice suddenly sharp. "You are right where you need to be."

Michael cried as he pushed against the bars. But Ella, summoning what strength she had, did not allow the turnstile to spin.

"You heard the announcement," she said. "The subway is arriving soon."

"But the numbers smeared," he said, his eyes radiant with fear. "Write them again."

"I don't have the marker with me," she said.

"Go get it."

"No, honey. You don't need those anymore."

"I'll forget the numbers."

"You won't. And even if you do, that's going to be okay too."

When the train arrived, the children, led by Nathaniel, moved toward it in a steady stream. There were more of them than Ella could count. They called out in their high, sweet voices. Ella felt the great, pulsing waves of the other adults as they crashed against the turnstiles and fell back. She held Michael's hand as the other children tugged and pulled and pulled and swelled. Again, the voice hovered above the roiling depths: “THE TRAIN WILL BE ARRIVING SHORTLY. PLEASE EXERCISE CAUTION AS THE TRAIN ENTERS AND LEAVES THE STATION.” She had made her decision but still she did not let go. She had him. She had him. She had him until the moment she did not, when the little vessel of their family finally broke and he was carried away from her.

XVII

MICHAEL DID NOT KNOW HOW LONG HE HAD BEEN ON THE SUBWAY. SOMETIMES IT felt like only a short while and sometimes it felt like much longer. There were many children and the subway grew around them, vascular and womb-like. Inside they kicked and twitched, their lives tethered to the cars and the cars tethered one to the next and the train tethered to the navel of the tunnel ahead. Every now and then, at mysterious intervals, they were shaken by torsions of steel and aluminum as the subway, a triumph of engineering, rearranged itself and made room.

In the car next to Michael's, there was a girl about his age who always slept on the same seat, leaning up against a blanket imprinted with the logo of their city's baseball team. When Michael first noticed it, he assumed that she also was from the Pale but when he asked her about it she responded in a language that he did not know. She had a deck of cards and she knew how to play hearts and she taught Michael and they played together often in the afternoons, or in the evenings, which were like the afternoons, or in the mornings. And sometimes they would hold hands and press their faces to the glass and once, when they did, Michael's sleeve slipped up onto his elbow and the girl saw the last remnants of his mother's writing and he said, "My family," and the girl, whose name was Naomi, touched his arm with her fingers and his hair stood on end.

When there were signal delays or trouble with the track, the train would stop for a minute, for three minutes, for an hour, for a day, and when that happened Michael would read what he could find or he would draw or he would fold airplanes in the way that Ethan showed him and throw them from the window of the subway. Sometimes he would walk the length of the train from car to car, with Naomi or with one of the other children or alone. The cessation of movement allowed for things that were otherwise impossible. A group of dancers, led by Dafna from the Pale, would perform a show. The ones who liked chess set up chess boards. Others would play soccer, using the subway poles as goals. The ones who liked to draw and paint would decorate the car that they always painted, a mural that changed many times over. There was a car toward the end where Michael went to get food. It smelled of broth and apples and the kitchen was managed by one of the older children who had recently celebrated his bar mitzvah. He had a jar of pickled tomatoes that was never empty, which he said he found abandoned on the night of the demonstration. He treasured the jar and would let no one see it, but once he showed it to Michael because Michael was one of the only people he knew who actually ate them. It was a special jar, a jar of miracles, and he said that it was through the power of the jar that the train remained stocked with food. Who could say? Michael nodded and walked on. That day it was a long delay and Michael made it all the way to the front of the train, where Nathaniel sat in a little booth, looking ahead and never speaking anymore. The children were scared of him and they said he was a ghost or a robot or a goy or a Jew who had come through the great hole in the Middle East. But Michael was not scared. He knew him and he thought he looked sad and lonely and on that day, when the signal trouble stretched on through the afternoon and into the evening (which was the same as the afternoon), Michael knocked on the door of the booth, a common enough dare among the children, but not something anyone did without running away. But Michael stood there quietly, his hands folded in front of his body. He heard the door handle turn. The door slid open and Nathaniel looked down at him.

"Do you want to look?" he asked. "Come here."

He lifted Michael into the driver's seat and stood over him, his hand on the metal lever that controlled the movement of the train, and said, "It won't be much longer," and a few minutes later Michael did feel the subway car lurch forward, haltingly and then steadily and then with great power. The headlights did very little and all Michael could see was a great darkness. He thought of his mother and of Ethan, and he tried to fix the sound of their voices in his mind even as they seemed to fly away from him, like his paper planes, swallowed quickly by the dark, or like the bulbs that here and there flashed along the walls of the tunnel. He pictured the lights of a city, somewhere above him, and the lights of the grand terminal where they had boarded the train, somewhere behind them and somewhere ahead.

After a few minutes, Nathaniel helped him down and Michael walked back to find Naomi. As he made his way from car to car he stopped several times to read the subway posters and the screens that were mounted above the windows. The screens were ever-changing. They were radiant with exclusive offers, alluring vistas, unfamiliar alphabets. They were promises of the next station, the new station. And he was not afraid.

ACKNOWLEDGMENTS

TO MY EXTRAORDINARY AGENT, JESSICA KASMER-JACOBS, AND TO MY EXTRAORDINARY editor, Lauren Wein: revising and polishing the manuscript with both of you, first for submission and later for publication, has been one of the great pleasures of my career. The book is immeasurably better because of your vision and judgment.

Jessica, thank you, in particular, for finding a home for this book when and how you did. You believed in it from the beginning and your dedication, wisdom, intelligence, and clear thinking, through very hard times for our people, amazes and inspires me.

Lauren, thank you for providing that home—working with you, Amy Guay, and everyone at Avid Reader Press is a true privilege.

Thank you to Tom McCafferty, my dear friend and most trusted reader for more than two decades now. You are one of the most gracious, poetic, and talented artists I have ever met.

Thank you to my teacher, Dr. Vivian Paley, ז״ל, who taught me very early on how to tell stories and why.

Thea Wieseltier, you saw this book early on and helped get it where it needed to go. Thank you.

Thank you to all of the cafes—particularly in New York, Chicago, and Jerusalem—where, for the price of coffee, I've had space and time for all these years.

Thank you to my community at the Pelham Jewish Center. I am honored to serve as your rabbi and thankful for everything you have taught me about what it means to be Jews in America.

Thank you to my parents, Kenneth and Raiselle Resnick. You gave me the twin crowns of a blessed childhood and *ahavat yisrael*, without which I would never have written this book.

Thank you to my sisters, Rebecca Kossnick and Hannah Resnick. Your presence in childhood and loving friendship in adulthood was and is a source of constant strength and joy.

I am lucky that my family has grown in size and richness over the years. Jane, Richard, William, David, Art, Marvin, Andy, and Julian—I am so grateful to have all of you in my life. You've shaped me in ways large and small.

To my children, Jonah and Gabriel: as my zeyde once said to my father, so I will say to you. When you step into a room you shine so brightly that sometimes I have to shield my eyes from the light. You are what emerges from every dark tunnel, my next stop and my future.

And, finally, thank you to my wife, Philissa Cramer, who sees my work, now and always, before anyone else. You are a reader of breathtaking intelligence, an editor of bracing precision, and a partner of astounding devotion. You elevate me in every way. Listing the endless ways that this book simply would not exist without you would be an impossible, lifelong task. I love you.

22 SHEVAT, 5784

ABOUT THE AUTHOR

BENJAMIN RESNICK is the rabbi of the Pelham Jewish Center in New York. Ordained at the Jewish Theological Seminary of America, he lives in Pelham with his family. *Next Stop* is his first novel.

Avid Reader Press, an imprint of Simon & Schuster, is built on the idea that the most rewarding publishing has three common denominators: great books, published with intense focus, in true partnership. Thank you to the Avid Reader Press colleagues who collaborated on *Next Stop*, as well as to the hundreds of professionals in the Simon & Schuster advertising, audio, communications, design, ebook, finance, human resources, legal, marketing, operations, production, sales, supply chain, subsidiary rights, and warehouse departments whose invaluable support and expertise benefit every one of our titles.

Editorial
Lauren Wein, *VP and Editorial Director*
Amy Guay, *Assistant Editor*

Jacket Design
Alison Forner, *Senior Art Director*
Clay Smith, *Senior Designer*
Sydney Newman, *Art Associate*

Marketing
Meredith Vilarello, *Associate Publisher*
Caroline McGregor, *Marketing Manager*
Nicholas Rooney, *Marketing Manager*
Emily Lewis, *Marketing Manager*
Katya Wiegmann, *Marketing and Publishing Assistant*

Production
Allison Green, *Managing Editor*
Jessica Chin, *Manager Copyediting*
Jason Chappell, *Senior Production Editor*
Alicia Brancato, *Production Manager*
Ruth Lee-Mui, *Interior Text Designer*
Cait Lamborne, *Ebook Developer*

Publicity
David Kass, *Senior Director of Publicity*
Alexandra Primiani, *Associate Director of Publicity*
Rhina Garcia, *Publicist*
Eva Kerins, *Publicity Assistant*

Publisher
Jofie Ferrari-Adler, *VP and Publisher*

Subsidiary Rights
Paul O'Halloran, *VP and Director of Subsidiary Rights*
Fiona Sharp, *Subsidiary Rights Coordinator*